CW00427990

Ron Ellis was study̶ Liverpool Polytechn̶ Merseybeat phenomenon. He imported records from America for The Beatles, ran an entertainment agency and finally took to the stage himself as a DJ, eventually becoming Promotions Manager for Warner Bros Records. In 1979, he made the New Wave charts with a self-penned song, 'Boys on the Dole', an ironic title when the *Sun* acclaimed him as the man with the most jobs in Britain. The eleven jobs included that of librarian, lecturer, salesman, DJ, actor (he regularly appears in *Coronation Street* and *Brookside*), broadcaster, photographer, journalist – and author!

Ron still lives on Merseyside with his wife and two daughters. He currently works on local radio and reports on Southport FC matches for the press.

EARS OF THE CITY, the first novel to feature DJ and part-time Private Eye Johnny Ace, is also available from Headline:

'Lively romp set against a wonderfully authentic Liverpool setting . . . Memorable characters, plenty of fast, throwaway dialogue and a realistic plot . . . More, please'   *Yorkshire Post*

Mean Streets

A Johnny Ace Mystery

Ron Ellis

HEADLINE

First published in hardback in 1998 by
HEADLINE BOOK PUBLISHING

First published in paperback in 1999 by
HEADLINE BOOK PUBLISHING

10 9 8 7 6 5 4 3 2 1

ISBN 0 7472 5943 7

Printed and bound in Great Britain by
Caledonian International Book Manufacturing Ltd, Glasgow

HEADLINE BOOK PUBLISHING
A division of Hodder Headline PLC
338 Euston Road
London NW1 3BH

Dedicated to

The staff of Sefton libraries and
the members of the Southport Writers Circle

Chapter One

It was Thursday night. I was having supper with Hilary in my flat in Waterloo Dock when we caught the end of the news. We'd been to see *Tappin' Harlem* at the Empire. I've always liked that Cotton Club era of jazz, Cab Calloway and the like, and the hoofing had been pretty good too.

I was just pouring another glass of wine when the phone rang. I ran to pick it up before the ansaphone checked in.

'Johnny Ace?' The voice was thin and reedy, that of an old man.

'Who wants him?'

'Is that you, Johnny? It's Bert here, Bert Hope. You remember me, son. Bradley's Dad.'

'I remember you, Bert. It's been a long time.'

'I need your help, Johnny. It's about our Bradley's murder.'

'What? Bradley murdered? I don't believe it. When? How?'

'It's been on the telly tonight. Haven't you seen it?'

'No, we've only just come in.'

'They dragged him out of the river this afternoon. Some bastard had stuck a knife through him.'

'Christ, Bert. I'm sorry. It must have been a terrible shock for you.'

His reply startled me. 'Not really, Johnny. I was fearful for something of the kind. Look, can you get round here tonight?' He gave me an address in Bootle.

'But surely the police are handling everything?'

'Never mind them. Can you come now?'

'It's a bit late now, Bert. Can't we make it tomorrow morning?'

'All right. But don't forget, will you? It's important.'

'I won't.' I replaced the receiver.

'It's here in the last edition of the *Echo*.' Hilary handed me the evening newspaper. I took it from her and scanned the front page. Beneath the banner headline was a photograph of a raddled man who looked seventy but was only three years older than me and two years younger than Paul McCartney.

'Christ, if that's what a life of strong drink, loose women and designer drugs does for you, I think I'll stick to Horlicks in future.'

I put down the paper and took a sip of red wine. I'd seen him on television the week before. They'd run a repeat of one of the old *Top of the Pops* shows and there he was, along with Dusty Springfield, Jet Harris and Heinz. I wondered what had happened to them all.

'He was on the telly only last week,' Hilary said.

'I saw him.'

'He looked so slim and young.'

'He was only nineteen at the time.'

'And so innocent, somehow.'

'That didn't last long.'

Not many of the Merseybeat bands from the Sixties made it and, of those that did, few stayed long at the top. The rest returned to the 'real world'. Gerry's still going strong with new Pacemakers but his brother Freddie now runs the Pacemaker School of Motoring in Formby whilst The Undertakers' singer is a school caretaker. A far cry from the London Palladium.

Bradley had lasted longer than most. As Bradley and The Baronets, they'd had three big hits before he dumped the group in a blaze of publicity, a sort of Pete Best and The Beatles in reverse. The fans weren't happy with this and his first solo record bombed in England. For some unaccountable reason, though, it was a hit in America.

Bradley promptly flew across the Atlantic to promote it, dressed up like a cheeky schoolboy in the cap and scarf that were to become his trademark and see him through half a dozen pop hits.

He stayed in the States, cleverly reinventing himself as a younger Tony Bennett, and so making the transition from teen idol to Las Vegas cabaret star almost overnight.

That was where the serious drinking started and the voice started to go. Undeterred, he moved to LA where he went into films. He scored a few roles as the middle aged macho guy who, incongruously, gets to bed a succession of young nymphets, a story-line he carried through to his private life.

Rumour had it that, behind the scenes, he also had a secret love tryst with one of his young co-stars, Jason Wall, and it was suggested that his increasingly gaunt countenance was a sign that he was suffering from Aids rather than alcohol poisoning. Tales of his capacity for snorting cocaine were legendary.

This lifestyle of debauched luxury saw him rarely out of the pages of the *National Enquirer* and other, less salubrious, tabloids, with the emphasis on his personal life rather than his career.

Inevitably, the career suffered and, after a series of disastrous movies, in which he played increasingly insignificant parts, he finished up in the Betty Ford Clinic. When he came out, his time had passed and Hollywood didn't want to know.

He went back to wearing his old scarf and cap, now a useful device for concealing his disappearing hair, and took off round the cultural backwaters of the Mid-West, singing his old Merseybeat hits to decreasing numbers of ageing fans on the Oldies circuit.

I put slices of Red Leicester cheese on two digestive

biscuits spread with Olivio, handed one to Hilary, and
refilled our wine glasses.

'Wasn't he married to that girl who was in that last
Robert Redford film?' she asked.

'Probably.' He'd had four wives and several live-in
lovers, many of them women. Nobody could say Bradley
Hope had not explored every spectrum of human activity.

'What did he do before he was famous?'

'He was an apprentice in the barber's shop in Walton
where I used to have my hair cut.' It seemed a lifetime
ago and I supposed it was. 'At night he played in a group
called The Suttons – Gordon and Roy Sutton's band. They
played a lot of Carl Perkins numbers.'

It was in the days when I'd started playing drums
in The Cruzads, round about 1962. I was just fifteen.
While Bradley wielded his scissors, we'd chat about the
latest American rock'n'roll records we'd heard on Radio
Luxembourg. We'd both been big Larry Williams fans.

Another Larry Williams fan was John Lennon, whose
group The Beatles had just signed with George Martin
and Parlophone Records in a deal that was to propel them
to stardom. Their version of *Dizzy Miss Lizzy* was almost
as good as Larry's original.

'His mother had a stall in Paddy's Market like Cilla
Black's mother,' I recalled.

'How come he made it and you didn't?'

'Because he was good, I suppose. Oh, make no mistake,
Bradley had talent. Not a great voice but he had charisma
and the girls loved him. He had that Bobby Vee "boy next
door" appeal. A real smoothie.'

'It obviously pays to be a smoothie,' grinned Hilary.
'What a pity you couldn't be one.' She stroked my thigh
affectionately.

'We used to call him "The Great Honeydripper", after
the Big Joe Turner record.'

'I remember you having him on your programme a few
years ago.'

'God, you're right! Do you know, I'd quite forgotten that.'

I have an hour's show on a local radio station, six to seven p.m.; Monday to Friday. I play records that I like rather than sticking to some computerised playlist dreamt up by marketing men with no knowledge of music who think Oasis is a fashion store at a holiday centre in the desert.

Often, things are said on the programme that upset the station bosses but the listening figures are high enough to keep me in the job. Nothing fuels the success of local radio better than controversy.

I don't get paid much for the show but, since The Cruzads' days, I've invested my money in property, buying old Victorian houses, of which there are plenty in Liverpool, and converting them into self-contained flats to rent out.

'He'd made a new record and was over here promoting it. You played it on the show.'

'I've still got it. It wasn't a bad song but it didn't do anything. Mind you, you wouldn't expect it to. He was a forty-year-old has-been and the charts were full of Dance music. Who the hell would buy it?'

'Wasn't he half drunk or something?'

'Plastered. I remember, he looked terrible. His cheeks were hollow and he wore this awful fake suntan. He had a stomach like a beached whale and he sweated a lot.'

'Probably a liver condition,' said Hilary, who is a nurse.

'And he seemed to have trouble getting his sentences out.'

'His brain must have been pickled by then.'

'He certainly wasn't one of Alcoholics Anonymous's biggest successes,' I agreed. 'What does it say about the murder?'

'A ten-inch stiletto blade through his heart.'

I picked up the *Echo* again quickly and read down the

page. It had happened in Liverpool. Although I thought
he was still in America, he'd been back in England for
at least a couple of months. It wasn't exactly clear
where he'd been living but his body was found floating
near the landing-stage at Birkenhead. A weight of some
description, that had been chained to his legs, had come
adrift and he'd floated to the surface. The skipper of the
morning ferry had spotted him bobbing in the water and
raised the alarm.

'Poor bastard,' I said. 'What a way to end up after a life
of fame and glamour! He had a mansion in Carmel at one
time, you know, where Clint Eastwood was Mayor.'

'And Sonny Bono.'

'No, Sonny Bono was Mayor of Palm Springs, not
Carmel.'

Hilary grinned. 'All right, smart arse. It's near enough!'

'They seem to be big on show-biz people in politics in
California, don't they?' I mused. 'Look at Reagan.'

'Nobody gave Bradley the chain of office though.'

That was true. 'I wonder who there could be in
Liverpool who'd want to kill him? I mean, he spent
most of his life in the States, didn't he? He wouldn't
have known many people here any more.'

'Has he no other family around?'

'I've no idea. Bert must be well into his seventies; I
don't know if his Mum's still alive. Bradley used to have
a Hornby Dublo train set. I remember going round to play
with it once, when he was in The Suttons, and his Mum
gave us connie-onnies, Nestlés Milk sandwiches. And old
Bert was a porter on the railways.'

'Do they still have those?'

'I haven't seen one for years. Maybe they do on big
stations like Euston.'

'I've never seen one on Lime Street.' Hilary finished
her last piece of cheese and took a sip of wine. 'I wonder
why Bradley came back from America?'

'I don't know. And we probably never will now.' I

read the rest of the article. 'Hey, it says here they've got someone for it. "Police have arrested a thirty-three-year-old man in connection with the death".'

'That didn't take them long. I wish they'd showed as much enthusiasm when my bike got nicked.'

'They'd want a quick result, wouldn't they, him being so famous? Big kudos for Merseyside CID. So that's that then, all neatly tied up. Neat and sweet.' I walked across to the sideboard to fill up our glasses.

'Are you doing anything on Saturday?' she asked. 'Only I thought we might have lunch in town and go round the shops. They should have the new holiday clothes in.'

In an unguarded moment, probably in the middle of wild sex, I'd agreed to take Hilary to Majorca for a week in June. Why, I don't know. Five things I particularly dislike are package holidays, sunshine, sea, sand and Spanish television so there won't be a lot down for me in Majorca but Hilary wasn't so keen on my own suggestion – a tour of the blues clubs in downtown New Orleans – so Majorca it was.

If I had to go on holiday with anyone, Hilary is the one person I'd take, yet we've never been on holiday together before, although I've been seeing her for the best part of twenty years.

We've lasted so long, I suppose, because neither of us has made any demands on the other. We enjoy sleeping together, we enjoy each other's company but we've both agreed to remain what I call 'loving friends'.

I don't know that the holiday has marked any change in the situation and I reckon the relationship will survive it.

However, shopping's another matter, apart from which, Everton were at home, as I explained to Hilary.

'Can't you miss one match?' she said.

'I certainly can't, even though they're playing Arsenal so it could be the most boring game of the season.'

'They'll be due for their annual win soon, won't they?'

Hilary grinned. I threw a cushion at her and we went on to talk about less inflammatory things until, by one o'clock, we'd finished the wine and gone to bed. By which time, Bradley Hope was long forgotten.

The news on Radio Merseyside the next morning provided a little more information. The thirty-three-year-old man was now named as Michael Mitchell, unemployed and of no fixed abode. The motive was thought to be robbery. Police were unable to confirm that Mitchell was under the influence of drugs at the time of the attack.

I didn't find this very convincing. No smackhead half out of his tree was going to go to the trouble of tying weights to his victim's legs and carrying the body down to the river. He'd just take the money and run and leave the poor bastard to die in the gutter. It didn't ring true at all.

'Why worry?' said Hilary, as she got ready for work. She was on the afternoon shift at the Royal Liverpool Hospital and looked very sexy in her uniform. 'It's not your concern.'

She was wrong. The murder of Bradley Hope was going to be very much my concern.

Chapter Two

Bert Hope was actually eighty-one now and lived on his own in sheltered accommodation, not far from the Bootle terraced house where he'd lived when I'd first known them. When I knocked on the door later that morning, he took an age to answer.

'Who is it?' he called out eventually.

'Johnny Ace.'

'Hang on.' A rattle of chains, undoing of bolts and turning of keys followed. I half-expected Beefeaters to appear. Finally, the door swung open to reveal an old man in an open-necked shirt and braces holding up loose-fitting trousers. 'You can't be too careful these days,' he wheezed.

He'd shrunk since I'd last seen him. He locked the door carefully after me, this time with just a mortice lock, and hobbled across the room with the aid of a walking stick.

'It's arthritis. I've got it in my knees and my back. Some days I can hardly get out of bed. I tell you what, Johnny, there's nothing down for you when you're old. You want to grab what's going while you're young enough to enjoy it.'

He eased himself on to a bentwood chair covered with a ragged cushion.

'Like your Bradley did, eh Bert?'

At the mention of his son, his face clouded over. 'When he started playing in that group, it was about 1959. He used to say, "This'll be my passport out of here, Dad." Liverpool was a dying city, even in those days. The cotton trade was gone, the docks were on the way out, there were no jobs for half the youngsters. Ten years after the war and they'd hardly started rebuilding after the Blitz. Bombsites on every corner.'

'Bradley got away though, didn't he?'

He sighed. 'You know what saddens me, son? We're nearly forty years on and things here are worse.'

'You can't say that, Bert. Have you been down the South Docks lately and seen all the new apartments and hotels and the Marinas?'

But he wasn't impressed. 'They're just posh squatters, outsiders. There's nothing down for ordinary Scousers like me. You expect everything to improve with time but it doesn't. Our Bradley may have got away but he ended up back where he started, so what good did it do him?'

'Oh, come on, you've got to think of the fun he had in between and what he achieved. He was a big star at one time. He travelled all over the world. Not many people get the chance of a life like he had.'

'But where'd it get him, eh? The bottom of the bloody Mersey.'

We were both silent for a moment as we contemplated this, then, 'Why did you ring me, Bert?'

'Oh sorry, Johnny. I'm being inhospitable. Let me make you a cup of tea.' He tried to struggle to his feet.

'You stay there. I'll put the kettle on.' The kitchen was sectioned off from the lounge by a small archway, covered by a curtain – it was what they nowadays call a studio flat. The cooker was a Baby Belling. I filled the old silver kettle through the spout and put it on the biggest ring. The place was clean and tidy and I guessed a home help came in a couple of times a week.

'I'm told you're doing a bit of investigating work on the side.' I detected a certain admiration in his voice.

The Liverpool working classes have always approved of
moonlighting.

'That's right, Bert. I'm a private eye now.' It wasn't
strictly true. About six months ago, I'd had some free time
on my hands. Matt Scrufford, the son of our singer in The
Cruzads, had been murdered and I'd fancied myself as a
detective, probably after watching too many episodes of
Frost and *Sharman* on TV.

Nonetheless, I managed to track down the killer before
the police, which rather gave me a taste for the work.

I haven't actually advertised yet, but then, with the
Liverpool grapevine in operation, who needs *Yellow
Pages*?

'I can't do everything on my own you see, especially
at my age.'

'When did Mary die, Bert?'

He looked grim. 'Over six years ago. She was run
over by this off-duty copper in an XR3.' Just like John
Lennon's mother. You wonder who trains these police
drivers. 'Goes without saying he was over the limit.
They did him for it, of course, and I believe he lost
his job, but it didn't bring my Mary back. It knocked
the stuffing out of me, I can tell you. I stayed on my
own in the house till the Social Services put me in this
place. They have a warden here and Meals on Wheels
come round with my dinner. Michael Winner wouldn't
eat it but it does me.'

'I'm sorry about Mary. A terrible way to go.'

'At least it was quick. That's why I want things
sorted out about our Bradley, for Mary's sake. She'd
have wanted it.'

'But, Bert, it said on the radio this morning the police
have arrested someone for Bradley's murder, a man called
Michael Mitchell.'

'That's bollocks.'

I had to admit I'd thought the same myself.

Bert went on. 'That's the law trying to look good.

Gives them breathing space, keeps the press off their backs. No, I want the people who really did for him but I'll need your help.'

'You said yesterday you weren't surprised that Bradley was killed. What makes you think he was in danger?'

He paused. 'Because, Johnny, Bradley was being blackmailed.'

'What!' I found this hard to accept. As so many of Bradley's indiscretions had been well-publicised by the press all over the world, I could see little opportunity for the crime.

Bradley was a self-confessed adulterer, sodomite and wife-beater. Blackmail victims are usually people who are anxious to appear squeaky clean in public. It could hardly have been a secret love-child, either. There must have been at least half a dozen of those little beggars running around that he'd happily admitted to. There'd have been more money in it for the blackmailers to go for the Pope. I said so to Bert.

'It was nothing to do with anything our Bradley did, it was a private family matter. Something that happened years ago. These people found out about it and they were putting the screws on Bradley because he was the one with the money.'

'So how long had this been going on?'

'Oh, months, so he said. He'd been paying what they asked but then his money ran out so they threatened to kill him.'

'Didn't he go to the police?'

'No. He didn't want them to know the secret and that's why I don't want them involved now. If it ever got out, it would ruin our family name.'

I didn't point out that Bradley's lifestyle had hardly qualified the Hopes for a visit to Buckingham Palace.

The kettle started whistling and I went across to make the tea. I found some round tea-bags in an old Craven A tin and a half-empty bottle of milk in the old Fridgedaire in the corner. I brought two mugs back, both red with the word OXO on them, and handed one to Bert.

'Please, Johnny. I'll make it worth your while.' He reached in his trouser pocket and pulled out a bundle of notes held together with an elastic band. 'Here's two hundred on account.'

'Put it away,' I insisted. 'I don't want it. I might not be able to find out anything.'

'Call it protection money. They might come for me next. I need a bodyguard.'

'Don't be silly, Bert. Nobody's going to come looking for you.'

I hadn't made any money from the last case either. Good job I had the flats and didn't need it. Bert's financial situation puzzled me though.

'How come you're still living round here, Bert? I thought the first thing pop stars did was buy their Mum and Dad a mansion in the country.'

'Because we didn't want one. We'd made friends in the neighbourhood. Didn't want to move again, and after Mary went, there was no point in me going somewhere on my own.'

'When did Bradley come back to Liverpool?' I asked.

'A couple of months ago. Just after Christmas, it was. He walked in out of the blue one morning. Said he was living in London. I'd not seen him before that for getting on for five years.' That would be about the time he'd appeared on my show. 'He said he had some business with this agent in Dale Street – David Warner. You must know him.'

'Doesn't everyone?' David Warner, variety agent, concert promoter and pop star manager, was a mythical figure in Liverpool folklore.

He'd started in the early Sixties, putting local groups into the church halls and beat clubs that had sprung up all over the city. He wasn't much older than the guys in the bands but he soon moved on to booking chart-topping acts into venues all over the country.

His 'big break' came when he booked The Tornados to play in Dundee. The group's manager had rung up to say they were ill so Warner sent a local band to fill in. Except he didn't bother to inform the promoter they weren't The Tornados.

Telstar was No. 1 at the time and all the groups played it anyway, but Warner was careful to pick one with an organist and a blond singer who could be mistaken for Heinz in the dim lights of a distant Scottish ballroom.

It worked. Nobody noticed the difference on the night and the promoter sent Warner a cheque for £200, whereupon he paid the group £40 and pocketed the rest.

Realising that a fortune awaited him in far-off backwaters like East Anglia, Mid-Wales and Scotland, he stepped up his operations. He had scant regard for the observation powers of the local inhabitants.

'Sheepshaggers,' he used to say. 'The stupid bastards couldn't tell the difference between Helen Shapiro and Long John Baldry.' Soon, five Tornados were appearing on the same night between Aberdeen and Aberystwyth.

The Cruzads once did a gig for him somewhere near Goole. When we arrived, we found we were billed as Emile Ford and The Checkmates.

'Christ, this is a bit much,' complained our lead singer, Mally, when he saw the posters. 'This is Al Jolson territory. I didn't know we had to bring our own boot polish.'

But, amazingly, nobody said a word. Mally sang *What Do You Want To Make Those Eyes At Me For?* and *Slow Boat To China* and we stayed for two encores.

Warner knew there was always the risk that, one day, one of the groups would threaten to expose him, especially when they realised that his share of the fee was often quadruple their own.

When it eventually happened, he dealt with it in a

simple way by dangling the hapless guitarist concerned by his ankles outside the first-floor window of his office. Word got around and nobody ever grassed.

'I don't know why some of those groups got upset,' Warner once grumbled to me, in later years when he'd forgotten I'd been in one of them myself. 'They made double what they were earning in Liverpool. The promoters charged a fortune on the door, so they made a profit too, and the punters went home satisfied, thinking they'd seen their idols who, let's face it, would never have gone to those godforsaken holes in a million years. So why wasn't everybody happy?'

He made it seem like he'd performed a public service.

I'd last seen him at a Variety Club luncheon a couple of years ago, drinking champagne at the top table with Ken Dodd, Derek Hatton, Pete Price and other local luminaries. He hadn't mentioned Bradley Hope then.

I took a gulp of tea. 'Did Bradley say what this business was?'

'No. I know Warner used to book them out occasionally in the old days, when they were Bradley and The Baronets. I assumed it was something to do with his music.'

'And was this when he told you about the blackmail, when he came up to see Warner?'

'Yes. He asked me if I'd told anyone about . . . about the secret, but of course, I hadn't. He said he'd been paying for months but he'd run out of money. They'd cleaned him out and now they were going to kill him in case he shopped them.'

'It couldn't have been Warner who was blackmailing him, could it?'

'Come off it – with his money! He's a crook all right but he's a con man. Blackmail's not his game.'

'I see your point. Tell me, why are you so sure it wasn't Mitchell that killed him?'

'Mitchell's only been out of prison a fortnight. He'd

been doing five years. I know his old fella from the
railways. The whole Mitchell family are a bad lot.' The
city grapevine again. Liverpool's more like a village for
gossip. 'The lad's a druggie.'

'Perhaps he killed him anyway, nothing to do with
the blackmail. They might have had a row in a pub.
Mitchell's had too much to drink, next thing he's flashing
his blade and Bradley gets in the way.'

'I can't see it, Johnny. The chains round his legs, it was
too planned for a Mitchell.' The old man suddenly looked
very distressed at the image he'd conjured up.

After a moment, I said quietly, 'Let's assume it *was*
the blackmailers, then. Incidentally, how do we know
it wasn't just one person?'

He thought about it, then gave a deep sigh. 'We don't
really, I suppose. Bradley didn't say one way or the other.
It could easily have been one man.'

'Or woman.' These were the days of equality, after
all. 'Where was Bradley staying, this last couple of
months? There'd not be room for him here, would
there?'

'Oh, he didn't stay in town. He kipped down here on
the sofa for one night then he was away, don't ask me
where. It was the last time I saw him.' His voice choked.
'He must have been in hiding somewhere.'

He hadn't hidden well enough. I wondered how long
he'd been back in Liverpool before he ended up in the
river. Everything pointed to a local villain rather than a
transatlantic one.

For a start, the Americans were more professional
about this sort of thing. If they'd organised Bradley's
demise, he'd be nicely tied up now in a seaweed sandwich
instead of floating to the surface like a badly wrapped
parcel. No, the answer lay in England and probably in
Liverpool.

'Who else knows about this family secret?'

'Nobody. Or so I thought.' He suddenly looked all

of his eighty-one years. 'But, obviously, someone's found out.'

'You'd better tell me, Bert,' I said gently. 'What it is, that's so terrible.'

Chapter Three

He told me the whole story and it was pretty harrowing.

Bert and Mary had had three children, Alison, Norman and Bradley – Bradley being a good bit younger than the others.

When she was fourteen, Alison got pregnant. She refused to name the father and none of her friends were able to recall a particular boyfriend. Being a good Catholic girl, abortion was out of the question but, to give them due credit, Bert and Mary stood by their daughter and made plans for the baby's arrival.

'Bear in mind, this was the 1950s,' explained Bert. 'It were a thing of shame then. Not like today when young girls are dropping babies like rabbits and sod getting wed.'

Alison died in childbirth. She was just fifteen years and two days old. The space for the father's name on the birth certificate was left blank.

Worse was to come. It transpired that her own brother, Norman, had been having intercourse with her, and blood tests proved that the baby's blood matched his. He was barely seventeen – sixteen at the time of conception.

Norman was despatched from the house and his parents never set eyes on him again. The baby was adopted. As far as the rest of the family and the world in general were concerned, Norman had left to join the Army and the baby's father was unknown.

Until now.

'Someone else must have known,' I pointed out to Bert, 'otherwise Bradley couldn't be blackmailed.'

'I've been racking my brains,' he said. 'But, apart from Norman, who is there?'

'You've really never heard from Norman since he left home?'

'Since I threw him out, you mean. No, not a word. Not even when his mother was buried.'

'Perhaps he didn't know she'd died.'

'Mebbe.'

There was a knock at the door. Bert jumped in alarm.

'I'll get it,' I said. 'You sit down.' On the doorstep stood a middle-aged lady, too fat to wear the floral leggings that were half-concealed by her long pink anorak. She held out a dinner plate with a battered silver cover from beneath which a spiral of steam escaped.

'Meals on Wheels,' she explained. 'Is Mr Hope poorly?' I stood aside to let her in. 'Oh, you're there. A visitor, eh, Bert?'

'Friend of the family, Stella.'

I smiled dutifully.

'He needs some company after the shock he's had, poor man. Worst thing that can 'appen to you, losing your own children.' She removed the cover from the plate to reveal some thick slices of fatty lamb, half hidden by coagulated gravy, a dollop of instant mashed potatoes and a clump of watery cabbage. I tended to side with Michael Winner.

'Get it eaten before it's cold,' she instructed. 'I'll see you Monday. Nothing you want, is there?' Bert shook his head. 'Shelley's on tomorrow. I'm off to my mother's for the weekend, she's been bad with her feet again.'

She rushed out to her next call, slamming the door after her.

'Another cup of tea, Bert?' I asked.

'There's a can of beer in the fridge,' he coughed. 'I'll have that. Help me wash my dinner down.'

It looked the kind of grub that would need some washing down. I fetched the beer and poured it into a pint glass from the cupboard. Bert took alternate mouthfuls from the plate and the glass, like a patient at the dentist's washing his mouth out.

'So, apart from Norman and Bradley,' I said at last, when Bert's progress was slowing down, 'nobody knew that Norman was the father of Alison's baby?'

'We moved soon afterwards. We used to live in the Dingle, in Powis Street – I don't know if you know it?'

I did. 'Off High Park Street.' Ringo Starr was born in the street behind, Madryn Street, before he moved to nearby Admiral Grove. I mentioned this to Bert.

'I used to drink at the Empress, where his mother served behind the bar. He did all right too, didn't he, little Richie? Just like our Bradley.' He dug some gristle out of his teeth with a fingernail. 'Anyway, I was telling you, after the trouble, we shifted across to Bootle where nobody knew us and started again, just me, Mary and Bradley.'

'When I first knew you, I thought Bradley was an only child. But someone from the old neighbourhood would have known he had a brother and sister.'

'So what if they did? Alison had died having a baby and Norman had gone into the Army. Nothing wrong with that. But the thing nobody knew, was that it were her brother's child.' He fixed me with a fierce glare. 'And you're the only person I've ever told, Johnny Ace. I'm putting my faith in you. It must never go out of this room.'

'So what exactly do you want me to do, Bert?'

'Find out who was blackmailing Bradley and who murdered him.'

'And if I do? Aren't you afraid the secret'll come out at the trial?'

He stood up and pushed away his plate, the meal

half-eaten. He cut a pathetic figure in his worn slippers, stained grey-flannel trousers, National Health glasses and wispy grey hair.

'There won't be a trial, Johnny. When you find him, I want you to kill him.'

'What! Don't be bloody ridiculous, Bert. Who do you think you're talking to – the Mafia?'

He shot me a malicious glance. 'Then just give me a name. I might be an old man but I've still got a few friends. They'll do the rest.'

I didn't like the idea of signing someone's death warrant but I found it hard to take Bert's threats seriously. Gangsters didn't usually wear button-up woollen vests. Time enough though, I thought, to worry what to do when I found the blackmailer.

I was certainly curious enough to want to investigate further so I promised Bert I'd have a go for him.

'I knew you wouldn't let me down, Johnny.'

'I'll be in touch if I find anything,' I promised.

'Make it quick, eh? Before they get me.'

'Give me one good reason why they should come for you, Bert.'

'I don't know, but since Bradley died I keep thinking I'll be next.'

I drove back into town and parked at the Albert Dock. The wind was pretty strong and there weren't too many people about. I went into Lucy's teashop for some lunch, taking a seat by the window overlooking the dock. A pleasure-boat was touting for tourists for the river cruise and, beyond, a gaggle of schoolchildren were queuing outside the Maritime Museum.

I sat back and tried to make some sense out of what Bert had told me.

My first thought was that Norman could have told everything to anyone in the world, assuming he was not ashamed of his role in the affair. Yet this was unlikely,

I decided, otherwise it would surely have become public knowledge long before now. The tabloids would have loved a story like that, about a high-profile star such as Bradley then was.

This didn't rule out the possibility that Norman himself could be the blackmailer. If he was resentful enough at getting thrown out, he might have been prepared to expose his father to 'shame' if Bradley didn't pay up.

Bradley was only seven when Norman was banished from the family home, so they were unlikely to have forged a close relationship that would have precluded Norman blackmailing his younger brother. But would he have gone so far as to kill him? I thought of Cain and Abel and couldn't make up my mind.

The waitress came over and I ordered the homemade tomato soup with French bread and a sparkling mineral water. She was about seventeen with a pale complexion and long dark hair. She reminded me of Maria.

I hadn't seen Maria for a few weeks now. We'd been going out quite regularly for some months but things had cooled off somewhat of late.

Having divorced one husband, Maria was looking for a return to suburban family life and that was not something that had ever been on my agenda. Since her son had left for college she'd been on her own, so maybe she thought that, at thirty-nine, she had time to start a new family with someone else. She'd not said any of this outright but the hints were pretty strong.

Unfortunately, no similar biological time clock was ticking inside me. Back when I was forty, I decided I could wait ten years or so before thinking about a family and now, coming up to fifty, I think much the same.

My freedom has always been the most important thing, which is why Hilary has lasted so long. She understands that.

When I reach seventy, I *might* consider settling down . . . although there may not be too many takers by then.

Bradley Hope hadn't made it to seventy. Remembering his photograph in the *Echo*, I did think that, even if he hadn't been despatched to a watery grave, he wouldn't have lasted too long on dry land either. He'd looked pretty rough.

One thing seemed certain: whoever I was looking for was likely to be someone from Bradley's past, after what Bert had told me. Also, had it been his Stateside 'friends' who wanted him removed, surely they would have done the job over there.

The Baronets would be obvious candidates, having been consigned to the dustbin of pop whilst their singer soared to stardom. They'd never had another hit record after Bradley abandoned them back in 1965. After two flops, their record company had dropped them and they'd broken up. How bitter were they? And would they wait this long for revenge?

The Baronets . . . where were they now?

I knew the whereabouts of one of them. Verity Kennedy, or Vezzy as he was known at the time, was now a famous racing trainer.

It hadn't done him any harm being dumped by Bradley Hope; indeed, he'd thrived. After The Baronets' demise, he joined a group called Greenfly who did very well on the Continent. Vezzy wrote most of their hits so, by the time he left them, he'd amassed enough money to buy a couple of racehorses which he trained himself on his farm in the Cotswolds.

He must have had a natural gift for it, because both horses started winning races and soon, other owners were bringing their charges to Verity Kennedy's yard. He took out a trainer's licence and never looked back.

Vezzy was married to the daughter of a successful National Hunt jockey. I remembered seeing photos of their house in *Hello!*. It seemed unlikely that he would resort to blackmail with an income like that, but the other members of the group would need checking out.

And what about The Suttons, Bradley's original group? Had he left them amidst similar acrimony? The Sutton brothers had moved out of town long ago, I'd not heard of them for years, but their old drummer, Ronnie Richmond, was still around and I had a good idea where to find him. He was playing in a rock'n'roll trio called Murphy and The Monotones. They usually gigged at pubs at weekends and, afterwards, drifted down to the Masquerade Club. I'd catch them there.

A different waitress brought my soup and I turned my attention to the meal. Truth to tell, I felt quite elated to be back on a case. Had I known then that it could end up with me being nearly killed, I might not have been so keen to get involved.

Chapter Four

By six o'clock that same evening, I was at the radio station for my last show of the week. Ken, my producer, was waiting anxiously for me. He's always nervous when I get behind the mike. It's a live show, you see.

'It's St David's Day tomorrow,' he fussed. 'Might be a good idea to play a Welsh record.'

'How about Harry Secombe sings *The Chemical Brothers' Songbook*?'

Ken scratched his head. 'Who's Harry Secombe?' At least his sense of humour was still working.

I started with *The Old Folks Home* by Vernon Oxford, a marvellous whining country song, guaranteed to make a few lonely pensioners reach for the barbiturates. I dedicated it to Stella and Shelley, the Meals on Wheels ladies.

I could see Ken making groaning noises behind his screen and I was tempted to put on Attila the Stockbroker's *Jingo Bells*, a brilliant poem/song about football hooligans, but I'd have been drummed off the airwaves for life. Maybe I'll play it on my last show. Attila is a big Brighton supporter but I've never held that against him. Brighton need all the help they can get.

Remembering Ken's request, I found a Bryn Yemm track. Bryn's a Welsh gospel singer who travels round the country doing stand-up singing sessions in major department stores, flogging stacks of personally signed records along the way. He probably outsells Tom Jones.

For the final record, I played Bradley Hope's last hit

and dedicated it to his father and late mother, with the added wish that I hoped the police would find the real killer eventually.

'Christ, what've you said now?' Ken's blood pressure seemed to have risen alarmingly, judging by his crimson cheeks.

Ken should have been a vicar rather than a radio producer. He's very earnest, totally conventional and highly moral. He wears boring brown-framed spectacles, tweed sports jackets, beige slacks with permanent creases and grey slip-on shoes. All that's missing is the dog collar. And he's only twenty-nine! It's frightening.

Needless to say, I horrify him. He'd have been happier working on *Thought for the Day*.

'The shit may never hit the fan,' I told him airily. 'When it does, then we'll worry.' I collected my post and drove back to my flat for a quick cup of tea.

I reached the Masquerade Club just after eleven. The club is situated in a back street behind the Pier Head and is a mecca for society misfits, gangsters, musos, foreign seamen and a sprinkling of young trendies who think it's daring to hang out among such company.

It was early for the punters but the owner, ex-bodybuilder and multi-racketeer Tommy McKale, was outside the iron front door, posing as one of his own bouncers.

'All right, Johnny?'

I noticed the ticket booth was empty. 'Where's Dolly tonight then?' For all the years I'd been coming to the club, the grey-haired old lady, rumoured to be Tommy's grandmother, had been there to take the entrance money.

'We had a bit of trouble last night. One of the punters turned nasty. It was an ambulance job in the end. He said we'd overcharged him so he tried to get his money back.'

'Not from Dolly's till?' I said. 'Did he know what he was risking?'

'Apparently not. Mind you, he was Danish.'

'Did Vince hurt him badly?'

'Oh, we didn't need Vince. Dolly keeps a lead paper-weight under the counter. Broke his wrist and four fingers. Just missed his thumb or she could have had a full house.'

'But she's all right?'

'Sparkling, but I gave her the night off in case he brings his chums back. She's eighty-four, Johnny – I can't let her get a taste for it. It's hard enough holding Vince back.'

I went inside. Vince was at the bar. He was wearing black nail varnish to match a beauty spot on his left cheek.

'What happened to the designer stubble?' I commented, as he poured my usual drink. Scrumpy Jack has its own site on the Internet now – there's progress for you.

'That's George Michael, Johnny dear. Very passé. It's the satin smooth oiled look now, no body hair.' He winked suggestively as he handed the glass over. '*Anywhere.*'

The camp camaraderie was deceptive. Vince was six foot two, muscular and a match for any of the roughnecks who might cause trouble in the club, beauty spot notwithstanding.

I took my drink and went over to the far corner of the club, where three guys were sitting in a moody group round a table.

A murmur of greeting rose as I pulled up a chair and joined them. They were all in their late forties, shabbily dressed in worn trainers, jeans and polo shirts in dull autumn colours. Two had greasy receding hair and the third was totally bald beneath a navy baseball cap with the outdated insignia *Euro 96*.

'No gig tonight then?'

'It's very quiet, Johnny. We've got the Albion in New

Brighton midweek, and that's about it. It's all Karaoke
and disco these days.'

This wasn't quite true. Karaoke had long since passed
its peak, as people grew tired of the same idiots getting
up every night to sing the same songs, and disco had been
superseded in many venues round the city by young bands
playing either Dance and Rap, or Sixties' guitar sounds
regurgitated as Britpop.

However, there was indeed little demand for the
Fifties' rock'n'roll churned out by ageing has-beens
like Murphy and The Monotones, none of whom had
held down a steady job in their lives.

'That's because you're still playing *Blue Suede Shoes*
and everybody's heard it now. Perhaps you should learn
a new song.'

'Fuck off.' Murphy lit a cigarette and took a swig
from his pint of lager. I noticed his polo shirt did not
quite cover the excessive swell of his stomach.

'How's the show going, Johnny?' Little Ian Byrnes
was the bass player, occasional part-time window cleaner
and serious alcoholic. 'Couldn't you get us on doing
a spot?'

'When Murphy's mastered his third chord, I might
consider it.' I changed the subject. 'Bad news about
Bradley Hope, wasn't it?'

'Yeah, what a turn up. Bottom of the Mersey. I thought
he was in Hollywood.'

'No, he wasn't.' The third member of the trio, Ronnie
Richmond, spoke through a shaggy moustache which
had filtered the froth from his beer to form a beige
crust over his lips. 'I saw him in town only a month
ago.'

'What did he have to say?'

'Nothing. He never saw me. He was walking down
Dale Street by the Town Hall. I was on my way to
the dole.'

'You played with him in The Suttons, didn't you?'

'Only for a short while. Big ponce he was. Nobody in the group liked him.'

'Any reason?'

'He was a poser. Thought he was a big star and he wasn't.'

'He soon was, though.'

This wasn't something Murphy and The Monotones wanted to be reminded about.

'I'd heard he was being blackmailed,' I said, watching to see Ronnie's reaction. There was none. 'Did you ever associate him with anything criminal?'

'Only his singing,' said Ronnie, wiping the foam off his moustache. They all laughed.

I tried another tack. 'What about The Baronets? What happened to them after Bradley dropped them?'

The three looked at one another blankly. 'Dunno,' said Murphy. 'Pissed off back to oblivion I suppose, like us.'

'We've been oblivious all along,' remarked Ronnie. 'Oblivious to fame, fans and decent fucking money.'

Little Ian Byrnes spoke up. 'He shit on them just like he done on everybody else. I used to know their drummer, Kenny Leatherbarrow, another piss artist like me. We went to the same AA meetings.'

'Didn't do you much good,' I said, pointing to his pint of lager.

'I only went for the biscuits but Kenny was in a bad state. DTs, blackouts – you name it, he had it.'

'When was this?'

'Oh, years ago, in the Eighties. I've not seen him since. He's probably snuffed it. He used to hang around the Bamalama Club in Toxteth. Not my scene.'

'Yeah, come to think of it, I've seen him in there a couple of times.' I've always had a taste for dives. 'Did he have a grudge against Bradley Hope?'

'Not a grudge as such, but I don't think he liked him. Blamed him for ruining his career.'

'He did the same to The Suttons what he done later to The Baronets,' said Ronnie. 'Just pissed off and left us when something better came along.'

In today's jobs marketplace, this would be recommended as a smart career move but obviously The Suttons and The Baronets had not regarded the upwardly mobile Mr Hope with the respect he might have deserved.

'So Gordon and Roy Sutton might feel they have it in for him then?'

'Hey, what is this?' said Murphy. 'You've been watching too much television.'

'Did you see them new fellas in *Dalziel and Pascoe* the other night?' asked Little Ian eagerly. 'Better than Hale and Pace, weren't they?'

'Fuckin' couch onion,' said Ronnie. 'All you ever do is watch the box.'

'I think it's couch potato,' I pointed out.

'Better than playing those bleedin' stupid computer games like you do,' retorted Ian.

'You're not saying the Sutton brothers did for him, are you?' said Murphy to me.

'Well, someone killed him,' I said. 'I was just wondering why.'

''Cos he was a shit, that's why. Obvious to anyone. You don't go round upsetting people like what he did without somebody giving him a serious seeing-to.'

'You couldn't get a more serious seeing-to than Bradley's,' I said.

'That's the way it is,' shrugged Murphy, matter-of-factly. 'Some people you don't mess around with.'

'Or you end up a floater. Very nice. No second chance to say you're sorry.' I drank down the last of the Scrumpy Jack. 'What happened to the Sutton brothers in the end? I've not heard of them for years.'

'They're running a secondhand car place somewhere on the Isle of Man. At least, they were the last I heard.'

The DJ turned up the volume as the punters started to drift in. It was eleven-thirty and the pubs were throwing out. Tommy had hired yet another new face behind the decks – Dave S., an old bloke, knocking sixty, with a grizzled beard, bad breath, sparse hair and a line of offensive patter aimed at his audience.

'Come on, you rat-faced bastards, get up and dance.' He put on a Kiss record and the familiar tired thump of Seventies' rock reverberated round the club.

'Hey, you two.' He pointed to a couple sitting side by side at a nearby table. They couldn't have been more than eighteen. 'Get your hands off his dick, darlin', and get over here.'

The young lad must have been tempted to go over and smash his face in, but he had the physique of an undersized pygmy whilst Dave S. stood over six feet tall and could have balanced a pint of beer on his stomach without spilling any.

I wondered what had happened to entertainment but consoled myself with the fact that the DJs never lasted long at the Masquerade; I didn't fancy Dave S.'s chances of finding his van intact when he came to pack up his gear at the end of the night.

'Isle of Man, eh? Have they been there a while?'

'Christ, yes, since the late Sixties. Done all right, so I hear. Always were sharp bastards, the Suttons.'

'Yeah.' I reckoned my best bet was to start with The Suttons and, if I got nowhere there, move on to The Baronets. David Warner, too, might be worth talking to. Bert said Bradley had had business with him. After that, a countrywide search for Norman Hope. It sounded all very easy, but I knew only too well it wouldn't turn out like that. Nothing is ever that simple in the end. Sod's Law.

For starters, would there be a boat going across to the Isle of Man in the middle of winter? The regular twice-daily service had long since disappeared along with

the trams, the original Cavern Club and the Overhead
Railway.

I'd found out as much as I was going to, but I got in
a round of drinks and let Murphy tell me why he hadn't
given up hopes of fame. 'I'm doing all right with the
acting. I done *Brookside* last week. I was a solicitor.'

The make-up department must have had a hard job.

I didn't point out that most of the extras on *Brookside*
came from the Job Centre because they work for less
money than Equity members. The man hadn't much in
life to hang on to, his self-esteem was pretty low as it
was. 'Did you get to speak?'

'No, but I had to pull a face at the camera. I had to do
a smug grin.' He pulled back his lips in a Billy Fury snarl
to illustrate his point. 'That means it's a directed part so
I'll get paid walk-on two.' He seemed well-satisfied.

I stayed with them for another round then decided
to call it a night. By now, the club was heaving, the
atmosphere resembled a sauna and Dave S. had moved on
to Sweet and Gary Glitter at full volume. The Seventies'
revival was in full swing: platform shoes and flares were
back with a vengeance.

I made my way to the door, pushing through a crowd
of Norwegian seamen arguing with Tommy about the
entrance fee. Scandinavians often got charged double. It
was Tommy's way of getting his revenge on the Danes
for invading us in the eighth century. Or so he said.

I was glad to get into the fresh air. I could just make
out ten past one on the Liver Buildings clock and the
streets were still full of clubbers.

When I got back to the flat, I checked the Isle of
Man Steam Packet Company timetable on the Internet. I
touched lucky. The boats ran at weekends out of season.
The *King Orry* was leaving Liverpool for Douglas at
6.45 p.m., which meant I could still catch the game at
Goodison Park before I sailed.

The snag was, the boat was due out of Douglas again

at Sunday lunchtime, which gave me just one morning on the island to find and talk to the Suttons.

I'd have to move quickly. If I missed the boat back, the next one wasn't for five days.

Chapter Five

Next morning I hit the phone to organise my trip. I managed to book a room at the Sefton in Douglas and fix myself up with a hire car without much trouble. March wasn't the busiest month for tourists.

I asked the girl at the car hire if she knew of the Suttons. I didn't know what the business was called but she was able to tell me there was no entry under *Motor Dealers* in the Isle of Man directory for the Sutton brothers or, come to that, any other Suttons.

Of course, they could have been operating under some company name, which meant a harder slog. On the other hand, the Isle of Man was a small place, thirty-three miles long by thirteen miles wide, so surely somebody there would know them.

In the end, I'd agreed to take Hilary for lunch before the match so we met in Lucy in the Sky with Diamonds in the Cavern Walks at noon.

The café was busy with Saturday shoppers but we managed to get a table outside in the mall, opposite the lifesize sculptures of The Beatles. Margie, the owner, came over to say hello. 'You've not managed to get him into town on a Saturday?'

Hilary laughed. 'Only till they kick off.'

'Football!' said Margie. 'You ought to be ashamed of yourself, Johnny. I hope you're taking her somewhere nice tonight.'

Margie is used to me dining with different ladies and she's always discreet but she's got a soft spot for Hilary.

Probably because she's been around the longest and she's got to know her.

''Fraid not. I've got to go to the Isle of Man.'

'What?' Hilary looked surprised. 'You never told me.'

'Only happened last night – a bit of business that's come up. I'll be back tomorrow teatime.'

Hilary has never been too keen on my private eye career, if you could call it that, so I felt no reason to mention Bradley Hope in connection with my trip.

'I'll have the chicken curry and rice,' I told Margie. I reckoned I needed more than a snack as I didn't know when I'd be eating again. The *King Orry* wasn't noted for its Cordon Bleu restaurant. Hilary ordered a cheese and tomato toastie. She didn't have to sit through a football match in the cold.

After the meal, I left her in town to do her shopping while I made my way to the ground.

Goodison Park was packed, nearly 37,000 in, and I was wrong in my prediction. It wasn't the most boring game of the year, just the worst I'd ever seen Everton play and, after over thirty years as a Blues supporter, that's saying something.

A depleted Arsenal side won 2–0. Everton had only one shot on target in the whole ninety minutes and played so abysmally, I wouldn't have given them much chance of holding down a place in the Vauxhall Conference. Southport would have hammered them.

'Bring back Mike Walker!' chanted the Gladwys Street end, sarcastically referring to the last manager, who had been ignominiously sacked in the manner of his predecessors. The final whistle blew and we all made our way out of the ground in relief.

I walked across to the Winslow for a cider, where the mood amongst supporters could be described as seething fury. 'Dixie Dean would have been ashamed to play in this team,' said one man, a pensioner, probably the only person in the pub old enough to have witnessed Everton's greatest player in his prime.

'*I'd* be fuckin' ashamed to play with them, never mind Dixie Bleedin' Dean,' said a young lad with a blue Everton FC baseball cap. 'None of those wankers'd get a game in our Sunday League team.'

I listened to the car radio as I drove home. Irate supporters were calling Alan Kennedy's phone-in on Radio Merseyside, demanding manager Joe Royle's head. I felt like ringing in myself but I had a boat to catch.

I'd probably write a letter to *When Skies Are Grey* instead and hope the editor of the Everton fanzine dared print it.

As it was, I just had time to collect my overnight bag from the flat and walk quickly over to the landing-stage before sailing time.

It was cold, dark and windy, just the weather for a trip across the Irish Sea, and I was glad I'd put on a thick waterproof parka over my sweatshirt and jeans. Good secondhand car-dealer gear.

The crew were getting ready to cast off as I stepped aboard. Most of the passengers had brought their cars but a couple of people walked up the gangplank alongside me.

I stayed on the top deck as far as the Mersey Bar, watching the Liver Birds fade into the distance; then the rain started and I retreated down to the saloon for the rest of the four-hour trip.

The strong wind and choppy sea made for a rough crossing. The *King Orry* swayed ominously a few times but I was able to hold down a couple of glasses of cider and a tuna on brown sandwich. The *Ellan Vallin* had sunk in this same Irish Sea back in 1909, but I assumed that shipbuilding would have improved since then.

Just in case it hadn't, I walked over to the bar for another drink. A group of men were having an animated discussion about motor-cycle racing. From the conversation, I gathered they were locals and I interrupted them.

'Excuse me, but do you guys know anything about garages on the island?'

'Not broken down before you get off the ship, have you?' They all laughed. The man who spoke was in his late thirties, already developing a beer gut and wearing a sloppy *TT Races* T-shirt beneath a cheap orange anorak.

'I'm looking for some wheels,' I said, adding hastily, 'four of them.'

He looked me up and down and decided I wasn't a candidate for a Ferrari. 'Something cheap, was it? A runaround?'

I couldn't visualise the Suttons holding down the Jaguar franchise so I nodded. 'Something like that. A friend told me about a couple of brothers on the island – the Suttons. Do you know them? Supposed to have a good selection of old bangers.'

They looked at each other. 'Sorry, mate. Never heard of them, but Nev's brother does a bit of dealing, he could pick something up for you that'd get you round. And at the right price.'

I took down his phone number and promised to call. The talk switched to motor bikes and I moved away to a seat in the corner for the rest of the interminable journey.

I had no real plan of campaign when I got to the island other than checking out the newspaper ads and driving around asking questions. Sunday morning was hardly the best time for this. Most people would probably still be in bed.

Despite the headwinds, the *King Orry* was on time. I went back up on deck to admire the view as we sailed into Douglas Bay. The curved vista of Victorian hotels along the seafront looked as impressive as ever.

If the Isle of Man had been blessed with Mediterranean

weather, Jersey wouldn't have been in the game. As it is, the tourist trade has plummeted since package holidays came along and British holidaymakers found it was almost as cheap and easy to go to Spain and Florida where the sunshine was guaranteed.

What has saved the island's economy is its offshore status, which has led to the burgeoning of the financial sector and an influx of bankers, investment managers and the like. Locals who would once have worked on the land or in the holiday trade have, instead, become bank clerks and secretaries.

If the financial sector ever pull out, I imagine the population will fall catastrophically but, judging by the number of new office building start-ups, that seems a pretty remote possibility.

My hire car was waiting for me at the landing-stage, a little Nissan Micra in bright red. It reminded me of a ladybird that had lost its spots.

The Sefton was only a couple of minutes' drive away and I was able to park easily at the back of the hotel. Being a Saturday night, there weren't many businessmen in and the lounge was quiet.

After I'd dumped my things in my room, I went down to the Harris Café Bar for a drink and a chat with the barman. I ordered a cider and we exchanged pleasantries. 'By the way, I don't suppose you know a Gordon and Roy Sutton?' I asked. 'I think they have a garage on the island.'

He shook his head. 'Names don't ring a bell.' He was in his early twenties and had a deep suntan which showed up against his short-sleeved white shirt and the bleached hairs covering his arms. He'd obviously had his winter holiday far away in the sun.

'In Douglas, are they?'

'Could be. Could be in Ramsey or Castletown just as easy.' Or Peel, or Port St Mary or Port Erin or Laxey. Suddenly, the island seemed a lot bigger.

'Have you looked through the papers?'

'No, I only just arrived a few minutes ago.'

'Hang on. I'll get them for you.' He left the bar and returned a few minutes later with the *Examiner* and *Independent*. 'Have a look through these. You might find something.'

I took a seat by the window overlooking the bay. I could see the lights of the *King Orry* alongside the landing-stage, ready to take me back to Liverpool in just a few hours.

There were lots of car adverts in both papers and also in the *Manx Courier*, a freesheet I'd picked up in the foyer. None gave any reference to proprietors named Sutton. I even read the small ads in case the brothers were posing as private sellers, a favourite dealers' trick, but struck no joy there either. By midnight, the print was beginning to swim before my eyes.

I drained the last of my cider and glanced casually through the rest of the pages of the *Examiner* before going up to my room. It was then I saw the article.

My search for the Sutton brothers was over.

Chapter Six

It was just a short paragraph – more of a picture caption, really – in the social column: *Roy Sutton and his wife Samantha together with Gordon and Jeannie Sutton enjoy a drink before the meal.*

The four of them were pictured in evening dress, cocktail glasses in hand, against a backdrop of a glitzy ballroom. The occasion was a golf club dinner in Castletown. There was no mention of cars.

So, I had a lead. I wouldn't have recognised Roy and Gordon Sutton from the photograph, but then I hadn't seen them for over thirty years.

In their dinner jackets, they looked a cut above the average secondhand car dealer, but there was also a general air of prosperity about the occasion itself. Their wives, whilst not exactly Baywatch Babes, were young enough to draw glances in most surroundings and were expensively clothed and jewelled. It looked a pretty exclusive golf club, full of the usual posers and social climbers and, maybe, even the odd sportsman.

I knew now where I had to go.

I was up for eight o'clock and enjoyed the Sefton's famous Manx kippers for breakfast, the first proper meal I'd eaten for nearly twenty-four hours.

On a clear day, from parts of the island, you can see across to Cumbria, Wales, Scotland and Ireland, but in today's morning mist and drizzle, I could just about make out the *King Orry* still tied up on the Pier.

I'd been tempted to pack just a change of shirt,

underwear and socks, but at the last minute, decided to include a sweater and slacks which was lucky as I didn't think jeans would go down too well in the golf club.

I picked up the Micra and set off for Castletown. There was hardly any traffic about and I did the journey in twenty minutes. After the lofty driving position of my Toyota RAV4, it was like being in a bubble car.

The Golf Links Hotel was at the end of a long winding road heading back out to the sea, so long that I was beginning to think I might need a lifejacket. The foyer was more like a golf club than a hotel, all wood-panelled walls, leaded light doors and a staircase leading to a balcony which ran across the far end of the room. Above a big gas log fire hung varnished boards, engraved with the lists of past captains and tournament winners.

I went down to the club room, past the cupboards full of silver trophies, to where a few golfers were gathered, and asked if Gordon or Roy Sutton were about.

'You won't get either of them here today,' said a man of military bearing. 'They'll be at their showroom.'

'Showroom?'

'On the road to Port St Mary. You can't miss it – it's a large white building with a big neon sign on the side: "The Isle of Man Bespoke Horseless Carriage Company" they call themselves.'

This didn't sound like a back-alley operation. I was beginning to revise my opinion of the Suttons.

'Their busy time, the weekends,' continued the Steward. 'Unless there's a big tournament on, of course, then Roy usually turns up for that. Gordon's more of a social golfer, if you follow my meaning.'

I thanked him, and five minutes later I was speeding across towards the cliffs of Port St Mary.

He was right about the showroom. You couldn't miss it – a 1930s-style Art Deco building, its back to the sea, two storeys high with curved windows and painted a brilliant white. John Betjeman would have loved it.

A row of gleaming cars stood along the forecourt, none of them worth less than ten grand, most of them around twenty.

I parked the Micra on the side of the road and walked into the glass-fronted showroom where a selection of the latest Mercedes and Daimler models were displayed.

A young salesman in a dark suit came over to me before I'd reached the desk. He wore brown-rimmed spectacles which gave him an inquisitive air and added ten years to his age. 'Can I help you, sir?'

'Is Mr Sutton in?'

'Would that be Mr Gordon or Mr Roy?'

'Either,' I said, 'or both,' confusing him. He went into a back office and a tall, grey-haired man came out with him. I recognised him from the photo, but I still didn't know whether it was Roy or Gordon.

He stretched out his hand to me. 'Roy Sutton. I believe you wanted to see me.' No trace of a Scouse accent there. He was immaculately dressed in a light blue mohair suit, turquoise shirt and handmade shoes. Hard to believe he'd ever sung *Roll Over Beethoven* whilst playing guitar behind his back and doing the duck walk across the stage of The Cavern.

But then, there'd been a few success stories amongst other Merseybeat performers. Chick Graham, who took over from Billy J. Kramer in The Coasters, went on to become a psychiatrist, and Steve Day, who started out as Wump and The Werbels, ended up as the MD of a shipping company.

And I own houses, so why should I be surprised?

Probably because, back in the Sixties, the Suttons used to be thick, foul-mouthed bastards who looked set for a career in petty larceny and worse. Obviously they'd been on the self-improvement courses.

I shook his hand. 'Last time we met, you were

singing *Matchbox* at the Orrell Park Ballroom. Johnny
Ace.'

He stepped back and looked at me then broke into
a big smile and gripped my wrist with his other hand.
'Good Lord, so it is! Johnny, how good to see you.
We often listen to your show on the way home from
the office. Come on in.' He gesticulated to the young
salesman. 'Reg, bring two coffees in, will you?'

He led me through to his office and waved me to a
leather chair in front of his desk. He walked round to
a similar chair on the other side.

'You don't live in Port St Mary then?'

'I live in Sulby and Gordon and his family are in
Foxdale.' Cynthia Lennon used to live in Foxdale,
in the days when she owned Bunters Restaurant in
Castletown. I couldn't visualise Yoko on the Isle of
Man. 'But what brings you over here? Where are you
staying? You should have let me know you were coming
over, Samantha would have been delighted to put you up
with us.'

I explained that I was leaving at one o'clock. 'It's a
flying visit, Roy. Maybe another time.'

'You won't stay for lunch then? That's a pity. So,
what are you doing on the island?'

'Believe it or not, I came to see you and Gordon.'

'You surely haven't come all this way to buy a Merc?'

'I came about Bradley Hope.'

'What!' I studied his face. He looked surprised but
nothing more sinister. 'Bradley Hope? But what's he
got to do with us?'

'You knew he'd died?'

'Of course. It was on TV and in all the papers.'

'I've been involved with tidying up things this end.
His old man's getting on now.' This was my new story.
I reckoned it sounded reasonably plausible and vague
enough to defy close scrutiny.

'Old Bert? I didn't know he was still alive.'

'Just about. He's eighty-one now and can hardly get across the room. I'm trying to trace the brother and sister and any other relatives.' I waited for Roy's reaction. Did he have any knowledge of the Hope siblings? His reply was instantaneous.

'Did he have any? I only ever saw Bradley with his Mum and Dad. I suppose there could be aunts and uncles and cousins though.'

I agreed. 'Once they think there's a few bob in it for them, I'm sure they'll all come crawling out of the woodwork.'

At this moment, the door opened and Gordon Sutton came in. Roy jumped up. 'Gordon, you know who this is?'

Gordon looked hard at me but no flicker of recognition crossed his face. He looked older than his brother, worry lines under the eyes and his skin leathered by too much sun. He wore a blue blazer with grey flannels, a white shirt and striped regimental tie.

I stood up and held out my hand. 'Johnny Ace. Remember The Cruzads?'

We shook hands. He was more guarded than his brother but his manner was friendly enough.

'The Cruzads. That's a name from the past and no mistake.'

'Johnny's come to see us about Bradley, Gordon. He's the executor or something for the will.' I didn't contradict him. 'He wants to ask us . . .' He stopped. 'What exactly was it you wanted to ask us, Johnny?'

'It's a bit of a strange thing, actually.' I spoke carefully. 'Bert seems to be under the impression Bradley was being blackmailed and he's asked me to look into it.'

A glance passed between the two brothers, only a brief one but enough for me, who was watching for it, to notice.

'Really. Who by?' Gordon spoke in a quiet monotone that pretended a polite disinterest.

'I was hoping you might have some idea.'

'Why us?'

'You used to know him well.'

'We haven't seen him for thirty years.'

'Precisely.' I adopted a confidential tone. 'That's probably when it started. Apparently, there was some big family secret, a real skeleton in the cupboard job, that Bradley was anxious to keep hidden for his father's sake.'

'What was this secret?'

'I've no idea,' I lied, 'but Bradley told Bert someone had found out about it and was putting the black on him. Unfortunately, he'd run out of money so Bert reckons the blackmailer killed him to cover his tracks.'

The Suttons listened to this and I could feel a sense of relief as I told the story. They were more relaxed.

'You're not saying we could have blackmailed him?' Roy seemed amused by the idea.

'Of course not,' I lied again, 'but like I say, you knew the family back in the Sixties. Did anything strike you at the time? Were there any rumours about family scandals?'

'I never heard any,' said Gordon, 'but then we never really knew Bradley that well. All right, he was our singer but we didn't mix outside the group and The Suttons were only going for a matter of months.'

'Did you know anyone who had a grudge against him at the time?'

'He wasn't popular. Thought himself a cut above everyone.'

'So it seems,' I agreed. 'I spoke to Ronnie Richmond yesterday. He seems to hate Bradley. Blames him for ruining his big chance of stardom by leaving the group.'

'He would,' said Roy. 'Ronnie was always a loser. He'd hate anyone who got on in life. What's he doing these days?'

'Still drumming. He's in a rock'n'roll band called

Murphy and The Monotones. They just play a few pubs round town.'

Gordon looked around his showroom with the rows of new Mercedes. 'At fifty,' he said, and his tone expressed his contempt. 'How sad.'

The young salesman appeared with two polystyrene cups. 'Sorry to be such a long time. I had to wait for the espresso machine.' He put them down on a brochure on the desk.

'I'll have one too, Reg, while you're at it.' Gordon pulled up a chair from the side of the room and positioned it alongside mine. 'So you're in the media now, Johnny? We get your show very clearly over here.'

'I own a property company too,' I said. I don't know why I felt a need to mention this, except maybe to let the Suttons know that they weren't the only ones to have prospered. Also, I knew they were the sort of people who would only respect anyone for their money. To them, it would be the one tangible proof of achievement. So I told them about the houses I'd converted into flats.

'We'd thought of it ourselves when we first came across, hadn't we, Roy? But the market wasn't there then, and by the time the finance people arrived, we were too much into cars.'

I glanced round the showroom. 'It seems to have been a wise choice, by the look of it.'

Gordon Sutton smiled. 'We don't do badly. There are a lot of rich people on the island who need to be seen driving a prestige vehicle.' He sounded like one of his sales blurbs. 'How do you find the property rental market in Liverpool?'

'There's always been a good demand in Liverpool because of the University.'

'Two universities now, with John Moores,' said Roy, as Reg arrived bearing another polystyrene cup. I felt Spode china would have been more appropriate.

'Quite.' I tried to steer the conversation back to the

matter in hand. 'So you say you haven't seen Bradley
Hope since . . .'

'Since he left the group,' finished Gordon, carefully
placing a coaster under his cup to protect the polished
surface of the oak desk. 'Once he'd joined The Baronets
he was away on tour with them most of the time.'

'You didn't keep in touch then?'

'No. Roy and I didn't hang around too long after that.
A lot of our bookings were cancelled after Bradley left.
Understandable, really. Neither of us could sing much
and Ronnie was drunk all the time. You could say we
weren't dedicated enough.'

'This was when you came over to the island?'

'There was nothing in Liverpool for us,' said Roy,
'except the dole queue. We thought we'd try our luck
here. We used to come on holiday when we were
kids.'

'It certainly paid off.'

'It was hard going at first but we correctly antici-
pated a market for luxury motoring and we've never
looked back.'

We talked a little while longer and I managed to avoid
drinking the awful coffee.

'You must come across again, socially,' said Roy,
as I got up to leave. Gordon agreed, a little less
enthusiastically, and shook my hand. Roy accompanied
me to my car, wincing when he saw the Micra.

'Hired for the day,' I explained, seeing his disdain-
ful glance.

'When you want a decent car, give me a ring and we'll
do you a good deal. Someone in your position should be
driving a Merc.'

I climbed awkwardly into the Micra, put it into gear
and waved as I drove through Port St Mary, past the
steam railway station and out towards Ballasella to pick
up the Douglas road.

Maureen, Matt Scrufford's mother, lived somewhere

near here and I'd promised to look her up when I
was on the island, but the day was getting on. Maybe
another time.

Instead, I stopped on the way to the ferry for a bite
to eat at the Lancashire Hotel. I sat in the front bar and
ordered a sandwich. The walls were made of Welsh
mountain slates which looked strange but I supposed
they kept the sheep out. At the end of the bar was a
fireplace below a moose's head but the logs appeared
to be there just for show. Whatever happened to real
fires in pubs?

Well in time, I checked in the Micra at the boat
terminal and boarded the *King Orry* for the four-hour
trip back. The weather was milder and the wind less
strong. I sat outside on the top deck, and since I had my
Walkman with me, I listened to Benny Green's show on
Radio Two.

Commercial radio could never put on a show like
Benny's. For a start, few of the Thirties' and Forties'
tracks he plays would make the playlist, and the station
bosses certainly wouldn't tolerate the rambling anecdotes
he tells about every song. But that's what gives the show
its charm. I love it and, in many ways, model my own
programme on it.

A lady of about sixty came walking past, smiled at
me and took up a seat along the deck. She wore a brown
woollen coat and a cloche hat. She took a pile of knitting
out of a canvas holdall and, gathering the needles, started
work on what looked like a striped cardigan.

Knitting is like breastfeeding – not something you
see very often nowadays in public. Victims, perhaps,
of the twin market forces of bottled milk and ready-
made knitwear. Or maybe it's a new mood of reticence
or political correctness.

When *Sing Something Simple* came on, I went down
to the bar and ordered a cider. I tried to work out
what my trip had accomplished. The Suttons genuinely

didn't seem to know anything about the Hope Family
Secret. Yet, there was something, I was sure, that they
were hiding.

The boat docked in Liverpool at five o'clock, just as
the *Mountwood* was crossing the river from Woodside.
The ferry boat looked small compared to the *King Orry*,
but the *QE2* had dwarfed them all when she had visited
the Mersey the previous year.

I walked back to the flat, trying hard to imagine
the Suttons as blackmailers. Like Verity Kennedy, they
seemed too prosperous to need the money for the
risk involved, but there had been something in their
exchange of glances that made me think they were
keeping something back.

Perhaps I would find out more from someone else who
had known Bradley in the Sixties. Little Ian Byrnes had
said that Kenny Leatherbarrow, The Baronets' drummer,
still hung out at the Bamalama Club. He looked my best
bet now.

I microwaved an Indian meal from the freezer and ate
it with a bottle of Scrumpy Jack. An episode of *Touch
of Frost* was showing on ITV, and I got caught up in
that, then I had a shower and changed into a khaki cord
jacket, T-shirt and denims ready for my night out.

At eleven o'clock, I took the RAV4 out on to the Dock
Road, headed south past the Liver Buildings and turned
into Upper Parliament Street.

I'd enjoyed watching David Jason as Frost but now
it was time for some real-life detecting.

Chapter Seven

I'd first visited the Bamalama Club back in The Cruzads' days, and often used to end up there after we'd finished a gig. The audience was mostly black and of all ages. The few white people who went in were usually hookers or musicians.

I loved the place. There was always a band on or sometimes, just a solitary singer, playing John Lee Hooker, Elmore James or Jimmy Reed stuff. The atmosphere was as near to a Chicago jump joint or New Orleans blues house as you'd get this side of the Atlantic, and I can't think of an English city other than Liverpool where you'd find anything like it.

Drugs have made many parts of the city a no-go area these days, and there are taxi drivers who'd think twice before collecting fares from the Bamalama. You can't reason with a man on smack or heroin, and the nostalgic memories of cordial race relations in the Sixties have become a dangerous myth in today's Liverpool, with shootings and gang warfare redolent of Chicago in the Thirties.

Nevertheless, I wound my way round the side streets until I found the tall house with the steps at the side leading down to the cellar where the club was held. A cracked, coloured neon sign at the side was missing the letter L.

I locked the car and ran down the steps to the big steel door at the bottom, rang the bell and waited. A sliding panel opened at face level and a black face

peered through some iron bars to inspect me before a
bolt was drawn back and the heavy door pushed open.

'Yo Johnny.' He would have dwarfed George Fore-
man. He stood about six five with a domed head, flattened
ear and broken nose, obvious relics of the boxing ring.

'Alex.' We slapped hands as I passed him and wan-
dered into the smoky darkness of the club. The people
at the counter turned one by one to check me out then
looked away again. Most had seen me before.

A couple of white women in their late thirties sat on
adjoining stools, one with long red hair and a low-cut
silver sheath dress, the other, a blonde, wearing a tight
tank top and a short leather skirt which had ridden up
her thighs.

Everyone else was black.

In the corner, on a low stage, an elderly man was
sitting on a chair, an acoustic guitar on his knee, wailing
a throaty version of Robert Johnson's *Standing at the
Crossroads*, tapping his feet to keep time. Several of his
teeth were missing, his jowls were heavy with age and
his petrel-blue suit was threadbare. But he sang like he
was in a cotton field beside the Mississippi.

'Johnny Ace! Man, where you bin these past weeks?'
A thin man, in his early sixties and wearing a pork pie
hat and a Harris tweed sports jacket, came out of a back
room, his arms held out in greeting.

'Jonas!' The owner of the Bamalama had a big smile
showing a lot of yellow teeth as he put his arms round
me in a friendly embrace.

'How yo' been doin', man?'

'This and that, Jonas, you know how it is.'

He nodded. 'Come on, let me buy you a beer.' I
didn't argue. Cider hasn't reached the Bamalama yet
and sometimes I suspect the beer is home-brewed in a
still out the back. Pure moonshine.

'I'm looking for Kenny Leatherbarrow,' I said after
we'd taken two vacant stools at the bar and got in our

beers. 'Do you know him? Used to be the drummer in The Baronets.'

Jonas did. 'Kenny comes in a lot of nights, not usually before twelve. He likes to get well sozzled first. Says he drums better that way.'

'He doesn't play here, does he?'

Jonas laughed. 'No, only on the tables. He keeps time with his fingers.' He tapped on the bar to demonstrate.

'He wasn't a bad drummer in his day.'

'Hah! One thing fo' sure, man, his day ain't coming back. You hang around, Johnny, you'll catch him.'

Sure enough, at two minutes past midnight, Kenny Leatherbarrow appeared, shuffling slightly as he made straight for the bar and ordered a beer. I went over.

'Hi Kenny, not seen you about for a long time.'

'Bloody hell, it's . . . don't tell me, you were a drummer too.' He screwed up his face and tried to drag my name from his memory. 'With The Cruzads, wasn't it?'

'That's it. Johnny Ace. How ya doing?'

I slapped his shoulder and offered him a beer. We drank a toast to Old Times.

'So, what are you doing now?' I asked. 'Still drumming?'

'When I can. I've nothing on at the moment.' I noticed his hands trembling slightly and thought he'd have a job holding the sticks.

'Shame about your old mate, Bradley.'

'Yeah, I heard about that. Sliced open, wasn't he? Serves the sod right.'

'You didn't like him?'

'I couldn't give a shite one way or the other. He left the band and made a packet, good luck to him.'

'I saw Ronnie Richmond the other day. He blamed Bradley for breaking up The Suttons.'

'Richmond? I know the name. Hang on, didn't they used to make pork sausages somewhere in Litherland?' The singer went into the intro to *Dust My Blues* and

Kenny began beating the side of his hands against the bar like a demented karate champion.

'Do you blame Bradley for leaving The Baronets?'

The flailing hands didn't miss a beat. 'Up to him, the gobshite!'

I kept trying, though I felt he wasn't altogether with me. 'Kenny, there are whispers about Bradley's past. Some dark secret. Did you ever hear anything about that?'

'Bradley? You must be kidding. Nothing was ever secret with that get. If he raped your kid sister or stole your old lady's purse he'd do it in front of you then sell his story to the papers.'

'A real upfront guy, eh?'

'An arsehole. Say, are The Cruzads still playing? Do you need a drummer?'

'No,' I said, and, 'I *was* the drummer.'

'Ride on,' said Kenny, and turned away from me to concentrate on the middle eight. I looked around. The dance floor was full, couples writhing against one another. Both the hookers had acquired partners. I put my mind to Bradley Hope.

I was running out of suspects. The Suttons seemed clean, Kenny Leatherbarrow incapable, Ronnie Richmond unlikely. None of them seemed to know anything about any secret in Bradley's past. I still had three more members of The Baronets to check out although Verity Kennedy, racehorse trainer, was the only one I knew where to find.

Somehow, I felt adrift of the case and I now realised why. I was missing Maria. When I'd been involved in the Matt Scrufford affair, I'd discussed things with her. She was a good sounding board for my ideas and often came up with her own suggestions for investigation. Maria and I had been an item for a time but I'd felt the relationship was getting too claustrophobic and I'd eased myself away to the point where I'd stopped ringing her. I missed her but I didn't feel ready for her level of commitment.

Hilary had never been interested in my private eye career, if I could call it that. She was there for fun and a good time which, generally speaking, was what I wanted myself.

I hadn't officially broken up with Maria, I'd just not rung her for a while. Ominously, she hadn't rung me either. I made a decision to call her in the morning and felt better for that.

'Hi, Johnny. Not seen you for ages.' The barmaid came across and put her hand on my cheek. She'd left forty behind and was on the plump side of curvaceous but her smooth skin gave her face a young look and jet black curls hung to her shoulders.

'Shirley!' I took her hand and kissed it and looked straight into her deep brown eyes. They were eyes I'd gazed into on a pillow on several occasions in the past, nights when I'd been drinking in the Bamalama till two in the morning and we were both alone and ended up at Shirley's flat. 'You look as lovely as ever.'

'Creep. I look forty and I know it.' But she didn't. She looked just like Mary Wilson out of The Supremes who is gorgeous. 'What can I get you?'

I handed over my empty glass. 'I'll have another beer and get yourself something.'

'So, why've you never been to see me lately?' she asked, as she returned with the drinks. She had a port and lemon.

'I took on another job,' I said. 'Kept me busy for a few weeks.'

'As if yo' ain't got enough with yo' wireless and yo' flats.' Occasionally, slight overtones of West Indian crept into her otherwise broad Scouse accent. 'Say, talking of flats, have you got one for me, Johnny?'

'You're not thinking of leaving Princes Avenue after all this time?' I had happy memories of Shirley's flat.

She had the first floor of a large Victorian mansion with
high ceilings, huge fireplaces and spacious rooms which
she filled with Oriental rugs and posters and ornaments.
Incense burned in the background and she hung luminous
stars from the dark blue bedroom ceiling. Suddenly, I
wanted to be there again.

'Could be. The place is really going down. The
landlady won't mend anything. She seems to have lost
all interest.'

'What are you doing after you finish, Shirl?'

'Going home as ever, what else would I do? Do ya
wanna come?' She smiled coquettishly and leaned across
the bar to give me a quick kiss on the lips.

'Why not? We can discuss the flat over breakfast.'

I hung around till closing time, had another beer or
two. It got quiet at about one-thirty and Shirley came
round from behind the bar to have a couple of dances
with me.

Jonas came over at ten to two. 'Why don't you guys
go on home? I'll clear up for you. Alex'll give you a lift.'
After the moonshine I'd put away, I felt he'd need to.

Shirley needed no telling. 'I'll just get my coat,' she
said, and reappeared a couple of minutes later in a striped
fur. 'OK, let's go.'

Her flat looked no different since I'd last seen it, which
was six or seven months ago.

'Patchouli,' I observed, sniffing the oil burning inside
a porcelain Buddha on the mantelpiece, spreading a heavy
scent over the room.

'Clever of you,' said Shirley, removing her coat. She
put an Aretha Franklin CD on her midi system.

'I used to wear it as an aftershave in the Sixties.
Summer of love and all that.'

I sat on a huge old settee which was covered in a
woven Indian blanket. Shirley lowered herself next to
me. She was wearing a silk blouse embroidered with
Chinese dragons and a long skirt slit up the side enough

to expose most of her long thighs when she opened her legs.

We kissed. She rolled her tongue into and out of my mouth, exploring it, finding my own tongue and licking it and mixing her saliva with mine. At the same time, her hand slowly slid up my thigh and stroked the front of my jeans.

I undid the buttons on her blouse. Her large, black breasts swelled over a white, half-cup bra, exposing the purple aureolas of her swelling nipples.

'Just a minute,' she said and reached over to her handbag next to the settee. 'I've got these chocolate flavoured condoms I'd like to try. See if they taste as nice as Black Magic.'

We never made it to the bedroom.

Chapter Eight

'The landlady's done nothing for months. She won't put central heating in and my clothes have been turning mouldy in the wardrobe. It's friggin' freezing in the winter, Johnny, even with an electric blanket. And, what with the electric fires, it costs me a fortune in heating bills. Maybe I'm getting old but I can't stand the cold like I used to.'

Maybe I was getting old myself. My back couldn't stand too many nights sleeping on couches. I'd had to hobble to the kitchen where Shirley had made us eggs and bacon for breakfast. 'Have you asked her about the central heating?'

'All the time, but she keeps saying she can't afford it, the tight sod. The money she's had from this place over the years. Now she says she's going to sell up and she wants us all out.'

'She can't make you leave. You were here before the 1988 Rent Act, you're a protected tenant.'

'I bet she'll have ways of making things uncomfortable though.'

'Maybe.' I turned over a few ideas in my mind.

'So, what about it? Have you anywhere for me?'

'Your dressing gown's open.' She wore nothing underneath it. Her ebony skin was glowing after her shower and it was taking my mind off my breakfast.

'Sorry.' She pulled it to and blew me a kiss. 'Well, lover, do I get to have you as my landlord?'

'As it were,' I replied. 'I think so, though perhaps not

the way you were thinking of.' I finished the last piece
of toast and wiped my mouth with the napkin. 'How
about if I buy the house? Then you could stay in the
flat and I'd do it up for you.'

'Oh, Johnny. That sounds wonderful. But it's in really
bad nick, you know. Come and look in the bedroom.'

I could smell the mustiness as soon as she opened
the door. Liverpool City Council have issued a video
showing that ninety-seven per cent of damp is caused
by condensation, but I knew this was part of the other
three per cent. Probably the house needed repointing; the
damp could be penetrating through the brickwork, or lead
flashings had gone on the chimney breast. Nothing that
couldn't be cured, at a price.

Shirley's bed was king size and covered with black
silk sheets. I'd never seen those before. 'Bad, isn't it,'
she said, referring to the damp.

'It could be fixed.' I noted the areas of fungus around
the skirting boards, and the window sills showed early
signs of wet rot. When I pressed a key into them, it
pierced the wood like a hot knife through butter. 'What
are the other flats like?'

'I've only been in the one across the landing where
my friend Rose lives. Hers is worse than mine. She's
got black stains all down one wall.'

'I'll see what I can do.'

Shirley was still standing beside the bed. Slowly, she
removed her dressing gown. I was still in my T-shirt
and boxers. But not for long.

'Why didn't we sleep here last night?' I asked. 'All
this opulence going to waste.'

'Something to do with your wild passion,' she smiled,
'or impatience.'

'I've never slept on silk sheets.'

'You won't be sleeping on these, lover,' she whispered,
reaching for me.

I finally got away around eleven. Before I left, Shirley

made me have a bath with patchouli bubbles so I smelt like a San Francisco hippie.

'This'll cure your back,' she promised. 'Aromatherapy.' Hilary uses similar potions.

I wrote down the name and phone number of Shirley's landlady and told her I'd be in touch when I'd made some enquiries.

Shirley rang for a cab to take me back to the Bamalama to pick up my car. I was glad to see it in one piece. I drove first to my office in Aigburth Road. Geoffrey was surprised to see me.

'It's not Tuesday,' he said, and sniffed. 'Bloody hell, you smell like a New Orleans brothel.'

Geoffrey looks after my flats. Since I put a sign on the door saying *Property Manager*, he's taken to wearing a shirt and tie which doesn't suit him as he has no neck to speak of, his head merging into his huge body like Superman in the comic strip.

'Do they smell different in New Orleans?'

'Yeah, English ones smell of Dettol.'

'I'll take your word for it.'

'What's up then?'

I gave him Shirley's address on Princes Avenue. 'Check this out for me. It's supposed to be owned by a Mrs Clarke. Here's her phone number. Ask around a bit and find out why she's selling, if she needs the cash or whatever.'

'You thinking of buying it?'

'If the money suits. I've not bought anything for a while.' I'd enjoy doing up the flats. Perhaps I should have been an interior decorator. I certainly wasn't doing so well as a private eye at the moment.

'I thought you were too busy trying to be Liverpool's answer to Philip Marlowe.'

'Doesn't stop me being Donald Trump the rest of the time. I'll see you tomorrow. No other problems?'

There weren't. Geoffrey was capable of sorting most

things. He could get rid of bad tenants almost by looking at them and he was cheaper to feed than a Rottweiler.

I stopped off at the Everyman Bistro for a quick lunch before driving back to my flat and I spent the afternoon sorting the mail and picking out the records for the show.

I played *Ain't Got No Home* by Clarence Frogman Henry for Shirley and I found another Bradley Hope record, the first smash he had with The Baronets. I played it then asked on the air for people to ring in if they knew the current whereabouts of the group.

The scheme worked. We had over a dozen calls at the station. Most of them were about Verity Kennedy, but three people rang to say that lead guitarist Simon Butterworth was, variously, a doctor, a bus driver in Santa Barbara and a vet in Australia. One lady assured me that Tony Pritchard, the organist, had died in Yorkshire only a short time ago.

The last item I could check in the papers in the Library. Which reminded me – I'd forgotten to ring Maria. Now I had a reason to ring her, not that I needed one. Or perhaps I did and had subconsciously been waiting for an excuse to call.

I went straight home after the show. I needed an early night for a change.

Nine o'clock the next morning found me in The Diner in the Royal Liver Buildings having breakfast and reading the morning paper.

The *Daily Post* headline announced that Littlewoods were selling their stores. It came as no surprise. Not only had they been under-performing but the football pools side of the business had been decimated by the Lottery. I did neither. The odds favour the wrong side. Them, not me.

I rang Maria when I got back to the flat. She sounded pleased to hear from me and delighted that I had another case to work on.

'I'll check Tony Pritchard in the Obituaries,' she said, when I'd explained what I wanted. 'He should rate a line or two somewhere. What about the others?'

'There's only Simon Butterworth I can't trace. I've been reliably informed he's in Australia, America and England and he's a vet, a doctor and a bus driver.'

'Versatile man.'

'Verity Kennedy is a racehorse trainer and quite famous, I can find him easily enough, but I'll need your help with Tony Pritchard.'

'I'll see what I can do. When do you want to know?'

'How about dinner?' I said.

'Love it.'

'I'll pick you up at eight. I'll book a table at the Blundelsands Hotel.'

'Sounds good.'

After I put the phone down, I had a thought and logged on to the computer. If Scrumpy Jack was on the Internet, then surely there must be something about Bradley and The Baronets.

I typed in the group's name on the Alta Vista search engine and came up with half a dozen entries. One was a record store, two were collectors offering and selling souvenirs of the group. The fourth was a town called Bradley somewhere in the States, the fifth a list of baronets in England and the sixth a fan club, Bradley's Babes.

I clicked on to the Babes and up came a news-sheet all about Bradley. There were pages of e-mails, epitaphs and tributes, most of them drivel but I read through them all.

Only at the end was there any mention of The Baronets. Obviously, they'd long been discounted by Bradley's legion of followers. But then, The Baronets had never had a hit in America, and most Internet correspondence still originated there.

This one, though, was an e-mail from a girl (girl? more likely a granny) in Iowa, calling herself 'a Baronette', who wanted to remind the world not to forget Tony, Simon, Verity and Kenny who'd made it all possible for Bradley Hope.

I immediately sent an e-mail to her, asking her to get in touch with me if she had any information on where the boys were today.

I thought of Kenny Leatherbarrow in the Bamalama. Had he any idea that he was on the Internet and that women in Iowa were singing his praises round the world? It seemed unlikely, and he probably couldn't care less anyway. Rumour had it that he'd even sold his gold discs to buy whisky.

Geoffrey had news for me when I drove round to the office after lunch.

'That house you told me to check out. Mrs Clarke's selling up, going to live in Gran Canaria with her daughter. She's in her sixties.'

'Has she only got the Princes Avenue house?'

'She had another two but they've already been sold.'

I wondered why the buyer had left Princes Avenue out of the deal but Geoffrey had the answer ready. 'They were a pair together in Edge Lane. She sold them to a Housing Association but they weren't interested in the other one. Too far out of town.'

'What's she asking?'

'A hundred and twenty grand. It's bringing in twenty-four grand a year.'

I made a quick calculation. 'I'll give her a hundred and ten top bat but try for ninety.' I was working on around four and a half times the gross annual rental as a maximum. 'It's not worth any more and when the new fire regulations are made mandatory, as they will be before too long, it'll be worth a lot less. Is it on the open market yet?'

'No.'

'Right. Then try and tie it up today.'

'Don't you want to see it?'

'I've seen all I need to see.' Assuming the other flats were like Shirley's, I'd be looking at five lots of central heating and double glazing to install, not to mention all the work for the new building regs.

'If you say so, boss.' He addresses me as if I'm a football club manager. 'Anything else?'

I queried a couple of outstanding rents but Geoffrey had already collected them. A couple on Housing Benefit had done a runner owing £300.

'Are you going to sue the bastards?'

I remembered my solicitor's advice. Sue for profit, never for principle. 'Waste of time. They won't have any money when we win.'

'I'd like to get my hands on them.' His expression suggested they wouldn't enjoy the experience. 'They're just laughing at us.'

'So would I, but they'll only sue us for assault and then they'll laugh even more when they win and we end up having to pay them.'

I went back to the flat to change for the evening. I put on my new mustard jacket, black shirt and black chinos to meet Maria but first I had the show to do.

A few people rang in about Tony Blair's latest statement that, if New Labour were elected, kids of ten to thirteen were going to be made responsible in law for their crimes. Everyone thought it was a good idea. A lady from Croxteth wanted it lowered to seven because a bunch of primary-school kids were making her life hell on her council estate. The return of the stocks was a popular option. Probably do wonders for the soft fruit trade.

I played a couple of old US Bonds tracks. You could see where Gary Glitter got the idea for the sound from. I also played a track from the new Radiohead CD, which critics say could be the sound for the new millennium. I couldn't see it myself, but what did I know? It was No. 1 in the charts.

I was at Maria's for eight. She came down to the door when I rang her bell and we drove straight off to the Blundelsands Hotel.

We had a corner table in the Mauritius Restaurant which had been redesigned in the style of the old liners. Maria ordered the chicken provençale and I settled on the spicy salmon with black bean sauce.

'Right then,' she said, as we waited for the starters. 'Tell me about the new case. Why are you trying to trace this group?'

Maria looked ravishing. She'd pinned up her long, black hair in a pleat at the back and wore a calf-length, sleeveless black dress. The sapphire necklace matched her earrings. I couldn't imagine her at the Bamalama Club.

'Sorry. I was just thinking how sophisticated you look.'

'Thank you.' She smiled. 'So do you. That's a new jacket, isn't it? It suits you. They had a lot of those bright colours when I was in Germany last year.'

'It's very fashionable,' I said. 'We're always two or three years behind the Continent.'

'True.' It had been a while. We had the small talk to get through.

'Perhaps we ought to go over to Berlin or Paris to do our shopping,' I suggested.

'Then we'd be first with the new look. Good idea.'

'Yes, the case.' I finally got round to the point. 'Well, you read in the paper, did you, that Bradley Hope had been murdered?'

'Who could have missed it?'

'I got a phone call the next day from his father.' I went on to explain about Bert and the subsequent events. Maria listened attentively until I'd finished. Bert had told me to say nothing but Maria was my confidante.

'So the theory is, the blackmailer killed him because he'd got all he could out of him?'

'Something like that. Basically, I'm trying to find out who might have known the family secret and I'm going to work from the point that it must be someone from the Sixties who knew the Hopes then.'

Maria stopped me. 'Hang on. There's a mystery here. All the things we know about Bradley suggest he's a bit of a bastard. He's an alcoholic, he's promiscuous, he's arrogant and he's a drug-taker. Right? Yet, here he is, allowing himself to be blackmailed just to protect his old Dad's feelings. It just doesn't add up.'

'Perhaps it shows there's some good in everyone. Besides, as far as the groups are concerned, it's probably just sour grapes.'

'Hah!' Maria was sceptical. 'Besides, it's not as if having this baby is so terrible by today's standards, even if it was her brother's.'

'I don't think Mary and Bert lived by today's standards. Bradley would have known it would probably kill his Dad if it got out.'

'Mmmm . . . I'm not convinced.'

'But why should Bradley say he was being blackmailed when he wasn't? He couldn't have been asking his father for money. Bert hasn't any money to speak of. It doesn't make sense.'

'OK, we'll leave that for a minute. What about the suspects? You say you've eliminated some of them?'

'Yes, and I can't see it being Verity Kennedy although I suppose I should check him out. I really need to trace the rest of The Baronets. How did you get on with Tony Pritchard?'

'I got something, but not very much, I'm afraid. Most of it came from the *Yorkshire Post*. He was an estate agent in Harrogate and he died six weeks ago falling from a third-storey window.'

Chapter Nine

Alarm bells rang immediately. 'That sounds very suspicious. What was the verdict at the inquest?'

'Open. There was no suicide note, he wasn't under the influence of anything, and there was no evidence to suggest anyone else had been in the room with him.'

'Did anyone see him fall?'

'It just said he was found on the pavement after falling from the balcony of this flat. He'd been waiting for a prospective viewer who never turned up. The report quoted friends as being dismayed; he'd no money problems and the business had been going for years.'

'What about his family?'

'He left a widow and two children. They were "devastated" according to the papers. Pritchard was a devoted family man. No suggestion of affairs or anything untoward.'

We sat in silence to consider this. 'We've no reason to suppose there's any connection with Bradley Hope,' I said. 'All the same . . .'

'Could be just coincidence,' said Maria, and then the starters arrived and we abandoned further discussion while we ate.

'Do you want to come back to mine for a coffee?' she asked when we'd finished the meal.

'I'd like that.'

Maria's flat was only five minutes' drive away. I hadn't been there for weeks but I felt quite at home when I walked through the door.

'You've changed the pictures,' I said, as we entered her lounge. The two Hockney prints had been replaced by two Victorian landscapes in gilt frames.

'And decorated the room.' I looked around and saw she'd changed the colour of the carpet and curtains to a bottle green. The walls were still white but a new green suite had taken the place of the blue one.

'It looks nice, cosier somehow. But isn't there some psychological reason why a woman changes her rooms around? She wants to change her life or something?'

I remember our old singer Mally Scrufford once saying that if a married woman bought a dog, he always knew she was available. 'It means her husband isn't paying her enough attention and she's seeking love and affection,' he explained. And, of course, Mally, being the archetypal ladies' man, was always willing to supply it.

'I don't know about changing my life. After all, I'm still at the Library and, despite the fact that I've not seen you for weeks, here you are again, back in my life.'

'I didn't know I'd been out of it. We've talked on the phone.' I sat on the new sofa and she brought over the drinks, coffee for her, tea for me.

'It's been nice tonight,' she said, 'being out together again. I thought I must have upset you.'

'I'm sorry. After the Matt Scrufford episode, I just drifted away from things. I needed some time on my own.' I didn't want to go into it in any more detail. I'd still seen Hilary during this period. The truth was, I was frightened of too much commitment with Maria. Sitting here now, though, I had to admit I was glad to be with her.

Would I have been so keen if I hadn't had Hilary as well?

I didn't stay the night. I judged it would be presumptuous after being out of touch for so long, but I promised to ring her later in the week.

When I got back to the flat, I switched on my laptop

and checked my e-mail messages. It was just after midnight but it was still mid-afternoon in Iowa. Could there be a reply already from the 'Baronette'?

There was.

Her name was Jane, she told me from across cyberspace. She'd helped run The Baronets' Fan Club back in England during their Sixties' heyday but now she was a farmer's wife in Iowa with five children. However, she'd kept in touch with two of the group.

Kenny had disappeared from sight about ten years ago, she said. I could help her out there. She'd stopped hearing from Vezzy but she knew he was training racehorses in England. As I did myself. Tony was in Yorkshire and had bought property with the money he'd made from the group. She hadn't heard from him for a little while. She wouldn't again.

Which left the one I was waiting for.

Simon was in regular contact with her by e-mail. They had kept up a correspondence over the years which was made easier than ever by the new technology. He was a surgeon, working at a hospital in the Lake District.

I immediately sent back an e-mail to Jane thanking her and giving her the sad news of Tony's death. I told her that I'd seen Kenny and that I'd pass on her regards to him, and I asked her to let me have any further information about Simon, leaving my phone number in case she might want to talk to me. And then I went to bed.

The second e-mail from Jane was waiting for me when I woke at eight o'clock. What efficiency! Not only did she give me an e-mail address for Simon Butterworth but she also included the name, address and telephone number of the hospital he worked at and a small photograph he'd sent her.

All this from Iowa in just a few hours and half the cost of a call to Directory Enquiries!

I studied the photo. Soon, I suppose, everyone will

have digital cameras and the only place you'll see a roll
of film will be in a museum.

It was obviously a family snapshot because a smil-
ing blonde woman and two small girls stood alongside
Butterworth, arms entwined. He was wearing shorts and
a short-sleeved shirt and appeared fit and sun-tanned. He
didn't look like a blackmailer but I should know by now
that appearances don't count for much.

This information didn't help solve my problem though.
Simon Butterworth appeared to have as little reason to
blackmail Bradley Hope as did Vezzy Kennedy or the
Sutton brothers. All seemed successful enough in their
chosen careers that they hardly needed to resort to crime
to augment their incomes.

However, I felt I ought to follow up every lead
and the Lake District was only an hour and a half's
drive away.

I made some breakfast, waited till nine o'clock then
rang the hospital. I was put in touch with Simon Butterworth's paging service who instructed me to leave a
message, saying he'd contact me in the near future.

I busied myself with some paperwork in the flat
and it was mid-afternoon when he finally got round
to calling. I explained who I was and told him I wanted
to interview him about his time with The Baronets for a
Tribute to Bradley Hope piece I was doing on my radio
programme.

He seemed quite amenable, which was what I'd hoped.
After all, he was keeping in touch with Jane from his old
Fan Club and who knows who else from his days as a
pop star? He obviously wasn't ashamed of his erstwhile
profession.

'I'm off tomorrow,' he said, 'if you can get up
here.'

We fixed up to meet the following morning at his
home. He lived in a village called Crook, on the road
between Kendal and Bowness.

I was looking forward to the meeting but first, I had a radio programme to do – and it turned out to be a lively show. A Conservative minister, David Evans, had said the previous day that he thought all rapists ought to be castrated or strung up. This had caused a bit of a storm in the media so I had a phone-in about it.

Most people who rang in agreed with him, although several woolly minded liberals thought Evans was the one who should be strung up for saying such awful things about those poor misunderstood rapists.

I tended to side with Richard Littlejohn's comments in the *Daily Mail*, that the real question was not 'Do you castrate them?' but 'Do you use a rusty Stanley knife?'

Then I played P.P. Arnold's *The First Cut is the Deepest*, which had Ken wincing in the other studio.

After the show, I went back to the flat. I decided I would ring Verity Kennedy and try to arrange a meeting for the weekend. His number was easy enough to find but the man himself was not so forthcoming.

'I've nothing I want to say about Bradley Hope. That part of my life is over.'

I explained that I was doing a tribute programme to Bradley on my radio show and was looking for some quotes from each member of his old group. 'You obviously prospered after the group split,' I said ingratiatingly but he wasn't impressed.

'So why don't we talk about Greenfly? That was a more successful band than The Baronets.'

I pointed out that as it was Bradley who had died, it was obvious that it was that aspect of his career I was interested in. 'What was he like to work with?'

'A shit. Thought he knew everything. Should never have been in a group at all. A group's a team effort.'

As someone who shared Bradley Hope's low opinion of teams, I wasn't impressed by Mr Kennedy's sentiments but I still wanted to meet him.

'Not interested,' he said, when I suggested a visit.

'When did you last see Bradley?' I asked, anxious to find something out before he put down the phone.

'Thirty years ago and I haven't missed him.' And this time he did replace the receiver.

I made myself a meal and pondered over the character of Bradley Hope. The man was an enigma.

The musicians who played with him said he was an arrogant sod, yet wasn't this just jealousy? His subsequent success had proved the wisdom of his decision to go solo.

He was supposed to be an uncaring libertine yet he allowed himself to be blackmailed to save his family's feelings. Or did he? Maria wasn't comfortable with that idea.

Who was the real Bradley Hope?

Maybe the answer lay in the Lake District with Simon Butterworth.

Chapter Ten

I set off soon after breakfast. The traffic on the M62 and M6 was pretty light, mainly large trucks headed for Scotland. I came off the motorway on the A590, by-passed Kendal and took the 'B' road that leads down to Bowness and Lake Windermere.

Crook is just a couple of miles along that road, a typical small Lakeland village with a few cottages and a pub. It was close to eleven o'clock when I arrived. A spiral of smoke rose from one of the cottage chimneys and a pale sun was shining from behind a row of poplars.

The Butterworths lived in a white cottage, set off the road, with pink clematis growing up the walls round the front porch, and room for five parked cars on the gravelled driveway.

A Mercedes 450 convertible stood outside the garage. I wondered if he'd bought it from the Suttons but the registration letters were SJB, not an Isle of Man numberplate, more like Simon Butterworth's initials.

Surgery was obviously paying well.

He answered the door himself. The photo I'd seen must have been recent because he looked the same except the shorts and shirt had been replaced by designer jeans and a cable-knit jumper, an outfit more suited to the March climate.

'You must be Johnny Ace,' he said. 'Simon Butterworth.' We shook hands and he led me through the hall to a dining-kitchen at the rear of the cottage, with patio windows overlooking a huge back garden. On the lawn,

a children's swing and a bird-table stood beside a row
of fruit trees, and in the corner was a rockery with an
ornamental pond set against a backdrop of the hills.

'We get herons,' he said, noticing my glance, 'eating
the fish.'

'It's a lovely spot, have you lived here long?'

'About three years. Ever since I took the job up here.
Before this we lived in London so the children thought
it was wonderful moving to the country. So do I, as a
matter of fact. Would you like tea or coffee?'

'Tea would be nice.'

He carried on the conversation as he filled the kettle.
'And you? You used to be a musician yourself at one
time, you said?'

He was making it easy for me. 'That's right. I played
drums in a group called The Cruzads. You've probably
not heard of them but we did all the usual clubs in the
Merseybeat days.'

He shook his head. 'No, I'm afraid not. Apart from
the drummer, Kenny, we were all from Manchester so
we didn't know that many Liverpool bands.'

I took out my portable cassette-recorder. 'If I can just
ask you a few questions on tape?'

'Sure, no problem.'

I set up the microphone and we took up positions side
by side at the kitchen table. 'How did you come to join
up with Bradley Hope originally?'

'It was our manager, Wendy Feld.'

'A lady manager? That was unusual in those days.'

'I suppose so, although Adam Faith had one.'

'Jewish as well, by the sound of it. All the right
ingredients for a successful career in show-business.'

Simon looked embarrassed at my political incorrect-
ness. I'd managed to be sexist and racist all in one go.
'I suppose so,' he said. 'Anyway, she wasn't keen on
the singer we had at the time, a guy called Howard
Wolstenholme. He called himself The Baron. And The

Baronets, you see. Wendy said he sang flat. She'd seen Bradley performing with The Suttons in Liverpool and signed him up to front our band.'

'How did The Baron feel about this?'

'Pretty brassed off, actually. Especially as we had our first hit less than three months later.'

So, I thought, another potential enemy of Bradley's, a deposed singer with a grudge. 'What happened to him?'

'No idea. I think he joined another Manchester band but I've not a clue what he did after that.'

That would be in 1963. Wherever would I find him now? And surely he didn't really stand up as a likely candidate to blackmail his successor. Living in Manchester, how would he have found out about the Hope family? He probably never even met Bradley. If there was anyone he would want to vent his wrath on, it would probably be Wendy Feld.

I decided to leave Howard Wolstenholme out of the equation until all the other avenues had been explored. I hoped this wasn't a mistake.

'Your career with Bradley didn't actually last all that long, did it?'

'No, only about two years. We had three hits then he buggered off to the States and that was the end of it. We had a couple more records released but they didn't do anything.'

'Did this upset you?'

'Me personally, you mean? No, because I was doing my A levels at the time. The music was only a hobby for me. I would have given it up to go to university anyway, even if Bradley had stayed.'

'Even if you'd carried on having hits?'

'Oh yes. I always wanted to be a doctor. The music, as I say, was secondary.'

'But you still stay in contact with your show-business days?' I explained how I'd got his number from Jane, his old Fan Club secretary.

'I'm one of those people who like to keep in touch with everyone. I enjoyed being one of The Baronets, all the more because I had my career, and the same applies now. I'd be quite happy to do a TV show with The Baronets or make another record, not that we're ever likely to be asked.'

He couldn't have put in a better plug if he'd bought advertising.

'I don't know about that,' I said. 'Look at The Monkees, they're touring again after all these years.' I brought the conversation back to Bradley. 'Unfortunately, it can never be Bradley and The Baronets any more.'

'A terrible loss.' He didn't sound mortified. 'He was a very talented performer.'

'How about the others in the group?'

'I'd known Verity Kennedy since we were kids. We went to the same school in Didsbury. Vezzy did pretty well after we broke up. He was in a group called Greenfly who had a few hits.'

'What made him give it up?'

'He was always mad about horses. As soon as he got a chance to make a living with them, he took it.'

'Do you ever see him?'

'Our families send Christmas cards and we meet up at odd times. He travels round the country a lot. Haven't seen him for a couple of years though.'

'And the others?'

'Tony's in Yorkshire somewhere. I used to be in contact with him when he was doing this surveyors' course in Leeds but he went to work for an estate agent in another part of Yorkshire, I'm not sure where, and I never heard from him again.'

He didn't seem to know Tony was dead and I didn't bother to enlighten him.

'Kenny?'

'I never knew quite how we came to have Kenny

in the group because he was from Liverpool and not many Scousers came up to audition for Manchester groups.'

'Is that what happened?'

'Yes, and we couldn't understand a word he said, partly because of his accent but mainly because he was always pissed.'

'He got the job though.'

'He was a bloody good drummer. Crazy, mind you.'

I smiled. 'I believe drummers often are.'

He looked at me. 'Of course, I was forgetting you were one. I didn't mean . . .'

'Just joking. So where did Kenny go next?'

'Back to Liverpool, once The Baronets finished. I suppose he's still there. He's not the sort who travels well.' He made Kenny sound like a parcel. 'Or who keeps in touch.'

'What about Bradley? Had you seen anything of him in recent years?'

'Never clapped eyes on him since the day he went to America and that was, let me see, 1965. Bradley was a person who moved on, and good luck to him.'

'I thought you liked keeping in touch with people?'

'Oh, I wrote to him once or twice but he never wrote back. But then, his career had taken off. He probably never received my letters.'

He smiled and looked me in the eye. It was a gesture he made several times during the conversation. I decided he'd been studying one of those American books on the art of successful social intercourse.

'You got on all right with him, then?'

'Fine. We didn't mix much socially, our interests were different, but we had no fights in the band. As far as I was concerned, it was a business; we all had our part to play.'

I made a point of switching off the tape-recorder. 'A couple of people, off the record, have mentioned some trouble in connection with Bradley, something to do with blackmail. Did you ever hear anything?'

His denial was swift and vehement. Maybe too much so, I couldn't tell. 'Ridiculous. Whoever said such a thing?'

'Apparently, Bradley had some dark secret that somebody had found out.'

He looked puzzled. 'You're saying someone was blackmailing Bradley? When was this?'

'Sorry, I didn't mean in the Sixties, this is within the last few months.'

'Has this got some connection with his murder?'

'Quite possibly, but I don't know what.'

The kettle reached auto-stop with a sharp click, steam pouring from the spout, and he stood up to make the tea. 'What exactly is your angle on this? I thought you were here to talk about the music.'

'I am. I was just curious, that's all. Bradley Hope didn't seem the type of person who would be blackmailed. I wondered what on earth he could have done. Perhaps something connected with his family, I don't know.'

'I never met his family.'

'Did you never see his sister?' A trick question.

'I didn't know he had one. I don't recall him ever mentioning it and I certainly never met her. We actually played very few gigs round Merseyside after Bradley joined. We had our first hit soon afterwards and started going on nationwide tours with Roy Orbison and Gene Pitney and The Beatles and the like.'

'Do you miss all that?'

'Of course, it was fun at the time, but I'd hardly be doing it now at my age, would I?' I thought of Murphy and The Monotones playing at the Albion. 'And I enjoy being a surgeon a lot more.'

We chatted quietly as we drank the tea. Simon showed little interest in any gossip surrounding Bradley and I found it impossible to believe he could be the black-mailer. I looked around the room at the mahogany Ercol dresser and dining set and, across the patio, the conservatory built out from the lounge. It didn't look like he needed the money. I made a move to leave.

'I've got a couple of songs I've written if you'd like to play them on your show. They're ones I've recorded at home but the quality's good. I've got an eight-track set up in my study.'

Perhaps he would welcome a night sitting in with Murphy and The Monotones after all. I took the cassette he offered.

'Shame about the way Bradley died,' he said, as he saw me to the door. 'Not an end you'd wish on anybody. They've got someone for it, it said in the paper.'

'So I believe,' I said noncommitally.

'Liverpool's getting like New York, isn't it? Mind you, it's the same anywhere. A Sister at my hospital was attacked in her own house last month and she lives in a little country village near Kirby Lonsdale.'

I thanked him for the interview and climbed into the Toyota. It hadn't been a wasted journey because I'd been able to eliminate another suspect, but it hadn't taken me any further in finding the right one.

I drove back to the village and stopped for a bite to eat at the pub. The Sun Inn was part of a terrace of cottages and had a slate floor, low wooden beams and whitewashed walls, on which were hung old prints, most of them featuring gundogs. Not the sort of pub you find in Liverpool.

I had the pea and ham soup with a hot white roll.

Instead of returning home immediately, I carried on to Bowness, parked alongside the church in the middle of the village and walked down to the edge of Lake Windermere.

It was very peaceful. I watched some swans gliding across the water close to the shore. Despite it being out of season, there were plenty of boats out on the lake. I wondered how many were lying on the bottom and whether they'd ever be found? Would Bradley Hope have ever been found if the weights tied to his legs had not come adrift?

How long had Bradley been in the water before he surfaced? That had never been mentioned. He could have been floating around for days. And where was he killed? I only knew he'd been found in Birkenhead. It didn't follow he was killed there.

I realised there were a lot of things I didn't know about Bradley Hope's death and maybe I ought to start finding them out.

Chapter Eleven

On the way back to Liverpool, I stopped off at Forton Services for a drink and phoned Geoffrey from the café. Nobody looks at you any more when you use a mobile phone in public. Probably because nearly everyone else seems to have one nowadays, even schoolkids.

'Any news on Princes Avenue?'

'Looking good, boss. I offered eighty-five k to start off with as a taster, just to see which way the wind was blowing.'

'And?'

'They made a lot of noise about insulting their client then they came back at a ton so I upped it to ninety and I think we might be in at ninety-five. They're getting back to me after lunch. Where are you?'

'Lake District.'

'I thought you couldn't swim.'

'Very funny. I'll be back in a couple of hours. See if you can get it tied up by then.'

'Before you go, Hilary rang to remind you to pick her up at the hospital after your show.'

I hadn't forgotten. We were going to see the new version of *101 Dalmations* with live dogs.

Driving back down the M6, I considered my next move. I felt that all The Baronets could now be ruled out. Two of them were rich and respectable, one was drunk and incapable, and one was dead.

What was it Winston Churchill once said? 'Never take dead men for granted.' Or was that Lazarus?

Maybe a visit to Harrogate might be in order. I should find out more about Tony Pritchard's demise and talk to his relatives, because the only suspect I had left other than him was David Warner – and he was a long shot at best.

An hour later I was back at the office. Geoffrey was grinning as I walked in; he held up his fingers in a cupped gesture.

'Go on, then,' I said. 'Tell me the good news.'

'Ninety-five – what do you think about that?'

'Brilliant. When do we take over?'

'First of May if the old girl doesn't change her mind.'

'Sounds good. I'll go round tomorrow to draw up a works schedule, then we can get the men started on the renovations.' I have a team of workmen on call to carry out repairs and maintenance on the flats. 'I take it she'll give me a key once we've exchanged.'

'You can ask her yourself. She wants to see you.'

'Me? Why? Can't the solicitor deal with it?'

'She wants to know her house is in good hands.'

'She can't care that much about it, otherwise she'd have spent some money and made it halfway habitable. I could have got chronic rheumatism after a night there.'

Geoffrey didn't enquire why I'd spent the night at Princes Avenue. He was used to my unconventional nocturnal habits and wisely kept his mouth shut on the topic. I'd spent the night in many of my flats over the years.

'Anyway, I made an appointment for you tomorrow at four if that's all right?'

I said it was. 'In the meantime, can you get me David Warner's number? He's the entertainment agent with an office somewhere on Dale Street.'

'I've heard of him. He's pretty big, isn't he?'

'As big as you'll get outside London.'

After his success with his dubious dealings in the

Sixties, Warner found a new scam for the next decade and by the end of the Seventies, he'd doubled his fortune.

Fans would pay to see The Incomparable Drifters, only to find they bore no relation to The Drifters who'd had all the hit records or, indeed, to The Original Drifters who were playing for Warner on the same night in several other towns, often on the same bill as The Original Temptations and The Fabulous Platters.

You couldn't do it today, not with pop music on TV at every turn, not to mention newspapers, magazines, videos and the Internet. People are too sophisticated and well informed now, but way back then, David Warner cleaned up.

'I created more jobs for young out-of-work blacks than the Labour government,' he used to boast. 'And some of them could sing too.'

He used the money wisely, investing it in his business until, by the Eighties, he turned legit. He put on pop and classical concerts at the Royal Albert Hall, managed several major recording acts and was part-owner of a chain of night clubs around the country.

So why, with all that going for him, would he suddenly take up blackmail?

However, I'd spoken to the others so why leave him out? And, unlike the others, I did know that he had seen Bradley Hope within a few weeks of his death.

'Here we are.' Geoffrey handed across the open page and I dialled the number. A secretary answered.

'Mr Warner, please. It's Johnny Ace.'

'Just a moment.' She switched me over to a recording of one of Warner's artistes wailing her latest record. It wasn't pleasant. I would have preferred that mechanical version of *Greensleeves* that other offices have on their phones.

'Johnny. Long time no see. How are you?' He spoke with the eager insincerity of an American Bible salesman on speed.

'Fine, David. And you?'

He was fine too. I told him my standard story, that I was planning a tribute to Bradley Hope and could I do a short interview with him? He didn't seem over-enthusiastic but I emphasised the publicity angle. 'Bring a few of your current records down and I'll give them a play.'

A silence, then: 'Yes, OK then. Why not? Tomorrow's Friday – how about eleven in the morning? Why don't you come to my office?'

'If you like.' We exchanged a few more pleasantries and I put down the phone.

'Not a man you'd trust with your life savings,' I said to Geoffrey.

'Back on the private eye job then, are you?'

'Something like that.'

'Not that it's any of my business, but you want to watch yourself. Some people can get nasty if you start interfering in their affairs.'

'If that happens, I might have to extend your duties to minder.'

Geoffrey clenched his fists like a white Mike Tyson and said he'd be happy to take on the job.

I picked up the phone again and dialled the Library. Maria was on duty and answered the phone herself.

'How do you fancy a weekend in Harrogate?' I asked. 'If you're not working, that is.'

'I am, but I think I can get someone to swap with me. Yes, that'd be lovely, but why Harrogate? Oh, don't tell me . . .'

'You've got it – Tony Pritchard.'

'But he's dead.'

'It's the family I want to talk to. They might know something. Do you think you could find an address for them? I presume his estate agency is still in business.'

'I think I should change my name to Watson. I'll do what I can. When are we coming back?'

'Sunday afternoon, if that's OK? I'll pick you up at yours about ten on Saturday morning.'

'I'll be ready. See you then.'

So that was it, meetings organised with my last two leads. If these produced nothing, I'd probably give up. It seemed less and less likely to me now that Bradley was being blackmailed, though why he should tell Bert a lie about it was beyond me.

I was at David Warner's office prompt at eleven the next morning but he kept me waiting in his reception area for fifteen minutes. Luckily, I was in a sanguine mood and the receptionist did make me a cup of strong tea.

It had been a good night with Hilary. We'd both enjoyed the film, although I couldn't see the idea of real animals replacing cartoon characters catching on in a big way. Imagine Mickey Mouse played by a brown three-inch-long rodent or a six-foot grizzly as Yogi Bear!

Afterwards, we'd brought fish and chips back to the flat and opened a bottle of Albert Etienne champagne which we enjoyed in bed.

I took note of the replica gold discs hanging round the walls between the framed photographs of Warner shaking hands with various luminaries of show-business. It all represented a lot of money.

On the coffee table were the latest editions of *Music Week*, *Variety*, *Billboard* and other trade magazines. I glanced through them. The Spice Girls were hoping to be the first group to score four No. 1 hits in a row with their new single. I didn't doubt for a moment that they would make it.

A buzzer sounded and the receptionist leaned across her desk. 'You can go in now, Mr Ace.' She had a small stud in her nose which glinted when it caught the light.

Warner was behind a huge mahogany desk on which were assembled a variety of phones, faxes and computers.

He stood up and stretched his arm through them to shake my hand.

'I heard you'd gone into the private eye business,' was his opening statement. I was taken unawares. 'So what are you investigating at the moment? Don't tell me. Bradley Hope was really killed by a well-known Liverpool drugs syndicate and you're hot on their trail.'

'Not quite, but he certainly wasn't killed by Michael Mitchell.' Gone was the pretence of conducting an interview about Bradley's musical career. I didn't know whether this was a good or a bad thing.

'And how do you know that?' Warner settled himself in his high-backed leather chair and lit a cigar. He didn't offer me one.

I avoided answering his question. 'There's a whisper going around about blackmail.'

Warner laughed heartily, a sound that lacked humour. 'Well, he didn't blackmail *me*.'

'You've got it wrong. It was Bradley who was the victim. Were you blackmailing him?'

He laughed even louder and this time he did sound amused.

'You are joking, aren't you? That little turd.'

'Why did he come to see you?'

'Why does anyone come to an agent? He wanted me to manage him. His career was on the rocks and he thought I could resurrect it for him.'

'And could you?'

'I told him, his only chance was to get himself killed and we could go to town on the Memorial Album CD Box Set.'

'Nice to see someone takes your advice,' I said drily. 'How did he react to your suggestion?'

'As you'd expect. Whined about his misfortune, how he should still be a megastar, blamed everyone but himself.' This didn't seem like the confident, arrogant Bradley of old.

'So you turned him down?'

'In a word, I told him to sod off.'

'And when did you next see him?'

'I didn't. Never heard from him again.'

'And that meeting took place when?'

'January,' he replied. 'My secretary'll have the exact date.' He stood up. 'Does that answer all your questions then, or are we going through a charade of talking about his music?'

'But, David, the name Bradley Hope must still have some box office appeal. After all, he was a big name for years. Surely you could have done something for him?'

'Johnny, I'm a businessman and, of all businesses, show-business is the last place you'll find sentiment. You're a DJ, you should know the score.'

'Yes, I do, but there's people who can build a whole career on one hit record. Ricky Valance is still making a living on the back of *Tell Laura I Love Her* and Wee Willie Harris never even had a hit record, yet he's still getting gigs.'

'Wee Willie Harris and Ricky Valance have an act. They can put on a show. Bradley Hope couldn't. He'd had it, he was washed up, he was a mess. He could no more have gone on stage and given a performance than Elvis Presley could have climbed out of his coffin to do the London Palladium.'

'That's funny. I heard Elvis was alive and well and working in a chip shop in Millom.'

'Oh, very good.' He rose to his feet as if to conclude the interview, but I remained seated.

'How did Bradley seem when he left?'

He paused to consider. 'Dejected, I suppose.'

'He didn't threaten you?'

'Good Lord, no.' I remembered what had happened to that guy who'd threatened Warner in the past. He'd been hung by his ankles from the upstairs window. At least his new offices were on the ground floor. 'He just shuffled quietly away. Never heard from him again. And now, if that's all, I have a busy schedule . . .'

He saw me to the door. He didn't say, 'It's been a long time, we must meet more often,' as we shook hands, and I felt as though I'd been dismissed as I stood on the Dale Street pavement.

I also felt there was a lot that David Warner was hiding.

Chapter Twelve

A steady rain was falling. I walked down to the Pier Head, keeping to the side of the buildings to avoid the spray from passing vehicles. Since privatisation, there seem to be a lot more buses on the road.

I stopped off for something to eat at The Diner. It was the height of the lunch-hour and the suits from the upper-floor offices of the Royal Liver Buildings had formed into two queues, the eat-ins and the takeaways.

I lined up with the diners and went for a mushroom omelette and a mineral water. All the tables were full but I managed to squeeze on the end of one, alongside two young trainees from an accountant's office upstairs. They spent the meal discussing self-assessment and the extra work they believed it would bring in to their profession.

I didn't listen to the details of their argument. I was too busy contemplating the results of my investigations over the last week. There was precious little to show for all my travels.

None of the musicians who might have had a grudge against Bradley Hope could be seriously considered as possible blackmailers. That much I did feel I'd established.

I wasn't hopeful of learning anything from my visit to Harrogate either, but I'd promised Maria the weekend away so I was committed to the trip.

Bradley Hope was an unlikely victim, therefore was

Bert Hope's story of his son being blackmailed a
figment of his imagination – or had Bradley been
lying to his father for whatever reason? Or had Bert
been lying to *me*?

I didn't know the answers and, without some insight
into the background of Bradley's last weeks on earth,
my chances of finding the killer, or killers, looked
non-existent.

I finished my omelette but the mineral water was
contaminated with peach flavouring and I left it. I like
water to taste of water not a perfumery.

I walked back to the flat to collect the car. My
appointment with the owner of Shirley's flat in Princes
Avenue was at four.

Mrs Clarke was exactly as I'd imagined – a hard-
bitten, streetwise Scouser who'd obviously come up the
hard way and wouldn't be an easy touch for anybody.
I was amazed Geoffrey had got the house for ninety-
five grand.

She was small and wiry and slightly stooped. She
wore a grey anorak and a pair of cream slacks. Her
face was sharp and heavily lined, with a Barbra
Streisand nose and a chin that reminded me of Mr
Punch. The crowning glory was her hair, an obvious wig. Nobody had golden curls like that in their
sixties.

'So you're Johnny Ace. I've heard your show.'

'I'm glad you like it.'

'I don't. You play some crap records. I prefer that Billy
Butler and Wally on the other station of a morning.' She
had a nicotine-stained voice that was badly in need of a
Zube and her accent suggested her formative years had
been spent in the Dingle.

'Everyone to their own taste,' I replied icily.

'I'm selling this house too cheap,' she said, as we
walked across the litter-strewn weeds to the front door.
'My solicitor says I'm giving it away.'

I observed the piece of cardboard covering a broken pane of glass in the front door that I hadn't noticed when Shirley had brought me here the Sunday before. Possibly because it was night-time then and the light bulbs in the hall had been missing.

I said nothing as she produced a set of keys and opened the door of Flat One. 'Let to two students,' she informed me, 'paying seventy pounds a week.'

It couldn't have been anybody else but students living there. The high lounge ceiling was painted black, fantasy posters covered the walls and there were books everywhere. I read the titles. They were mostly history and psychology, with a good sprinkling of science fiction, horror and fantasy plus the obligatory Steinbeck and Kerouac.

'No central heating?' I asked, affecting surprise.

'Don't need it,' she retorted. 'There's an electric fire in here and in the bedroom.'

Two mattresses lay side by side on the floor of the bedroom, half-covered by unmade bedclothes. A packet of Mates lay on the faded Axminster carpet next to several empty beer glasses; ominous patches of black mould obscured the woodchipped walls in several places.

'Calor-gas heaters,' she said, noticing my glance. 'That's what causes the condensation. I tell them not to use them.'

'They obviously don't feel your electric heating's adequate,' I said, 'or they can't afford it, though I think you'll find that it's actually rising damp. What are the cellars like?'

They were like dungeons and wet through into the bargain. Furthermore, as we progressed round the property, I noticed there was settlement in the gable, probably caused by rotted joists collapsing.

The old chimney-stacks needed dropping, both front and back walls needed repointing and, judging by the addled plaster and ruined decorations in the top flats, a new roof was needed.

I let her show me round the other five flats. Two of the tenants were in and I was introduced as a builder. 'They get nervous if they think you're selling up,' Mrs Clarke explained, 'and give notice. Of course,' she added quickly, 'if you wanted it empty . . .'

I hastily reassured her. 'No, I want to keep all the tenants.'

Shirley was out. I smiled as I was shown round her flat. Mrs Clarke described her as a professional lady with a job in the city. The blue dressing gown with yellow moons was hanging behind the bedroom door and the familiar smell of patchouli still permeated the atmosphere.

'I think ninety-five's a fair price,' I said, as we completed the tour. 'There's a lot of work needed to bring it up to scratch, not to mention all the new fire and building regulations.'

When I mentioned the building regs, she went quiet. 'It's getting too much for me at my age,' she murmured. 'I've sold the others. This is the last one. They was my husband's, you know, but he died five years ago. It's been a struggle for me to keep them going. I'll be seventy next birthday.'

'You're better off out of it,' I said, and I meant it. 'What will you do when they're gone?'

She told me about her daughter in Gran Canaria. 'I'll miss it round here, mind. I've lived here all me life. I were born not two miles away, down the Dingle, in Powis Street. Do you know it?'

Did I know it? Powis Street was where the Hopes used to live, where Bradley's sister died and the whole business first started.

'You didn't by any chance know a family called Hope, did you?'

'Bradley Hope, you mean, the singer?' I nodded.

'He's been murdered, you know,' she said thoughtfully. 'Something funny there if you ask me.'

'You did know them then?'

'Course I did. Bert and Mary Hope lived across the road from us when I were a girl. Lovely couple, they were, but they had an awful tragedy with their daughter.'

'How do you mean?'

'Well, their Alison died when she were just fifteen. She were having a baby and something went wrong.'

'At fifteen?' I feigned ignorance. 'She couldn't have been married.'

'She wasn't.'

'Did they know the father?'

'If they did, they never let on. All sorts of rumours was going round, as you'd imagine. The lads round there was a wild bunch, even in them days, before they had teenagers as such like they do today.'

'What year would it have been?'

'Let me see, I think it were 1952, the year King George died. Young Bradley were only a nipper at the time. And then the other brother ran away from home. To join the Army his parents said, but everyone thought it were to get away from the Law. He were no good, was their Norman.'

'In what way?'

'Stealing, bullying, sagging off school, that sort of thing. He'd got in with a bad crowd. There'd been a lot of burglaries round about. Anyway, the family left the district soon after, went to live up Bootle way. We never heard of them again, until their Bradley became famous, of course. He did well, did little Bradley. Always was a happy little soul. Cocky with it, mind you, but he always had a smile.'

A smoothie, I thought, even as a kid. 'And you never knew where Norman went?'

'No. He'd gone for good – although funnily enough,

I saw one of my old neighbours the other day and she mentioned Norman Hope. Said she'd heard he were living out in Kirkby in one of the tower blocks. Hey,' she added, as if the thought had just come to her, 'you've not said how much you're giving me for the furniture.'

She was trying it on, of course. I'd have been lucky to get two hundred pounds for the lot at the auctions and told her so.

'All those sofas and beds are illegal now, they're not fireproof. But I tell you what, as a gesture of goodwill, I'll give you two hundred and fifty if you'll give me the keys and let me start the work once we've exchanged.'

She agreed to that. 'Very nice to have met you, Mr Ace. I hope you can find some better records for your programme.'

I offered her a lift home as it was still raining but she declined. 'It's all right, I've got the Merc parked round the corner. It doesn't do to let the residents see it. My husband used to collect the rents on a push bike.'

I climbed into the RAV4, wondering if I should change it for a Lada to prevent unrest amongst my new tenants.

I drove straight to the radio station. I needed a couple of hours to catch up with paperwork, fill in playlist forms, deal with requests, sort out new CDs etc.

I thought about Norman Hope. If he was really in Kirkby, there was every chance I could find him. I wondered if Bradley had found him and, if so, what that would have meant.

But before I went looking for Norman, I needed to rule out Tony Pritchard's involvement.

Just in case she listened to my programme for once, I played Shakin' Stevens's *This Old House* for Mrs Clarke, then I dug out Wee Willie Harris's *Rockin' at the 2 I's* – one of the better British efforts at rock'n'roll which should have been a mega-hit but wasn't. I dedicated that to David Warner 'who'd always enjoyed Willie's stage act'. Perhaps someone would hear it and book him for the Empire. I also played Della Reese's *Someone To Watch Over Me*, which had just been re-released after twenty years and still sent shivers up my spine. I could imagine her singing it in the Bamalama Club.

After the show, I went straight home and had a quiet evening in alone. I grilled myself some liver and onions, mashed some potatoes and opened a can of Scrumpy Jack. Over the meal, I played Simon Butterworth's cassette and heard nothing that made me think he should swap his scalpel for a microphone although the melodies themselves were not unpleasant.

When I'd eaten, I went over to the piano, the white Steinway grand that fills up half the lounge, and tried improvising the tunes. It's the best way I know to relax.

After an hour of this, I went to bed. I wanted to make an early start for Yorkshire.

The rain had stopped by morning and the sun was shining over the Mersey as I picked up Maria at Blundelsands. I took the road through Southport and picked up the A59 towards Skipton.

We stopped for a break at the Little Chef on the way. From the window we could see the silhouette of Pendle Hill and I wondered if any witches still lived there.

'How's the case going, then?' Maria asked.

I brought her up to date with events so far.

'So if nothing pans out with the Tony Pritchard connection,' she said, 'is that it for the music side of things?'

'I reckon so. I've seen all the people from the groups he played in and drawn a blank every time.'

'What do you hope to find out from Mrs Pritchard?

After all, her husband couldn't have been the blackmailer. He'd been dead over a month when Bradley
was found.'

'He was still alive when Bradley came back at
Christmas.'

'That's true. If it was him, do you think Bradley had
him killed?'

'Why would he?'

'If Tony Pritchard was blackmailing him, he could
have pretended to be buying the flat and, when Tony
arrives to show it, Bradley pushes him out of the
window.'

'Maybe. But then, who killed Bradley and why?'

'Mrs Pritchard's hardly likely to tell us if her husband
was a blackmailer.'

'If she knew.'

'Mmmm.'

We reached Harrogate by noon. I decided to go straight
to the estate agency in case they shut for the afternoon.
Maria had found the address; the office was on the edge
of the town centre at the end of a tree-lined road of
detached stone houses.

Tony Pritchard – Estate Agent and Valuer said the
sign over the door. We went in and asked to speak
to whoever was in charge. A young man in a dark
suit with hair over his collar came forward. 'Can I
help you?'

'I'm trying to get in touch with Mrs Pritchard.'

'Mrs Pritchard?' He sounded surprised. 'She isn't
involved in the business.'

'I know. It's a personal matter.' He looked unsure.
'To do with Tony. I think she'll want to see us.'

'I suppose it will be all right.' He wrote an address
and phone number on a compliments slip and handed
it over.

'You're keeping the business going then?' I asked
conversationally.

'For the time being.' He didn't look old enough to be running it and I guessed the two middle-aged ladies in the office were only part-timers. It looked to me like a business ripe for a takeover.

I thanked him and we went back to the car. 'Lunch first, do you think?' I suggested.

'I think so,' replied Maria.

We drove back into the town centre and I managed to find a parking space by the old Pump Rooms.

'You need a parking disc,' said Maria, pointing to the sign.

'This'll do.' I produced one I had in the car from a visit to Whitehaven years ago, set the time, and left it on the dashboard. We walked round the corner alongside the gardens and came across The Blues Bar next to Betty's Tearooms.

'How about this?' I suggested. 'Looks OK.' We pushed our way in through the lunchtime crowds. An Elmore James record was playing loudly in the background, the sound of the slide guitar cutting through the buzz of conversation; a mural of assorted blues legends covered one wall.

We found a seat on a raised balcony in the window. 'I think I'll have an Italian Airforce Sandwich,' said Maria, studying up the menu.

'Whatever's that?'

'It says here it's bacon, melted mozzarella, tomato and courgettes.'

I looked over her shoulder. 'In that case, I'll go for the Cockadoodle Dandy and we can mix and match.'

'I don't like asparagus.'

'I'll ask for it with pineapple instead.'

They had Scrumpy Jack on draught so I was quite happy. By the time we'd finished the meal, the music had changed to B.B. King. We hurried back to the car before the time ran out on the disc and continued with our quest.

Mrs Pritchard lived in a detached pseudo-Tudor house situated in what her late husband, the estate agent, would have described as a 'desirable leafy suburb'. It had leaded light windows and rose bushes in the front garden.

One ring of the 'Avon' chimes brought her to the door. She was in her late forties, plump with short curly hair and wearing a cream cardigan over a high-necked white blouse and a cream Crimplene skirt. She could have stepped from the cover of a 1950s knitting pattern.

I had the story ready.

'Mrs Pritchard? My name is Johnny Ace and this is Maria. We've come about the murder of Bradley Hope.'

She opened the door wider. 'You'd better come in.' We followed her into the sitting room and sat on the sofa as directed. Mrs Pritchard took the chair opposite.

'In what capacity are you here exactly?' she asked.

'I'm a private investigator working for Bradley Hope's father.'

'How does Bradley Hope's death affect me?' she asked.

'Do you know if your husband saw him at all in the weeks before he died?'

Her lips tightened. 'Why do you ask?'

'Bert Hope, Bradley's father, maintains that Bradley was being blackmailed, and that the blackmailer might have killed his son because Bradley was no longer able to pay . . .'

I stopped because Mrs Pritchard was reacting in a most unexpected way. She was laughing.

'I'm sorry,' I said. 'Have I said something?'

She took a handkerchief from the sleeve of her blouse, removed her glasses and wiped her eyes.

'You must be joking,' and her laughter was turning

into tears as she spoke. Maria ran forward and put her arms round her as sobs racked her body but she pushed her away and her mood changed to anger.

'Bradley being blackmailed, you stupid man? Nobody blackmailed Bradley Hope. Why do you think my husband killed himself? Why?' She screamed the words at us. *'Because Bradley Hope was the one who was blackmailing HIM!'*

Chapter Thirteen

Once she quietened down, Mrs Pritchard told us the whole story. About five years ago, Bradley had turned up at her husband's office. His career in the States had reached an impasse after troubles with drink and drugs, but he was now clean. He'd decided to give up show-business and he wanted to return to England.

Tony had felt sorry for him and offered him a job. His estate agency business was prospering and he'd been thinking of expanding so he took Bradley on.

'How come there was no publicity?' I asked. 'After all, Bradley was a big name.'

'In the States he was, but once you're finished in America, you're dropped like a stone. Besides, he'd returned to Britain and nothing that happens in Britain ever gets reported in America. He might as well have been in Outer Mongolia.'

'So he was here in England for the last five years?'

'As far as I know, yes.'

He'd stayed at the estate agency for a few weeks, supposedly learning the business, until one day he disappeared. With him went a lot of documents relating to certain planning permissions, mortgage applications and property purchases that would have put Tony Pritchard behind bars for several years, were they ever to reach the right authorities.

His ex-keyboard player had been either very careless or very trusting. The evidence was totally incriminating and he'd left it there for Bradley Hope to find.

'Tony was no worse than a lot in his profession,' protested his widow. 'What he did was going on all the time – property is a very grey area in law. All the estate agents were doing something of the kind.' I couldn't see the Halifax or the Nationwide arranging fake mortgages but I didn't say so to Mrs Pritchard.

'So what happened next?'

'Nothing for a few months, then Bradley turned up again out of the blue and wanted five thousand pounds. I was all for turning him over to the police, but Tony was frightened of the consequences. He said he couldn't stand the shame a prosecution would bring, and the thought of going to jail terrified him. So he paid up.'

'And Bradley came back for more?' A bit like Oliver Twist.

'Yes. Not immediately, but after twelve months or so. Another five thousand. And then again the next year.'

'Almost like an annuity,' I said. 'Tony kept on paying, I take it?'

'Yes, until this year. Bradley turned up in January and said this would be the last time. He wanted twenty thousand pounds and he would hand over the documents.'

'Did he say why he suddenly wanted twenty thousand instead of the usual five?' Perhaps he was taking early retirement from the extortion racket.

'He didn't give any reason.'

'And did Tony pay?'

'Tony hadn't got twenty thousand. Since this last recession, the housing market has been in the doldrums. Business has been terrible. We've had to remortgage this place to keep going.'

'So how did Bradley react when Tony told him he couldn't pay?'

'He gave us a week to find the money or he'd send all the papers to the police. We didn't know where to turn. Tony tried to borrow it, we went to all the crooked moneylenders we could find but we'd no security so nobody would lend.'

'No possessions you could sell?'

'Second-hand televisions and videos may fetch a good price at car boot sales but they fall well short of twenty thousand pounds.'

One thing was puzzling me. 'In the report of the inquest, Mrs Pritchard, it said Tony's business was prospering.'

'You don't advertise your misfortunes to the world, Mr Ace. The business was solvent. I saw no reason to broadcast the fact that we'd remortgaged to keep it afloat. I didn't want people to know my husband might have a reason for suicide.'

'How do you know he really did kill himself? He could have fallen or been pushed,' I said very gently. 'Bradley had a strong motive. He might have felt he had to murder your husband to stop him going to the police.'

'Tony posted me a letter the afternoon he died. I received it the following day. I didn't tell the police.'

I didn't need to ask the contents.

'It was easy enough for him. Alone in a third-floor flat to meet a non-existent viewer. Nothing unusual – they often don't keep appointments.' I knew that myself from letting my own flats. 'He opens a window and leans out to see if he can spot anyone, and loses his balance.'

It sounded fair enough. Too suspicious to be accidental death but, without evidence to the contrary, no coroner would have brought in anything other than an open verdict.

She stood up. 'So there you have it. That's turned your enquiries upside down, hasn't it? I wonder how many other people Bradley Hope was blackmailing.'

I wasn't able to give an answer but I was pretty sure there were more victims and that prompted another question.

Which of them killed him?

I thanked Mrs Pritchard for all her help and we quickly departed.

'Well, that was a shock,' I said to Maria as we drove back to town.

'You think Tony Pritchard wasn't the only one Bradley was blackmailing?'

'My guess is he was doing them all – Butterworth, Kennedy and Warner. They all had money.' He obviously thought he'd make more money that way than working in an ordinary job. And he probably resented their success now his own life had failed so spectacularly.

'But what hold would he have over them?'

'They were all self-made men, started with nothing, so it's a fair bet there were a few corners cut along the way, just like with Pritchard. Bradley would have wormed their secrets out.' Now I had to do the same.

Maria looked smug. 'I always said I didn't see how Bradley could be blackmailed, didn't I?'

'Fair enough. But why tell his father he was? That's the big question.'

'What about who killed Bradley?'

'Well, we've got a few candidates now, haven't we? Mrs Pritchard for starters. She had a motive. Revenge for her husband's death.'

'I can't see her coming to Liverpool to stab him.' Maria sighed. 'The poor woman. She'll end up losing the house and everything.'

'No, she won't. He'll have been well insured or they wouldn't have lent him the extra money. And she'll be able to sell the agency. No, she'll be quids in.'

'That doesn't mean she'll be happy though.'

'Who said she'd be happy? Having money is nothing to do with being happy. Happiness is within yourself. It's how you react to circumstances, not the circumstances themselves, that determine whether or not you'll be happy.'

'I didn't know you were a philosopher,' said Maria.

'I have my moments.'

We reached the town centre and I guided us through the Saturday afternoon traffic to the last vacant space in the Crown Hotel car park.

'I'm going to have a shower,' said Maria, 'and get changed.'

I carried the cases in. We signed the register and went up to our room.

It was four o'clock. I switched the radio on to Five Live and heard the bad news. Everton were losing 1–0 at Leeds. I realised I was only a half-hour drive away from Elland Road but I wasn't tempted to go. I wasn't that masochistic.

'There's an Indian we passed that looked quite nice,' said Maria, emerging from the shower. 'I think it was called Shebab. Do you fancy going there tonight?'

'Sounds good.' I decided to have a bath rather than a shower. The bath must have been built in Victorian times along with the hotel. Most baths are only five feet or five feet six inches long and I have to lie with my knees up to my chin to fit in. This one was over six foot and deep. It was like bathing in a small swimming pool.

It occurred to me that if Hilary had been with me, we'd have ended up making love in the bath.

The meal at the Shebab was excellent. We had a couple of bottles of wine with the food and walked at a leisurely pace back to the hotel.

'I don't know whether I want to do this,' said Maria as we undressed.

I stopped in the act of removing my new Calvin Kleins. 'Do what?'

'Sleep with you.'

'I only booked the one room.'

'I feel there should be more, I don't know, not

commitment exactly but . . . continuity. Would that be a better word? I don't see you for weeks then you turn up and I'm supposed to carry on where we left off, as if things are just the same.'

'Aren't they?'

'I don't know. They couldn't have been what I thought they were, otherwise we'd have carried on seeing one another.'

She looked beautiful at that moment. She had on a lacey white bra with matching high-cut knickers which contrasted with her sallow complexion. Her long black hair cascaded over her shoulders and I reckoned that if she'd been around at the time of the Cleopatra auditions, Liz Taylor wouldn't have got a look in.

Yet, in that same moment, I knew why Hilary and I would be together long after Maria had gone her own way. Hilary never set any itineraries or made any conditions. We had fun, we went out, we made love and nothing had to be explained. We didn't have to give reasons for anything, make apologies or feel guilty. We just WERE.

'What did you think they were?'

She hesitated. 'I thought we were a couple. An item.'

Just like I am never part of a team, I am never part of a couple. I am ME. I belong to me, answer for me and suffer for me. I am not an US person. I am not a joiner.

But I couldn't explain this to Maria. For one thing, it sounds terribly selfish, which it probably is, and for another, I didn't want to be in a position where I had to win some sort of debating contest just to have a fuck.

'If you feel like that,' I said. 'Fine.'

'What?'

'I wouldn't want to force myself on you.'

'I didn't mean it like that.' She started to unclip her bra.

'No, if you feel uncomfortable with it, that's OK. I'll sleep at one side of the bed, you sleep at the other.'

'Now you're being silly.'

'Being silly would be offering to sleep on the floor or in that uncomfortable-looking armchair.'

She laughed and threw her bra across the room. 'I'm sorry,' she said. 'I wasn't meaning to be awkward. Of course we can do it. I'm sorry, Johnny.'

I took her in my arms and kissed her. 'That's all right.'

And it was. We made love and afterwards slept with our bodies entwined but part of me was somewhere else, somewhere where Maria could never reach and I wondered how long we would go on seeing each other.

Maria wasn't the sort of girl who'd be content to be just a friend; she'd have regarded such a suggestion as an insult. And yet I had to admit that I didn't like to think of a time when I'd never see her at all.

We woke about nine, in plenty of time to catch the substantial hotel breakfast. Then: 'We can't come to Harrogate without going to Betty's Tearooms,' Maria said. She was happy again and fulfilled. I thought she'd make someone a wonderful wife.

'Will they be open on a Sunday?' Was she really hungry again already?

'I don't see why not. Everybody opens on a Sunday nowadays.'

She was right. After breakfast, we put our luggage in the car and went for a wander round the gardens and Spa, ending up mid-morning at Betty's for tea and toasted teacakes.

'What's the next step with the case?' she asked, as the white-pinnied waitress lowered the silver teapot and strainer on to the table. We might have been in the nineteenth century.

'I want to go back and talk to all the people I've already seen.' I stopped and corrected myself. 'Maybe

not all of them. Kenny Leatherbarrow would be a waste
of time, and Ronnie Richmond. They're both skint.'

I thought about the reactions of the Suttons and Simon
Butterworth when I'd mentioned the word 'blackmail'.
At first they'd been quick to rebuff the idea, until they
realised I was referring to Bradley Hope as the victim, not
the blackmailer. Then they'd relaxed, obviously aware
that I was completely on the wrong tack.

It would be interesting to see their reactions next
time round.

David Warner, too. He'd denied he was being blackmailed before I'd even asked the question. A case of
getting in his denial first?

'It's like Mrs Pritchard said, isn't it?' Maria poured
the tea into the china cups. 'It's turned the case upside
down. You were looking for blackmailers when you
should have been looking for victims.'

'Which means,' I said, taking up her train of thought,
'that the people who were in the clear because they were
too rich, now become the most likely victims.'

'And thus become the most likely suspects for murder,
because they'd have the motive for killing Bradley
Hope,' she finished. 'You can't just go round and ask
them if they were being blackmailed, Johnny.'

'Why not?'

'Because they're hardly going to tell you, are they?'

'If they're innocent, why shouldn't they? If they won't
tell me, I'll know they've got something to hide.'

'Well, obviously they've got something to hide, or
he couldn't have blackmailed them! And they won't like
you asking questions,' she pointed out, 'which means
things could get dangerous. You're talking murder here.
Whoever killed Bradley won't hesitate to kill again if
they think you're on to them.'

It was a sobering thought. Why was I doing this?

I took the motorway route for the journey back,
picking up the M62 at Leeds. We had a late lunch

at the Birch Services and it was mid-afternoon when I dropped Maria off at Blundelsands.

'Be careful if you go to the Isle of Man,' she said as she got out of the car, 'and let me know what happens.'

'I will.' I was well aware that my enquiries could put me in some danger. If Mrs Pritchard was right, everyone I was going back to see could have had a motive for killing Bradley Hope.

I was glad to get back to the flat and have some time to myself. Shirley was on the ansaphone, asking about the house. I'd not told her yet that I was definitely buying it. I'd get round to it eventually.

I heated a chicken and vegetable pie for tea and thought about the case. Another week of travelling lay ahead. The questions I had to ask were better done in person than by phone. I wanted to see the reaction on people's faces.

I switched on Radio One for the Top 40. The Spice Girls had made their fourth No. 1 as predicted. I was pleased for them, but not enough to watch them on the *Clive James Show* later.

I switched on the box and watched a few minutes of *Coronation Street* but the excitement was too much for me. All those affairs and secret liaisons in one back street. The only woman Ken Barlow hasn't done it with is Ena Sharples and we'll probably find out she was really a man all the time.

I find it very difficult to concentrate on television.

In the end, I put a *Fifties' Greatest Hits CD* on my juke box and opened a can of cider whilst listening to my favourite doo-wop group, The Skyliners, with Jimmy Beaumont singing *Since I Don't Have You*. Pop music doesn't get any better than that.

I was as happy as I'd been all week, but trouble was on the way.

Chapter Fourteen

David Warner did not seem pleased to hear from me when I rang him at ten the next morning.

'Give me a chance to get in, will you? What is it now?'

'It's about Bradley Hope again.'

'I didn't think there was anything more to say about Bradley Hope.'

'Something's come up,' I said, 'and it concerns you. I think you ought to hear it.'

'Can't you tell me on the phone?'

'I wouldn't like to risk it. You never know these days, with scanners and authorised bugging. Remember Charles and Camilla?'

He didn't chuckle. There was a pause. 'All right. Come over now,' he said irritably. 'I'll give you five minutes.'

The walk took me fifteen minutes and, this time, the secretary showed me straight into his office. Warner dispensed with niceties. 'Right, what is it you want now?'

I didn't care for his tone and felt like asking who the hell he thought he was, but there was no point. 'Bradley Hope was a blackmailer. One of his victims has committed suicide. I think he was blackmailing *you*.'

He didn't even pause for breath. 'Are you suggesting I've done something illegal, that I should be open to blackmail?'

I thought his choice of 'illegal' was significant. Most

people when blackmail is suggested tend to think more of moral indiscretions like adultery or interfering with Boy Scouts.

'I wasn't suggesting anything.'

'That's a good job, or you'd be hearing from my solicitors.' Warner had obviously come a long way from his window-hanging, Sixties' days. Now it was the Robert Maxwell–James Goldsmith method of 'Counter Attack by Lawsuit'.

'You weren't the only victim. I'm sure there were others too.' It had been five years ago when Bradley had first approached Tony Pritchard, so I guessed he'd have first seen the others about the same time. 'Why did he come to see you five years ago when he was in England?'

'I didn't know he was in England five years ago.'

'He was on my show promoting his new record. His father said he'd called to see you.' He was hardly likely to check it out with Bert.

'His father's mistaken. Or lying.'

'So you are saying categorically—'

'I'm saying that if anyone tried to blackmail me, I'd have them arrested on the spot – right? So you may get out of here and I don't expect to hear from you again. If you take my advice, Johnny Ace, you'll stick to being a disc jockey.'

I left his office unconvinced. For all his bluster, Warner was just the type of person open to blackmail, a man whose life had been built on frauds and shady deals that could come back to haunt him.

But getting him to admit it was another matter. He'd had years of practice at covering up. I decided I might as well forget him for the moment and move along down my list. Another trip to the Lake District was in order.

I picked a chicken tikka sandwich and a fourpack of the new Strongbow Smooth cider at Tesco's Metro Shop in Clayton Square and took them back to the flat for a working lunch. I'll try anything once.

When I rang his hospital, Simon Butterworth was in the theatre. I left a message for him to phone me on my mobile.

I was wary of trying to make an appointment to see Verity Kennedy after my last rebuff. On the other hand, if I ran into him on the racecourse I might be able to gain his attention.

I dug out the *Sunday Times* and checked the sports section for details of the week's race meetings. The problem was to find the venue he would be at. It would be pretty annoying to drive all the way to Ayr, only to discover that he was in Towcester.

I needn't have worried. It was Cheltenham Festival week and every trainer in the country would be up for it, or so it seemed. Thursday was the Gold Cup, highlight of the meeting, so that seemed the likeliest day to catch him.

I rang Shady Spencer, my colleague on the radio station. Shady used to work on the docks where he wrote poetry in his spare time. His poems were subversive, rude and often didn't rhyme, which made them very popular amongst university students trying to throw off their conventional middle-class shackles.

Shady toured the pubs, giving readings in a breathless drawl suggestive of an emphysemic coal miner trying his luck at the 100-meter hurdles. Someone in the media heard him and next thing he had his own radio show, spouting his muse between discs.

'Hi, Shady, it's Johnny. Can you do the show for me on Wednesday and Thursday?'

'If I have to. What's on that I'll be missing?'

'I'm going to Cheltenham for the Festival.'

'I didn't know you were into the gee-gees, Johnny. Got any tips?'

I glanced quickly through the runners and picked out

a name. 'Mister Mulligan for the Gold Cup.' It sounded suitably Irish and I knew the Irish always did well at Cheltenham.

'Inside information, is it?'

'Something like that.'

'Worth a few quid each way?'

'Put your shirt on it,' I advised.

'Then I'll do the show for you. But you better watch out if it loses.'

'No poems this time, Shady, either.' Last time he did my show, he read a poem which brought in seven telephone complaints and a letter from a local headmaster decrying modern broadcasting standards.

I checked my diary. If Simon Butterworth was available, I could drive up to Crook and back in the morning. Which left the Isle of Man and the Suttons. I could sort them out later.

The phone rang almost as soon as I put it down. It was my solicitor, wanting to confirm I was going ahead on Princes Avenue and asking if I was organising a structural survey.

'You know I never bother with them, Alistair. Jack's had a good look round and we've got a fair idea what state it's in. It's not going to fall down in the immediate future.' Jack's the builder in charge of my team of workmen. 'And I'm borrowing the money against other deeds so the building society won't be sending any surveyors round.'

'Well, you know what you're doing. Come in on Friday and I should have the papers ready for you to sign and exchange. I believe you're starting the work before you pay for it again?'

'Always do.'

'One of these days, someone will back out and you'll have wasted all your money doing their house up for them.' I could imagine his hands trembling with horror at the thought of it and spilling ash from his cigar on to the shiny sleeves of his old black suit.

'I'll have their deposit though, won't I? Don't worry about it. You're always fussing. It's about time they retired you.'

I'd hardly finished my sandwich before the phone rang again.

'Johnny Ace? It's Simon Butterworth. You rang. Is it about the tapes?'

I didn't want to waste time discussing his deficiencies as a singer-songwriter. 'Er – not exactly. Look, can I come up and see you in the morning?'

'I'm afraid I'm on duty at eight and I'll probably be at the hospital all day.'

'When will you be free?'

'Is it so urgent?'

'Yes, it is, as a matter of fact.'

'You could come up tonight if you're not doing anything.'

'I've got my radio programme till seven. I wouldn't be able to leave before then.'

'You'd be here for half-past eight. That'd be fine by me.'

'If you don't mind me interrupting your evening.'

'No. We'll have finished dinner so you can join us for coffee.'

I put on a suit and tie in anticipation of this invitation – an outfit which caused Ken to make a few comments at the studio.

'Going to a carnival, Johnny?'

I think it was the tie that did it; black with bright orange flowers.

'A funeral, actually, Ken.'

It was another lively programme. People had been ringing in about paedophiles. Should they be listed? Should they be tagged? If they moved to a new neighbourhood, should the residents be informed?

I said I thought they ought to be immersed in a permanent blue dye when they were convicted, then they could easily be recognised on release if they moved out of town. This had the airwaves jumping with the usual spate of horrified protests, although a few callers, probably followers of Attila the Hun, thought it a brilliant wheeze. Wonderful stuff to get the ratings soaring.

I then played Billy J. Kramer's *Little Children*.

The rush-hour traffic had long since dissipated by the time I started my journey north, and I was able to race up the motorway without much trouble. The journey to the Lakes took me less than ninety minutes.

Simon answered the door when I arrived at the cottage in Crook and led me into the dining room. They were just finishing the dessert so I was in time for the coffee.

'This is my wife, Emma.' She looked no older than in the computer photo with her bobbed blonde hair, smooth complexion and slim figure. She would have passed for forty anywhere but I knew Simon was ten years older.

'Hello.' She stood up to shake hands and enquired if I wanted tea or coffee.

'Tea if I may.' There was no sign of their two daughters. I guessed they were in bed.

Emma went off to make the tea and I sat down with Simon.

'I didn't expect to see you back so soon,' he said. He obviously wanted to get the matter dealt with whilst his wife was out of the room.

'Didn't you?'

He looked uncomfortable. 'What do you mean?'

'When I mentioned to you last Thursday that Bradley Hope was involved in blackmail, you reacted pretty strongly.'

'Did I?'

'Yes – until you realised that I meant it was Bradley who was on the receiving end.'

'I don't understand . . .'

I went for broke and looked him directly in the eye. One of his own tricks, except I didn't smile. 'Simon, how long had Bradley Hope been blackmailing you?'

Chapter Fifteen

His face crumpled. 'You know, don't you?'

I nodded.

He rose from the table and went over to the drinks cupboard where he poured himself a large malt whisky.

'It started over four years ago,' he said wearily, 'when I was a surgeon at one of the London hospitals. One night, I got a phone call from Hope. I'd never heard a word from him since he went to America, I think I told you.'

'You didn't tell me he rang you though.'

'No.' He took another gulp of Glenfiddich. 'No, I didn't. Anyway, he said he was back in England, he'd been drying out in some clinic and had come home to recuperate. He'd nowhere to stay, could we put him up?'

'And you did?'

'I felt sorry for him. Emma never liked him – women's intuition, I suppose. We were renting a flat in West Hampstead at the time. He'd been staying with us for a few weeks – observing us would be a better term – until one day he suddenly asked me for five thousand pounds.'

The same amount he'd demanded from Tony Pritchard. Bradley was nothing, I thought, if not consistent.

'What had you done?'

'How do you mean?'

'That he had a hold on you.'

Simon gave a deep sigh. 'The Health Authority I was working for had a rule that you worked only for them.

The children were babies, Emma wasn't working, the extra money came in useful.'

'So . . .'

'So I started to do foreigners.'

'Foreigners?' I thought it was only people like car mechanics and plumbers who did foreigners, although I suppose plumbing and surgery have a certain amount in common.

'On my day off, I'd race over to Nottingham to do an appendectomy, that sort of thing.'

'Pay well, did it?'

'Up to five hundred pounds and all in pound notes.'

'Sounds reasonable.' More profitable than playing guitar for Murphy and The Monotones. 'So what went wrong?'

'I was removing someone's gall bladder. There were complications and the patient died. Not my fault, you understand – he was seventy-nine and had a dicky heart, but if my hospital had got to hear about it, I'd have been sacked and my career prospects would have been scuppered.'

'How did Bradley find out?'

'Total carelessness on my part. I never thought to hide from him the fact that I was doing these operations at the weekend. I'd no reason to – he had nothing to do with the hospital.'

I thought of Bradley quietly watching Tony Pritchard and learning about his estate agency fiddles.

'And the dead patient?'

'I must have referred to it at some time or other, probably in some other context.'

'And he assimilated all these bits of information and strung them together till the picture was complete and he had enough to threaten you with.'

'That's about it. I'd made notes, as well, and kept diaries. He'd found those.'

A blackmailer's dream. It's a wonder Butterworth

hadn't kept videos of his operations. 'So what did you do?'

'I gave him the five thousand and he said he wouldn't bother us again and left.'

One of the Great Lies of All Time. 'How did you get the money?'

'I withdrew it from our building society account. We were saving for a deposit on a house.' My opinion of Bradley Hope was getting lower by the minute. 'That's when we decided to get out of London and hope he wouldn't find us. I started applying for jobs and this one came up just a few weeks later.'

'But this cottage . . . you'd no money.'

'I had some left. Surgeons are quite well paid and Emma's father died shortly afterwards. We were able to get this place with the money he left her. Her mother was already dead and she was the only child.'

'I see. And how long did Bradley take to catch up with you?'

'Two years later, he appeared at the front door one night. I refused to let him in, there was a big row. I could willingly have killed him . . .' He stopped.

'But you didn't. At least, not then.'

The implication was not lost on him. 'You can't think I had anything to do with his murder!'

'You had the perfect motive.'

'But he died in Liverpool! I haven't set foot out of the Lakes for weeks.'

'Can you prove that?' I sounded like the police. 'If it ever came to it,' I added.

He didn't reply but sat with his head in his hands. 'You didn't need to pay him any more money,' I pointed out gently. 'You'd left the Authority.'

'They might have told my new bosses. We like it here. I was frightened to risk it.'

'So you paid?'

'I'd no choice,' he said heavily.

'And when was the last time Hope visited you?'

'At the beginning of this year. He wanted twenty thousand and promised he wouldn't bother us again.'

'How could you believe him?'

'I didn't – but what else could I do? I was in the running for a senior position in the hospital. Any whiff of scandal and I'd have been ruled out.'

'So you paid? And did you get the job?'

'Yes to both of those, but it nearly broke us finding the money. I had to take out a second mortgage.'

'You must have been very relieved when you read of Hope's death in the paper.'

'Overjoyed is more the word. We actually opened a bottle of champagne.'

'And who did you think might have killed him?'

'I can honestly say, I never gave it a thought. I suppose I assumed it was some other poor bastard he'd been screwing for money, but I never got round to thinking who it might be.'

The door was pushed open and Emma came through with the tea. 'Would you like some cheesecake?' she asked. 'There's plenty left.' She cut a slice and put it on a plate for me.

'Johnny knows about Bradley Hope,' said Simon. Emma paled.

'It must have been an ordeal for you,' I said. 'Never knowing when he'd next turn up.'

She stood and looked at me, a great sadness on her face but anger in her eyes. 'It's been a nightmare. I just wish he'd been murdered five years ago. If I'd known it was going to go on this long, I might have done it myself.'

'You didn't, though, did you?' I tried to make it sound a jokey throwaway line.

'Oh, you don't think I meant it?' She became thought-ful. 'I might have wished it and I can't pretend I'm sorry that it's happened. I don't even regret the way he died –

he deserved it – but I could never do anything like that myself.'

'Apart from that,' added Simon, 'neither of us has been away from here for weeks.'

If I wanted to check anyone's alibi, I needed to know the exact date that Bradley Hope had been murdered, which could be very different from the date on which his body was found.

'What is your involvement in all this?' asked Emma Butterworth. 'I thought you came to interview Simon for your radio show.'

'I've been doing some work as a private investigator,' I confessed. 'The radio show doesn't take up too much of my time. Bradley Hope's father hired me to find out who killed his son. It was he who told me Bradley was being blackmailed.'

Emma laughed hollowly. 'That's a joke.'

'Where does all this leave us?' asked Simon.

'I'm only interested in Bradley's murder,' I reassured him, 'not in your moonlighting. So if you didn't kill him, then it leaves you in the clear.'

They both looked relieved. I couldn't see them as the killers, but then, I believe Dr Crippen was quite good company at parties.

'Have you found any other people he's blackmailed?' asked Emma.

'I certainly have,' I said. I told them I could think of at least three, and related the story of Tony Pritchard. They both looked horrified. There but for the grace of God.

'I can't believe Tony's dead,' said Simon. 'He was a really nice guy. I often wondered what happened to him.'

'Well, now you know. He killed himself rather than be exposed by Bradley Hope. So you see, you weren't Hope's only victim. The big question is,' I concluded, looking them both full in the face, 'which one of them killed him?'

*   *   *

I was back in Liverpool shortly after midnight. At last I felt I was getting somewhere with the case.

The picture emerging of Bradley Hope was not an attractive one. It wasn't surprising that he'd been murdered. Most people he'd been in contact with would have been relieved at his demise. But at least it looked as if I could cross Simon Butterworth's name off the list of suspects.

However, Verity Kennedy and the Sutton brothers were back on it, and David Warner was definitely in the frame.

All potential victims with every motive for murder. Warner had already denied Hope was blackmailing him, but I didn't believe him and I wanted to speak with the other two.

I'd already arranged my trip to Cheltenham. Maybe afterwards, I could fit in a quick visit to the Isle of Man.

Chapter Sixteen

Geoffrey was arguing with the council tax department when I walked in the office the next morning.

'Of course it's not furnished,' he was saying. 'One tatty horsehair armchair left behind by the last tenant? It's hardly bleedin' *House and Gardens*, is it?'

I let him finish. He won the argument. 'We don't have to pay any council tax on that empty flat in Livingstone Drive.' He smiled proudly.

'Well done, Geoff. Now, how are we getting on with Princes Avenue?'

'Should be exchanging this week. That Mrs Clarke rang up and said you can go round the place anytime. She must have taken a shine to you.'

'I'll let you have her, Geoff. I think she's looking for a toy boy.' He blushed.

I decided to go over to Livingstone Drive to check out the empty flat. It gave me something to do whilst I considered my next move in the case.

I thought back to when I'd last seen Bradley Hope. It was five years ago, when I'd interviewed him on my show and he'd looked a physical wreck.

The record he'd had out at the time, the last he'd ever made as it turned out, had bombed. He'd not done any live shows in Britain and I'd assumed he'd returned to the States.

Obviously I was wrong. He'd stayed in Britain to embark on his new criminal career.

I took the road through Sefton Park. The grass still

glistened with overnight dew and early horse chestnuts were giving the first signs of coming into bud.

There weren't many people around although it was late morning. Of course, the park was in the wrong place. It should have been in the city centre. The planners in London and New York knew what they were doing. Hyde Park and Central Park are much more accessible.

The empty flat was on the ground floor of the four-storey house. As I reached the front door, the tenant from the floor above was coming in with her morning shopping.

'Hello Johnny, coming up for a cup of tea?'

'Hi, Pat. How's your Mum?'

'Same as ever.'

Pat Lake was in her early forties and shared the flat with her elderly mother. Pat was a teacher, one of those gentle women who, a hundred years ago, would have been a perfect village schoolmistress.

Unfortunately for her, she'd landed in the 1990s in an inner-city school near Croxteth where she was verbally abused, spat on, and assaulted on a daily basis until her health gave way and she ended up on extended sick leave.

'The children are frightening,' she used to tell friends, 'really cruel and vicious. I dread to think what they'll be like by the time they're ten.'

She was given counselling but, in the end, couldn't face returning to the world of violence and drugs that passed for life in a British primary school. She accepted early retirement and a small pension and devoted her life to looking after her elderly mother.

Mrs Lake, spared now of the effort of getting out of her chair to turn on the television, treated her daughter as a servant.

I held the door open for Pat and helped her carry the shopping up the stairs and into her flat. She went to put the kettle on.

'How's the poetry going?' I asked. She belonged to a local Writers' Circle and had had poems read out on Radio Merseyside.

She beamed proudly. 'I've just won the Spring Competition at our circle. Do you want to see it?' She fished the manuscript out of a bureau in the lounge and handed it to me.

It was called *The Ties That Bind*. I read it carefully.

> Mother, I know that it's lunchtime
> and Dorothy's coming at four,
> but I've still got to finish the kitchen
> and Hoover the dining-room floor.
>
> Thank God for the microwave oven,
> the meal will be ready on time
> and I'll still do the afternoon shopping;
> relaxing's a serious crime.
>
> What chance my degree now at Oxford
> since Father decided to die,
> and leave you alone in your wheelchair
> with no one to mind you but I?
>
> A lifetime devoted to caring.
> A daughter condemned to a life
> of bedpans and pills and unlikely
> to ever be somebody's wife.
>
> If only desire for grandchildren
> could have inspired you to let
> me go out and find me a husband
> instead of a life of regret.
>
> Too late for me ever to change things,
> a victim of life so unkind.
> Succumbed to emotional blackmail,
> strangled by ties that bind.

It certainly wasn't the sort of poem that Shady Spencer

would write. I looked up at her. She wore a long, pleated, navy skirt and a blouse and cardigan and her prematurely grey hair was shorn and brushed back. She was thin to the point of anorexia. She was also twenty years younger than Joan Collins, but I knew who I'd prefer to take to bed – which made the poem all the more harrowing.

The sentiments in the poem revealed a deep personal and private emotional wound. I felt embarrassed and struggled for the right words to say. 'It's brilliant, Pat, very moving.'

She took the paper. 'Thanks.'

I watched her walk over to the bureau. The room was filled with her mother's furniture, mostly Victorian. A chaise longue in the corner, a huge gilt-framed mirror over the marble fireplace, a square mahogany dining table with four matching carved chairs and two rocking chairs with antimacassars. The ambiance reeked of faded gentility. I sat on one of the dining chairs.

'Mother's still in bed,' she volunteered. 'She doesn't get up till lunchtime.' She went into the kitchen and brought back two mugs of tea. I took one and she joined me at the table.

'Bought any more houses?' she joked.

'Funnily enough, I'm just buying one in Princes Avenue. A big Victorian one like this.'

'I hope the ceilings are thicker than these. That man upstairs, Mr Mountbatten, keeps me awake till three some nights with his rap music. Can't you have a word with him for me some time, Johnny? It's upsetting Mother too.'

'Badger, you mean? I'll have a word with him now.' Neville Mountbatten, who lived on the top floor, was a university graduate whose hairstyle had given rise to his nickname.

'He's away this week. Gone to Trinidad on holiday.'

The exotic lives of some of my tenants never failed to amaze me, but Badger had always had a substantial private income, reputedly from dubious sources.

'When he gets back, then. I suppose you're more into classical music, are you, Pat?'

'Actually, I prefer heavy metal – Guns 'n' Roses or Bon Jovi, though I never play it loud. You have to think of other people when you live in a flat.'

I'd always thought of her as a docile and celibate spinster, spending her nights listening to Bach rather than Black Sabbath. So much for misconceptions based on appearance. Probably an uncontrollable lust also lurked within Pat Lake's emaciated frame.

It certainly seemed a waste of a life for her, stuck in this flat every night with her mother. On the other hand, Bradley Hope had had glamour, money and fame and she wouldn't want to swap places with him.

'Did you read about Bradley Hope?' I asked, by way of conversation.

'Oh yes. Wasn't it awful? I remember their records, Bradley and The Baronets. I was at school when they were in the charts.'

'They won't be in them again, that's for sure.'

'Mother used to know his mother.'

'Mary?' I was surprised. I would have put the two families in a totally different social class. 'How come?'

'I think they were in some charity organisation together during the war. I remember her telling me about it when I bought the records. My friends at school were very impressed.'

'But I thought Mary Hope had a stall in Paddy's Market?'

'She may well have done, but people did different things for the war effort.'

'I must have a word with your mother some time.' I wondered what else Mrs Lake could tell me about the Hope family. Had she heard any whispers about the

'Family Secret'? Did it even exist? I resolved to call again when she was up and about.

'Come after five,' suggested Pat. 'She's always up in time for the soaps starting.'

We chatted awhile. I promised once more to speak to Badger about the noise then, after sending my good wishes to Pat's hibernating mother, I went back downstairs to inspect my empty flat.

It wasn't a pretty sight. The horsehair armchair was not the only furniture, Geoffrey had been lying, but the bed and three-piece suite would have to be chucked out and replaced with new fireproof ones, and the smell from the fridge almost knocked me out. The last tenant had turned the power off and left the door shut. The wallpaper was ripped in several places where Sellotaped posters had been removed, and all the light bulbs were missing.

I went back outside, locked up the flat again, and called Geoffrey from the mobile to remind him to organise a cleaner and put in some new furniture.

'There's been a punter on the phone wanting a flat,' he said. 'I told him about Livingstone Drive and he wants you to meet him outside there tonight.'

'I'm doing the show till seven, don't forget.'

'I told him that. He says he'll be there at eight.'

'Fine.' I trust Geoffrey to do everything except let the flats. That's down to me and my gut instinct. And I never trust references. Other landlords will give a glowing testimony to get rid of their troublesome tenants.

'Something a bit odd though. He asked if you'd be there personally to show it.'

'So?'

'Nothing. Only, it's unusual, that's all. Your name isn't in the advert, so how does he know to ask for you?'

'Probably got the number from one of the tenants. Nothing sinister about that.'

'Mmmmm.' Geoffrey didn't sound convinced.

'Chances are he won't turn up anyway.' On average, only three out of five callers ever keep the appointment.

I put the mobile back in my pocket and drove into town. I had a few hours to kill before I was due at the radio station so I went round the record shops checking out new CDs I might have missed, spent an hour in the free reading room in Church Street that doubles as W.H. Smith and snatched some lunch in C & A.

The show turned out to be quite lively again. All the morning papers had carried the story of Peter Sutcliffe, the Yorkshire Ripper, who'd been stabbed in the eye by a fellow inmate at Broadmoor.

Complaining that doubtless he'd be mended at the taxpayer's expense, I suggested, on the air, that the Government would be able to knock off at least tuppence in the pound from income tax if they brought in capital punishment for rapists and murderers, thus obviating the need to keep them year by year in prison luxury.

Furthermore, I maintained, if they had the executions at Wembley, they could charge £10 a head for spectators and straightaway, on the first day's takings, they'd have £1,000,000 in the kitty towards refurbishing the railways. Hang the drug-dealers as well and you'd have the London Underground rebuilt within twelve months.

The response was amazing, with seventy per cent of my callers in favour and just four complaints.

Sometimes I think I should be an MP!

I even had time to play a few records as well, including a Hawkwind track for Pat Lake.

I drove over to Livingstone Drive after the show. I was hoping to fit in a few minutes with Pat Lake's mother before the appointment and find out what she knew about the Hopes.

'Twice in one day,' smiled Pat, as she opened the door. 'We are honoured.' She led me into the lounge. 'It's Johnny, Mother. I think it's you he's come to see.'

The old lady turned round in her armchair. She was positioned next to the gas-fire, two feet away from the television. *Eastenders* was just finishing. 'It's *The Bill* in a minute,' she said accusingly, pulling a rug over her knees. With the central heating on as well, the temperature in the room could have supported an orange grove.

'I'll talk quickly,' I promised. 'Pat tells me you knew Bradley Hope's parents.'

'I knew his mother, Mary. We did voluntary work together during the war – helping in the air-raid shelters with the ARP. A nice woman but very dominated by her husband.' She clicked her dentures disapprovingly and ran a liver-spotted hand through her blue-tinted hair. I couldn't imagine Pat's mother being dominated by anyone, least of all a husband. 'I never knew Bradley Hope. I'd lost touch with her by the time he was out of his pram.'

'But you'd know the other children, Bradley's brother and sister?'

'They were only babies. Let me see, what were their names? Norman was the boy . . . now, what was the little girl called?'

'Alison.'

'Alison, that's right. Pretty little thing. She was about seven or eight when I last saw her. Spoilt rotten, she was. You see, Mary couldn't have any more children after Alison.'

'What about Bradley?'

'Oh, Bradley was adopted, didn't you know? No, I suppose not. It never came out. I only knew because I'd seen Mary in hospital after the operation. Something had gone wrong and she was never able to have proper relations after that, if you get my meaning. But nothing was said. They were a very private family.'

I thanked her for the information although I wasn't quite sure of its relevance. I just felt that, somewhere along the line, something from the past had some bearing on the case. Maybe this was it. I needed to work out the angles.

I glanced at my watch as I said goodbye to Pat. A minute to eight. My prospective tenant would soon be arriving to view the flat downstairs.

I reached the front gate. There was nobody about. I walked to the kerb. My RAV4 was parked round the corner. Just then, a car turned into the Drive and came towards me. I stayed on the pavement, expecting it to be my appointment but the car didn't slow down!

From then, everything happened too quickly. Instead of braking, the driver accelerated and headed straight at me. I stood transfixed as the headlights bore down, too shocked to move.

Just as it was about to hit me, a figure came hurtling from round the corner and threw me to the side, away from the wheels but smashing my head against the windscreen before I fell to the ground.

I didn't remember any more.

Chapter Seventeen

'I think he's waking up.'

I heard the voices as if they were inside a cave. I opened my eyes. I was in bed, but not my own bed. Hilary, in her Sister's uniform, was standing beside me and next to her was Geoffrey, looking anxious.

'What happened?' I asked. I tried to sit up but a pain in my head stopped me. I felt dizzy and fell back on to the pillow.

'Lie still,' said Hilary sternly. Her hand reached for mine. 'You had an accident but you're going to be OK.'

I struggled to remember but couldn't.

'You tried to take on a BMW,' said Geoffrey. 'The BMW won.'

I tried moving my legs and arms and was relieved to find they all worked. 'What have I damaged?'

Geoffrey answered. 'Nothing important, just your head.'

'You were unconscious when they brought you in,' said Hilary. 'Then you slept all night.'

'I'm in hospital?' I looked blearily round the room. The sun was shining in through a window behind me on to a trolley filled with medical paraphernalia parked at the other side of my bed. There were screens round us. 'What day is it?'

'Wednesday morning.'

'Hang on, it's coming back.' I closed my eyes and tried to concentrate. 'I was in Livingstone Drive, waiting to show someone a flat.'

'I told you there was something dodgy about it,' said Geoffrey smugly. 'And I was right.'

'Geoffrey saved your life,' said Hilary. 'He pushed you out of the way of the car just in time.'

I turned to Geoffrey. The movement caused spikes to stick into my brain, or so it seemed. 'What were you doing there?'

'You wanted a minder, didn't you?'

Hilary put her arm round me. 'Good job he was there or you'd be dead.'

I remembered the headlights coming straight at me as the car accelerated and I shivered. Whoever had been driving was out to do more than frighten me.

'What happened to the car?'

'Smashed into the wall. Unfortunately, the driver lived. The car was a bit battered but he was able to reverse and take off.'

'Did you get the number?'

'Hang on, I'm not bloody Columbo. Anyway, it was dark.'

I ran my hand over my head. A thick bandage was wrapped round it but I was able to feel a large lump above my left temple.

'Don't mess with it,' instructed Hilary.

'Are you here in your official capacity,' I asked her, 'or just passing through?'

'Both. Kate North was on Casualty when the ambulance brought you in last night. She told me what had happened so I thought I'd check you were still breathing before I go off-duty.'

'You're going off-duty now?'

'In a few minutes.'

'Good. You can take me home.'

'You can't go home. You're under observation.'

'*You* can observe me. If I stay here much longer, I might have to eat the hospital food.'

I answered flippantly but beneath the banter I was

disturbed. Whoever had tried to kill me would know they had failed. They would try again. The big questions were, who were they and why? Obviously, it was connected with the Bradley Hope case. I must have got too close to the truth somewhere along the line, but right now I was in no condition to think about it.

'Where's my car?' I asked.

'Still at Livingstone Drive,' said Geoffrey.

'Can you drop me off there?'

'If you say so, boss.' He looked at Hilary for confirmation. She shrugged her shoulders.

'That's settled then. Tell your people I'm discharging myself.' I started to get up but the sudden effort produced only a wave of nausea and I laid down again. Hilary smiled at my helplessness.

'I'll take him home with me,' she told Geoffrey. 'Can you get him dressed? I'll be back in twenty minutes.'

I slowly raised myself to a sitting position. Geoffrey ran round to put pillows behind me. 'I'll go and fetch your gear. How's your head?'

'Aching, but nothing that a couple of aspirin won't cure.'

Half an hour later, I was in Hilary's Peugeot 306 on our way to her cottage near Heswall on the Wirral and by lunchtime, I was safely ensconced in her living room beside a coal fire with her tortoiseshell cat purring contentedly on my knee.

'I see Pepper's made herself comfortable,' said Hilary, carrying in a tray. She laid the plates on a coffee table. 'You'd better get some food down you, it'll help you get your strength back.'

'What were the results of the tests the hospital did?'

'You haven't fractured your skull and there's no brain damage, but you've got concussion which means you need rest.'

Rest was something I couldn't afford. Tonight I wanted to be in Cheltenham to see Verity Kennedy.

I started on the bowl of mushroom soup. 'I'll be fine.'

'You must stay here tonight.'

'I'm supposed to be in Cheltenham. I'm going to the Festival.'

'Well, that's out for a start.'

'It's the Gold Cup tomorrow, Hil. I've got a hot tip.'

'I've never known you interested in racing before.' She didn't ask any more questions. 'Anyway, you shouldn't be driving all that way.'

'I'll be OK.' But I wasn't entirely convinced. In the end, I agreed to stay the night at Hilary's and leave first thing in the morning.

'What about your car?' she asked.

'I'll get Geoffrey to bring it round later.'

'You'd better come to bed when you've finished your lunch. I'll put you in the spare room then I won't wake you when I get up to go to the hospital tonight.'

I slept more or less continuously until seven the following morning. Hilary was still at work, coming to the end of her night shift, as I made myself some breakfast. There was a note on the kitchen worktop. *Feed Pepper. Salmon in fridge. Take care. Hope you win! Ring me. Love, Hil.*

The RAV4 was in the drive outside and Geoffrey had pushed the keys through the letter box. At eight o'clock, I climbed in and set off on the 150-mile journey.

The lump on my head had gone down, leaving an ugly black bruise and, although my headache had disappeared, I felt totally drained. I was also apprehensive. How soon would it be before the next attack on my life?

Cheltenham was packed for the biggest race day in the National Hunt calendar. The traffic on the motorway going down was heavy enough – I got the usual M6 bottleneck around Walsall – but when I left the M5 and reached the outskirts of the town, it was nose-to-tail past the big Georgian terraces.

Near the racecourse itself, it seemed that every field for miles was being used as a car park. I was directed into a spot a good half-mile from the course itself. By the time I gained entrance to the stands, the first race was already underway.

The ground was so crowded, it took me a full twenty minutes to queue for a sandwich and I didn't even attempt to try to buy a drink in the Cottage Rake bar. No wonder people preferred to watch the meeting on television. Most of the accents I heard were Irish and there were an amazing number of brown trilbies worn – an item of clothing I hadn't seen on the streets for decades.

Hats, like pipes and cycle clips, seem to be an endangered species.

I bought a racecard and fought my way down to the parade ring. Verity Kennedy had a runner in the next race and the horses were being led in. I'd had a vague plan that I would be able to wander casually up to Kennedy at some time during the meeting, but I now realised the futility of this. Security men were everywhere, and to get near any of the owners or trainers was impossible without a pass.

I went back to the bar and jostled my way slowly to the front until, several minutes later, I was able to buy a plastic glass of warm cider for double the price I'd have paid for it in the Winslow.

There was a space to stand near the back of the bar, alongside a group of revellers noisily celebrating their success in the last race with glasses of champagne.

I pondered on my new problem. If I couldn't get near Kennedy here on the racecourse, and he wouldn't agree to a meeting, where *would* I be able to reach him?

Suddenly, the man standing next to me slipped on the wet floor and grabbed my shoulder to prevent

himself from falling. As he lurched forward, a bunch
of fifty-pound notes fell from his fist and I helped him
retrieve them.

'Yurra fine fellow,' he said, stuffing the money into his
back trouser pocket. 'Have some champagne with me.'
He picked up a half-full bottle from the table. 'Where's
your glass, now?'

I held out my cider. 'I'm OK. I've just got this.'

'Horse's piss,' he said dismissively, and taking the
glass, threw its contents on the floor, splashing his
brown Hush Puppies. He was about thirty, with a ginger
moustache and two days' stubble. His brown suit was
crumpled and his trilby askew. 'Have this, my friend –
Holy Water blessed by the Pope himself, so it is.' He
filled the tumbler to the brim and handed it to me.

'Cheers,' I said, sipping the silver liquid. It was
pleasantly chilled. By way of reply, he took a long
swig from the bottle.

'Are you at the Queens yourself?' he asked me.

'No, I drove down today. Is that where everyone stays,
the Queens?'

'All the boys are down there. There'll be some fuckin'
party tonight, especially when Danoli wins the big race.
We'll be singing till morning.' He took another swig and
the champagne dribbled down his chin. 'Here, let me top
up your glass, friend.'

I drank some more. 'Is that where the owners and
trainers go, the Queens?'

'A lot of them do.' He suddenly turned away from me
and started a chorus of *Danny Boy*, retitled *Danoli Boy*,
which his compatriots took up in a discordant wail. He
made Shane McGowan sound like Daniel O'Donnell. I
sidled off and fought my way through the crowds to
the Tote where I put £10 on Danoli to win the Gold
Cup.

My head was beginning to ache again and the champagne wasn't helping. I put down the half-full tumbler

and returned to the parade ring. The next race was taking place out on the course so there were seats available down at the front beside the rail. I was glad of the chance to rest. The sun was shining and it was exceptionally mild for the middle of March. Some people in sheepskins looked uncomfortably hot.

The ring soon filled up around me as the race ended, and the first four finishing horses walked in to the cheers of the crowd.

The jockeys dismounted and carried their saddles to the weigh-in room whilst the owners and friends gathered round to pat the steaming animals and congratulate each other on their success.

Eventually, these horses left the ring and, one by one, the Gold Cup runners made their entrance, led round by their stable lads and girls.

I read the names on the armbands as they came by and noticed Mister Mulligan, the horse whose name I'd picked up in the paper. It looked half-asleep – the sort of creature that would have been more at home pulling a milkcart. I wondered if Shady Spencer had backed it and was glad I'd put my money on Danoli, an altogether sleeker animal.

The jockeys came in wearing their newly changed silks and exchanged words with their owners and trainers before climbing on their mounts. After a couple of circuits round the parade ring, they headed out in line on to the course for the big race.

The crowd surged after them, anxious to get a good view of the winning post. I stayed at the parade ring on my stool, content to follow events on the giant TV cameras.

There was no sign of Verity Kennedy in all this. Obviously, he hadn't got a runner in the race and was probably seated in someone's private box.

The race began. Apart from the Grand National, which is held in Liverpool, I've never taken too much interest in racing so it came as no real surprise to me when Mister Mulligan romped home the winner.

The subdued reception the horse received when it made its triumphant entrance back to the ring, suggested it hadn't been a popular choice with the punters. I wasn't the only disappointed one. I saw a lot of betting slips being torn up.

I waited until after the presentation, when the crowd had subsided, before making my way out and walking slowly back across the field to the car.

Luckily, because there were still some races to go, I extricated myself from the car park without much trouble and drove the two miles into the centre of Cheltenham.

The Queens hadn't a spare bedroom in the building but I managed to find a quiet seat in the lounge and book an early table in the restaurant. All I had to do then was wait and see if Verity Kennedy showed up.

In the meantime, I could speculate on who had tried to kill me. David Warner was the only person so far who'd denied he was being blackmailed. Simon Butterworth had admitted it and offered an alibi for the time of the murder. He and his wife were in the Lake District.

The time of the murder . . . That was something I needed to clarify.

I still didn't know if the Suttons or Kennedy were being blackmailed, and I was now beginning to agree with Maria that asking them outright wasn't, perhaps, the best way.

However, I'd come this far to see Kennedy. No point in turning back.

I picked up a copy of the morning's *Times*. It contained an obituary for LaVern Baker, the Fifties' R & B star, who'd just died of diabetes. She'd been to Liverpool only a couple of years ago when she was well into her sixties, and she gave a brilliant performance.

At seven-thirty, I took my seat in the restaurant. It

was the first proper meal I'd had for days and I ate my way through four courses.

After I'd finished, I joined a group of noisy punters at the bar, keeping an eye on the doorway until I saw the ex-Baronet-turned-racing-trainer make his entrance.

A cheer went up: 'Good old Vezzy!' which he acknowledged with a wave of his hand as he took his seat in the restaurant with his companions – two ladies and a man.

I realised it was going to be a long night. By now, my head was throbbing badly. I had no accommodation lined up and I'd been awake a good fourteen hours. Hilary would be horrified at the neglect of my convalescence. I wasn't too thrilled myself.

I was just about to order another mineral water when I saw Kennedy excuse himself and make his way to the Gents. I seized the opportunity and followed him. Luckily, we were the only two inside.

'Excuse me,' I said quickly before he had a chance to reach the urinal. 'Could I have a quick word? I'm Johnny Ace. I rang you last week from Liverpool about Bradley Hope's death.'

'What!' He stopped in his tracks and turned round angrily.

I didn't waste time. 'I have reason to believe Bradley Hope was blackmailing you.'

'Who the hell are you?'

'I'm a private investigator. I have evidence that Hope was blackmailing both Tony Pritchard and Simon Butterworth who played in The Baronets with you. I don't know if you are aware of this, but Tony Pritchard has killed himself.'

Verity Kennedy stood still for a full minute before speaking. 'I have had no contact with Bradley Hope for thirty years or more. Not since The Baronets broke up.' He uttered the words with deliberation, as if he was reading out a press statement.

'Do you deny he contacted you five years ago, demanding money?'

'Yes, I fucking do. I don't know who you're working for, pal, but let me tell you this. You come near me again and I'll have you . . .' there was a split second delay before he said, '. . . arrested. Now piss off. Hope's dead, end of story.'

He turned away and went to relieve himself at the furthest stall, leaving me standing there, defeated.

It had been a mistake to come. Maria had been quite right. There was absolutely no point confronting people like Warner and Kennedy. If they were being blackmailed, they'd deny it and, if they *had* had anything to do with Bradley Hope's death, then I was putting myself in danger.

If they were innocent, I was just making a fool of myself.

I returned to the bar. The atmosphere was becoming very lively. Two groups of people were vying with each other, singing different Irish drinking songs, whose melodies, if not the words, I recognised from *The Dubliners' Greatest Hits*.

I made my way out into the night. Although it was warm for March, it was still chilly enough for me to be glad of the heater in the car as I set off on the long journey home. I played The Cramps at full volume to help keep myself awake but it didn't work.

By Birmingham, I was nearly falling asleep, so I pulled off at the Hilton Park Services for some refreshment. It was coming up to midnight. I bought a cup of tea and sat in the nearly deserted cafeteria.

What was my next plan of action? There were still the Sutton brothers to investigate, but I realised I had to approach them differently. I should be looking for evidence that would make them blackmail targets – some wrongdoing in their past. I would need at least a couple of days on the Isle of Man, digging around and asking questions. But no more confrontations.

Then again, even if I found they were being black-mailed, it wouldn't necessarily follow that they'd murdered Bradley Hope.

I washed down a couple of aspirin with my tea to stop my headache.

Something Pat Lake's mother had said had caught in my mind, but I couldn't recall it. Should I be looking more into Bradley's family and his early life, rather than sticking to the blackmail angle?

I decided I would pay another visit to Bert.

Finishing the last of the tea, I set off up the M6 on the final lap of what had been a wasted journey, knowing that waiting for me in Liverpool could be my potential killers who would not want to fail a second time round.

Chapter Eighteen

I slept through till eleven the next morning, when I was woken by the warble of the bedside telephone.

'I've been ringing since nine,' said Hilary.

'What day is it?'

'It's Friday. Are you all right?'

I told her I'd never felt better. It wasn't quite true although the headache had gone and I was refreshed after the night's rest.

'How was the Cheltenham trip? I believe you backed the winner.'

'What?'

'I listened to your show, or rather, Shady's show. He gave your tip out on the air.'

'Oh, he did, did he?'

'I thought I might go down to the club tonight after work. I'm off at eleven.'

'Good idea. I'll see you down there.'

Shady phoned soon afterwards to thank me for putting him on to Mister Mulligan. He'd won over £200. He said his two shows had gone well. He didn't mention poetry.

I called Geoffrey at the office to reassure him I was still alive. There was no word about the BMW.

'Are you getting the Law in?' he enquired.

'Waste of time. We've nothing to give them. Put it down to some tenant we've upset.'

'If you say so, boss.'

'I'm signing the contract for Princes Avenue today

so make sure Jack's ready to start there on Monday.'

'Don't worry. The tiles have already been delivered. The boys will be on the roof first thing.'

I sat down and thought. The time had come with the Bradley Hope case for me to go back to the beginning and talk again to his father. Why had he asked for my help? Why did Bradley lie about being blackmailed? Or was it Bert who was lying? And why had Bert been frightened? That was something I hadn't given much thought to before, but now I remembered the locks on the door. Yet who would want to harm him?

I made myself some breakfast then drove out to Bootle. The Meals on Wheels lady, Stella, was leaving just as I arrived at Bert's bungalow.

'You again,' she said.

'How is he?'

'Same as ever, luv. If you're quick, you can help him out with his dinner.'

It was corned beef mash and he was welcome to it. 'There's tea in the pot,' said Bert, between mouthfuls, pointing across the table. 'Can you get yourself a cup?'

I went over to the cupboard and fetched myself a mug.

'I see that Paul McCartney's been knighted,' I said, indicating an article in the *Sun* which was lying on the table alongside his plate.

'Never mind all that, where've you been? I haven't heard from you. What have you found out?'

'Not very much. The fact is, Bert, I'm not convinced your Bradley was being blackmailed at all.'

He stopped eating. 'What do you mean?'

'It's turning out to be rather the opposite. Bradley was putting the black on other people.' I poured out the tea and added a soupçon of milk.

'Rubbish!' Bert regarded me scornfully. 'He was skint, hadn't a penny to his name. He told me.'

'All the same, I've been making enquiries and I can name you two people who've paid your son several thousands of pounds over the last five years, and most of it as recently as this year.'

'Are you saying he lied to me?'

'Either that or you're lying to me. One or the other. But I can't work out why.'

The corned beef was forgotten as he put down his knife and fork. 'Johnny. My boy was murdered. All I want before I go to my grave is to get justice for him.'

Or revenge, I thought, remembering his original proposal.

'What I'm saying, Bert, is that Bradley was probably killed by one of his victims. Who did he see in Liverpool that you know of, besides David Warner?'

'He never mentioned anyone. He only went to see Warner for work.'

'Or so he said.'

'Why else would he visit that toe-rag?'

I didn't say 'to blackmail him'. Bert resumed eating his dinner. I took a sip of tea and tried to recall my conversation with Mrs Lake.

'You never told me Bradley was adopted.'

'How did you find that out? Not that it's a secret.'

'It might not be a secret, but it's certainly not been referred to in any of the articles I've read about him over the years, and you didn't mention it to me.'

'It's a private family matter. It doesn't concern anyone else.'

'Did Bradley know?' He didn't answer. I said, 'Mary couldn't have children after Alison was born.'

'I didn't want her to have the operation but she went ahead. It as good as finished her.'

'So you decided to adopt another child?'

'Why shouldn't we? She always wanted lots of kids.'

How ironic, then, that after Alison died and Norman

had been banished, the only child left at home was not her own flesh and blood.

'I don't know how much more I can do for you, Bert. You still insist Bradley claimed he was being blackmailed?'

'How many more times?'

'What about Norman? Have you really never seen or heard from him since you kicked him out?'

'No, and I don't want to.'

'Right.' I stood up. 'And the only thing these supposed blackmailers had on Bradley was this incest thing between Norman and Alison?'

'Isn't that enough?'

I guessed it had to be. I put my cup in the washing-up bowl along with his empty plate and pushed across the dish of thick rice pudding that had been left for him. It looked like congealed sick.

'I've got to go now. I'll be back to see you when I've any news, Bert.'

'Maybe you will,' he said, 'if I'm not dead by then!' He rose to his feet. 'I'll lock that door behind you.'

'Nobody's going to harm you, Bert. Why should they?' I blame the media. All these stories about violent crime must scare most pensioners shitless.

It had been an unsatisfactory meeting. I was still, I supposed, officially working for Bert but the questions I was asking were not the ones he wanted the answers to. And who was it he was so scared of? Why should Bradley's killers be after him?

I dropped the car off at my flat and walked over to the Bluecoat in Church Street for some lunch.

I still had the trip to the Isle of Man to arrange and wondered, after all, if I should take Maria. It was easier asking questions as a couple, people were less on their guard. Also, I liked having her around to bounce my ideas off about the case. Or was I looking for excuses again to see her?

I called the Library from a kiosk in Church Street using my chargecard.

'I wondered what had happened to you,' she said. 'I was getting worried.'

'With good reason.' I told her about the BMW and she was horrified.

'You'd better leave this alone, Johnny.'

'No chance. There's a lot more to this case than first appears but I haven't a clue what it is. I thought of going over to the Isle of Man tomorrow to check out the Suttons.'

'Oh, no. I wanted to come with you.'

'Fine, I'll book the plane for two.' I couldn't face eight hours on the *King Orry* again.

'But I can't, that's what I'm saying. I'm working in the morning and Robin's coming home for the weekend from university. I'll have to be there.'

'Oh.' This, of course, was the downside of having more than one relationship on the go. You couldn't expect someone to make themselves always available for you, if you weren't always available for them. And I'd gone a few months without ringing Maria.

'Let me know how you get on, though, won't you? Have there been any other developments?'

I told her about Simon Butterworth being blackmailed. 'But David Warner and Verity Kennedy both denied it. And I went to see Bradley's old man this morning. He says he's frightened they're going to kill him next, but he didn't say who "they" were.'

'I always said there was something fishy about his story.'

'I think you're right, but I'm not sure what it is. And that's about it. After I've checked up on the Suttons' story, I reach a dead end.'

'I'm sorry I can't come with you, Johnny. Shall I see you next week?'

'I'll ring you,' I promised.

My solicitor's office was not far from David Warner's in Dale Street. Eunice in Reception smiled as I walked in.

'Come to buy us all a drink, Johnny, with your winnings?' She was a tall woman in her late fifties but of stately bearing. It was her habit to wear frocks more suited to a ballroom than an office, and I'd never seen her without full make-up and carefully coiffured hair.

Unmarried, she'd been here as long as I'd been a client and I imagined the practice would fall to pieces without her.

'You've been listening to Shady, Eunice, haven't you? Do you fancy Ribena or Lucozade?'

She laughed. 'Alistair's expecting you. You can go straight up.'

I walked over to the quaint old lift with its ornate iron gates, wood-panelled interior and stained-glass dome on top like a miniature cathedral. It held no more than four people at most and was probably unchanged from the turn of the century when Isaac Goldberg and Bernie Davidson first went into partnership here in 1898.

Since then, the descendants of the original families have long disappeared from the company records, although the firm still trades as Goldbergs, a diminution of Goldberg Thorpe, after one of the many takeovers and mergers that have occurred over the years.

Alistair Crawford is the senior partner, the only one on the premises who can remember a living Goldberg or Davidson in the office.

He's one of the old school of solicitors who believes in crossing every 'T' and reading every codicil which makes my maverick approach to conveyancing very difficult for him.

'Late as always,' he greeted me from across a giant oak desk that held two telephones, an inkstand, a bound ledger, a decanter of whisky with two glasses and several piles of papers bound with ribbon.

He pushed these aside to lean across and shake my hand.

'The busy world of commerce, Alistair.'

'From what I hear, you're more likely to have need of our criminal department these days.' He wore a thin black suit, horn-rimmed spectacles and his white hair, thinning on top, curled over his ears and round his collar, giving him an almost frivolous appearance. But he doesn't miss a trick. 'How is the world of detection?'

'Not as profitable as being a property magnate,' I replied.

'But probably not as dangerous. Nobody likes land-lords. I've told you about making a will, haven't I?'

'Constantly. Maybe I'll get round to it one day if I can find someone to leave it all to. Now, have you got those papers?'

He produced the documents and I duly signed them. 'The gas certificates and tenancy agreements will be given to you on completion,' he fussed. 'Remember, the property is not officially yours until the end of next month.'

He reached for a cigar from a wooden box and made a big show of pricking and lighting it. The smoke hung over the desk like a mushroom cloud. 'I suppose you've started work already?'

'The old roof will be off by Monday teatime. I'm thinking of making the cellars into flats eventually.'

'Remember to get planning permission first.' He coughed with the smoke and his yellowed dentures moved in time to the rhythm of his jaw.

'When did I ever not?'

'I take it you are keeping the tenants on?' he asked, and I nodded and thought I must get round to telling Shirley. 'You realise,' he continued, in his formal voice, 'that nobody else buys houses this quickly.'

'That's because they have to apply for their loans and

wait for surveys and valuations. Good job I don't have those problems.'

The transaction completed, we shook hands and I went back to the flat to sort out some records for the show.

Down at the station, Ken seemed pleased to see me for once. 'We've had a load of people ringing in for your selection for the National,' said Ken.

'The National what?'

'Very impressed with you picking that Mister Mulligan. No one else thought it had a chance. Even the station's expert tipster never mentioned it. I wish I'd put more than a tenner on it, now. Have you got any more good tips?'

''Fraid not,' I said.

'Did you win a packet?'

'I never back horses, Ken. Don't believe in gambling. A pity really, what with me having second sight and all.'

'Shady left you a poem to read, by the way. He slipped a couple in the show himself and a few listeners phoned in to say they'd enjoyed them.'

'Really,' I said acidly. 'I've heard about Shady Spencer's poetry.'

But Ken was quite enthusiastic. 'Not my taste, of course, I prefer Tennyson but people seem to like it. Have a look.'

He handed me a typed sheet of A4, entitled *The Last of the Lake Poets*.

I'm the Last of the Lake Poets.
Who said the Last of the Lake Poets shouldn't
come from
Liverpool, anyway. The Atlantic's a lake innit?
That Grasmere and
that Windermere are just piddling puddles.
Besides, Wordsworth spent half his life poncing
about

France and Tintern Abbey, and Coleridge was so
out of the game he didn't know where
the Hell he was most of the time.
No, come fifty years from now, they'll be standing
*   by my grave at*
the Pier Head, all them Yanks with loud
*   clothes and*
loud mouths and fake degrees in English Poetry,
*   and they'll*
point their Japanese cameras at the inscription
*   on my headstone –*
'WHO DO YOU THINK YOU'RE LOOKING AT, PAL?'

'I think I'll stick to Keats,' I said. 'Were there many complaints?'

'None at all. Perhaps you should try your hand at a bit of verse.'

'I think the racing tips will do for now,' I said, and I played George Jones's *The Race Is On*, to thank Shady for doing the programme for me for the last two days. As a tribute to LaVern Baker, I played her version of *Saved*, which features the young Phil Spector on guitar, and talked about her last visit to Liverpool.

After the show, I picked up an Indian takeaway and ate it back at the flat along with a can of the new Strongbow Smooth I'd bought. It certainly tasted different. I wondered if it would catch on.

I wasn't sure, now, about going to the Isle of Man. The fiascos with David Warner and Vezzy Kennedy hadn't inspired me with confidence, and there was Everton's home game with Derby County on Saturday afternoon that I wanted to see. But I think the main reason was, I'd rather have gone with Maria.

She was right about Bert Hope. Something was wrong with his whole story, but if he was lying, what was the point of hiring me?

I wished I was seeing Maria tonight; I was looking forward to being with Hilary, but I've always believed that you need different people for different things, and at that moment I would have preferred to have been meeting Maria.

I tried to explain this to Tommy McKale at the Masquerade.

'You know what other people do,' he advised. 'They stick to one woman and mould her to what they want, or they make compromises.'

'But that's why so many marriages fail,' I argued, 'because one person can't satisfy another's every need. I mean, I like eating chicken, but I'd get fed up with it if I ate it all the time. I'd be longing for salmon or roast duck for a change. And it's the same with women. I need the stimulus of different companions.'

Tommy shook his head. 'What you've got to realise, Johnny, is that you're basically a loner. You come down here of a night to a place full of strangers and you chat to a lot of people and sometimes you have a woman with you, sometimes not, and it suits you. You don't join things because, if you did, you'd be drinking in the same golf club every night with the same people or maybe you'd be on the square, but as sure as hell, you wouldn't be down here.'

'You reckon?'

'Yes. You're a free spirit, so why not accept that and enjoy your own company? Nobody's forcing you to change. It may have disadvantages and you may have the wrong woman sometimes on the wrong night, but there's just as many plusses.'

'Except, when it comes down to it, if I don't belong to anyone then nobody belongs to me.'

'You've got to have commitment for that, something you lack, so you can't expect it back.'

'So ultimately, I end up on my own?'

'Christ, you can't take a travelling companion with

you past the grave. They don't make double coffins so you might as well get used to it and forget that claptrap they give you about being alone in your old age. Everyone's on their fucking own. The rest is an illusion.'

'So I'm lucky, really – is that what you're saying?'

'How can I put it?' said Tommy. 'You get around and know a lot of people but you're never one of the crowd. You're rather like the photographer at a wedding, in the thick of the action but not really part of it. Have you read Colin Wilson's *The Outsider*?'

I had, but I never had Tommy McKale down as a philosopher and told him so.

'Why not?' he snapped. 'Just 'cos I run a club, do I have to be stupid? It's a dangerous thing, you know, putting people into pigeon-holes.' I thought of Pat Lake and her heavy metal music. 'Just 'cos I left school at fourteen and I run a few rackets doesn't mean I'm thick.'

'Of course not,' I said quickly. Anyone suggesting that any of the McKale family was not *Mastermind* material ran the risk of a long stay in Walton Hospital.

'Tell me, Johnny, we've known each other a long while, but what do you really know about me, eh?'

'Well . . .'

'You only ever see me here in this place, surrounded by gangsters and perverts. We have a drink together and we discuss events and we're friends of a kind, but what do you *really* know about me? My family, for instance?'

'Dolly, you mean?'

'Forget Dolly. I have a wife who's a teacher in Gateacre, we live in a fucking big house in Blundelsands, my son's at Oxford and our two teenage daughters go to Merchant Taylors. Now then, that's shut you up, hasn't it?'

'But—'

'Why do I spend my time down here? That's what

you're going to ask, isn't it? Because I belong here, that's why. These are my people, they're who I grew up with. They're not my children's kind of people, they'll have their own lives, but my life is with club people.'

He nodded across to Dolly to let two women through. They were in their late forties, running to fat with heavily made-up faces, bleached hair and painted toenails. Doubtless they would fulfil the Guinness-induced desires of several foreign sailors, to their substantial pecuniary advantage, before the dawn broke.

'Which is what I'm saying. Live your life the way you need to. Why change it?' He looked down the street to see if there were any customers on the horizon. There weren't. 'Come on in and I'll buy you a drink before someone mistakes me for a fucking priest.' He laughed at the thought.

We went inside and it wasn't long before Hilary joined us.

'Your boyfriend's getting moody, sweetheart,' Tommy told her. 'Cheer him up a bit, will you?'

'He should still be in hospital,' she said, slipping her hand in mine.

'Hospital? You never told me.' He peered at me closer. 'Christ! I see what you mean. That's a nasty bruise you've got.'

'He was knocked down by a car, on purpose.'

Tommy shot me a swift glance. 'Are you in bother again?'

I never got the chance to answer.

'Can I have a word with you in private, Johnny?' The man who approached me was tall, six two maybe six three, with grey cropped hair and a stern expression. Detective Inspector Jim Burroughs didn't need to flash his warrant card to let people know he was a policeman.

'Hello, Jim. How's things?'

He didn't return the greeting. 'It's official business, I'm afraid.'

'You can use my office,' offered Tommy McKale obligingly. 'Hilary here can tell me all about your adventures whilst you two talk.'

The office was small, with just enough room for some bookshelves, a desk and a pile of stacked plastic chairs taken from the club. But we weren't sitting down.

Jim was watching for my reaction when he told me the news.

Bert Hope had been battered to death.

Chapter Nineteen

'Where were you between the hours of three o'clock and five o'clock this afternoon?'

'Christ, Jim, can't you pinpoint the time of death any better than that? What are Forensic playing at?'

He wasn't amused. 'I don't know how you come to be involved in this, Johnny, but I hope you're not trying to play detectives again.'

He was wearing a new three-piece charcoal suit with a high collar, a style currently popular with fashionable young men but which stretched uncomfortably round his middle-aged girth.

'I didn't know I *was* involved.'

'Your name and phone number were on a pad beside the telephone.'

'So? He wanted a request playing on the show.'

Jim Burroughs's lips tightened. 'And the Meals on Wheels lady identified you. According to our information, you had lunch with the old man today and you're therefore the last person we know of to see him alive, before he was beaten to a pulp this afternoon.'

'Between three and five,' I repeated. 'The last person to see him, Jim, would actually have been the killer, and that wasn't me because I was with my solicitor at the time as you may confirm with him.'

'I know you didn't kill him, Johnny, but what the fuck were you doing there?'

'Went to pay my condolences, Jim. I used to know

Bradley in the old days.' I saw no reason to tell him any more.

'Bullshit. And talking of the late Mr Hope junior, I gather you're not happy about the man we've arrested, or so you told the whole nation on the radio last week.'

'I'm not *un*happy. All I said on the show was, I hope you find the real killer one day.'

'What makes you think we haven't?'

I explained my reasons, about the premeditation with the chains and Mitchell's state of mind. I didn't mention anything that Bert Hope had discussed with me. Jim Burroughs said nothing. 'No one else in the frame then?' I asked innocently.

He didn't take up the challenge. 'Why should there be?'

'No reason.' I changed tack. 'Who found Bert?'

'The Meals on Wheels lady. She called at teatime to collect some dishes, couldn't get an answer so she fetched the warden. They found him lying on the floor just inside the entrance. Whoever he opened the door to, he didn't stand a chance. They just walked in, clobbered the poor sod to death and shut the door after them.'

'It's supposed to be secure sheltered accommodation, with wardens and alarm bells.'

'Means fuck all. People get murdered in hospital beds and nursing homes these days. How long does it take? A few seconds – maybe time for one scream. If anybody hears it, they'll stop and listen, and when they don't hear another one, they'll assume it was a cat howling or a car screeching and forget about it.'

'Nothing stolen then?'

'No attempt to make it look like burglary, you mean? No.' Then he realised. 'Hey, I'm the one asking the questions.'

'Do you think there's any connection between the two killings?' I asked, ignoring him.

'Christ knows. But it's just what we don't want, a

high-profile case like this with half the world's press crawling round the place.'

'Who's the next of kin?'

'There's an older son, Bradley's brother, but we haven't been able to trace him. And a sister but she died in her teens.'

The police had obviously been doing their home-work. However, Jim made no reference to anything strange about Alison's death and it wasn't up to me to enlighten him.

'Do you remember Bradley yourself, Jim, from the Sixties?'

He relaxed a bit on mention of his heyday. Personally, I like to think my heyday is always tomorrow, yet to come.

'Vaguely. He used to play with The Suttons to begin with, didn't he? We played with them at St John's in Bootle for Dave Forshaw. They were crap. We blew them off the stage.'

'Was Bradley crap?'

'When he did slow numbers he was OK, he had the girls screaming. But he couldn't sing rockers. Mind you, The Suttons could hardly play two chords between them and the drummer was always pissed.'

'Ronnie Richmond?'

'Was that who it was? They soon split up when Hope joined The Baronets. I never saw him after that till he was on the telly.'

'How's The Chocolate Lavatory doing?' Jim had played in a group himself in the late Fifties and they'd recently reformed to do charity shows for Merseycats.

'We're doing a gig next Friday in Crosby. We're hoping to donate another Sunshine Bus to the children's hospital this year. I'm doing a few vocals now as well as playing bass.' I supposed the worthy cause justified the horror of Jim Burroughs inflicting his untrained voice on the public. 'We're on with Johnny

Guitar and The Hurricanes.' I remembered when it was
Rory Storm.

'Getting back to Bert Hope,' I said. Any minute now,
he'd be trying to sell me a ticket to his performance.
'I'm surprised the Meals on Wheels woman recognised
me. She never said anything.' Usually, they ask for a
dedication on the show.

'She didn't. We showed her a photo when we saw
your name on the pad.' He stood up.

I waited for the killer question. The police always
do that. I think they've copied it from television. Just
as they're leaving, and the subject has relaxed his
guard, they casually throw in a loaded question to catch
him out.

'Did you go through to Bert's bedroom at all?'

'No. Why should I?'

'There was an old tin trunk in the corner that'd been
forced open. It contained mostly personal papers but it
was only half-full, as if some had been taken. I don't
suppose you'd know anything about that?'

'No. I told you, I never went in the bedroom. Anyway,
I thought you said it wasn't a burglary.'

'It wasn't, not in the true sense of the term. His video
and telly weren't taken and neither was £200 in banknotes
he kept in a drawer in the sideboard.' The money he'd
offered me to take on the case.

'So what's the motive if it's not robbery?'

'Perhaps the old man knew something about Bradley's
murder and they wanted to shut him up?'

'That only works if you accept it wasn't Mitchell
because he's been safely banged up in your custody all
the time. You have charged him, I take it?'

'We wouldn't be holding him otherwise. Anyway,
Mitchell could've had friends who killed the old man,'
he protested, but he sounded unconvinced.

'Has he confessed to killing Bradley yet?'

Burroughs looked uncomfortable. 'He says he can't

remember whether he did it or not,' and he proceeded to tell me the story.

What had happened, apparently, was that Mitchell was sighted in the early hours of the Thursday morning, staggering round the back streets of Birkenhead; he was picked up by a patrol car near the docks. The officers searched him and found a bloodstained knife in his pocket. It was the one that had killed Bradley. He was taken to the station and charged.

'Did he say how he came by the knife?'

'At first he said he found it in a litter bin, but later he said he might have used it on someone, he wasn't sure.'

'After police questioning, you mean?' Knowing what could happen to suspects in custody before the interview tapes were switched on, it wouldn't have surprised me if Mitchell had confessed to the IRA bombing in Manchester while he was at it.

Jim Burroughs ignored the question. 'To be honest, Johnny, he's not rowing with both oars in the water.'

'He's a smackhead, Jim.'

'He's got the right form. GBH, assault, a nasty piece of work, but—'

'But he could have genuinely found the knife in a litter bin, which would mean he didn't kill Bradley Hope?'

'Maybe he did, maybe he didn't, but now there's his old man's death to consider, which could throw in the proverbial spanner if not the whole bloody toolbox.'

'No theories?'

He shook his head. 'There's got to be a connection, but I don't know what it is.'

'Who inherits?'

He looked sharply at me. 'That's an odd question.'

'I thought it was the first thing you're supposed to ask.'

'Well, in Bradley's case, his last wife, I suppose. I don't know. We've not seen the will yet, but the word

is, Bradley was skint anyway. Blew the lot on drugs,
drink and alimony.'

And replenished it with the proceeds of his blackmail
operations, but the police weren't aware of that branch
of Bradley's entrepreneurial activities.

'That's been common knowledge for a while.' Didn't
Jim Burroughs read the tabloids? 'Who cops for Bert's
little lot with Bradley dead?'

'Assuming he hadn't made a will to the contrary, the
elder son, Bradley's brother. Not that there's likely to
have been anything to leave.'

'So it doesn't look like money was a motive. Any
trace of this mystery brother?'

'Not a dicky bird.'

'Do you think he could be expecting a few bob with
them both dead?'

'He'll be disappointed if he is. You've seen the place
yourself.'

'Funny nobody's heard from the brother. It's been in
all the papers.'

'He might be in bloody South America for all we
know, with Ronnie Biggs.' He sighed. 'Christ, if only
the old man hadn't got himself killed, this'd all be sewn
up now.'

'Very inconsiderate of him,' I said. Whatever happened
to sensitive, caring policemen, or was *Dixon of Dock
Green* really a propaganda series on behalf of the Home
Office? 'But I'm sure you'll be able to find some jobbing
housebreaker to fit up for the job.'

'Anyway, I'll want you down at the station first
thing in the morning to make a statement as the last
person to see Herbert Hope alive. That we know of,'
he quickly added.

He stopped for a moment and took a small bottle from
his trouser pocket; he shook out a small white tablet.
'Indigestion,' he explained. 'I seem to get a lot of it
these days, and no wonder.'

'You want to relax a bit, Jim. Too much stress is bad for you at your age.'

He popped the tablet in his mouth and swallowed it. 'Relax in this job? You must be bloody joking.'

'Are you stopping for a quick one now's you're here?'

'I'm on duty, Johnny,' he said, 'but you're right – why not? I'll just have a half with you and your good lady.' He paused by the door. 'By the way, who's that rather attractive woman I saw you with in the Blundelsands last week? Looked like Cher.'

'God, there's nowhere you can go in this city and not be seen by somebody who knows you.'

'The penalty of fame.'

'That was Maria, and we don't mention her in present company.'

He grinned maliciously as we rejoined Hilary and Tommy. 'Don't be late tomorrow, then.'

Chapter Twenty

I was at the police station in St Ann Street at ten the next morning. Hilary had driven home to Heswall after we'd had breakfast.

'This is Detective Sergeant Carol Page,' said Jim Burroughs, indicating the lady police officer present in the interview room.

'You got rid of that slob you used to have working with you, then?' Carol Page looked more like a librarian than a policewoman. Her straw-coloured hair was pinned up in a bun and she wore a lightweight navy suit which suited her trim figure.

'If you're referring to Kevin Payton, he's on second-ment to another station.' He indicated a plastic chair beside a table and I sat on the opposite side to them. Jim assumed his serious 'investigating officer' expression and switched on a tape machine. 'Ten-o-five Saturday March the fifteenth 1997. Detective Inspector James Burroughs and Detective Sergeant Carol Page present at the interview with Johnny Ace.'

He turned to face me. 'When did you last see Herbert Hope alive?'

I gave precise details of the time of my visit of the previous day. I didn't mention that I'd been to the house before, and reiterated that my reason for going was to pay my respects to the old man after his son's death.

'Left it a little late, didn't you? He'd been dead a fortnight.'

'I'd rung the week before,' I said, thinking quickly. 'That's why my number was on the telephone pad.'

Burroughs made a theatrical performance of pulling a piece of paper from his pocket and reading from it. 'Wait a minute, there's a statement here from the Meals on Wheels lady that you visited the deceased the week previously.'

The devious sod, I thought. He'd never mentioned that in the Masquerade Club.

'I called round last week, after I'd rung, and said I'd look in again to make sure he was OK. Nothing sinister in that.'

'What did he say to you?'

'Nothing much. He ate his lunch, I had a cup of tea with him, told him I was sorry about Bradley. Bradley used to be my barber when we were both teenagers, so I was a sort of friend of the family.'

'Did he give any suggestion he knew anything about his son's death?'

'None at all.'

'Did he say how often he'd seen Bradley over the last few years?'

'Only that he'd been home at Christmas and it was the first time he'd seen him for five years.'

'Did he give the impression of being frightened?'

'He had plenty of locks on the door but most old people are frightened these days. I never took it seriously. It's the society we live in. Perhaps if there were more policemen on the beat . . .'

'All right, that's enough.' Jim Burroughs didn't look satisfied but there was nothing he could say and the interview was terminated.

As he walked with me to the door he said, 'By the way, we released Mitchell this morning.'

I couldn't resist a jibe. 'But he did it, Jim, you told me so yourself only last night. Is it a good idea to let him loose on the unsuspecting public? He might kill again.'

He wasn't amused. 'Fuck off. I said he was a nutter at the time.'

'And only a sane and sensible person would have killed Bradley Hope, you mean? I quite agree. Anyway, how do you know Mitchell didn't do it? I thought he confessed.'

'Forensic. We've just had the latest tests back. The body had been in the water a couple of days and Mitchell was locked up in the cells at the time for vagrancy and drunk and disorderly.'

'What was that Peter Sellers film where they break out of jail to commit a crime?' I asked innocently. '*Two Way Stretch*, wasn't it? With Wilfrid Hyde-White.'

'Don't go making things difficult.'

'So when exactly was Bradley killed?'

'Some time on the Tuesday. He was knifed first, chained up then dropped in the river. He floated up with the tide and surfaced when the chains came off.'

'But you said you found the knife in Mitchell's possession.'

'He could have picked it up anywhere. In a litter bin, even.'

'So who's next on the suspect list?'

He ignored the question. 'Are you sure his old man never said anything to you when you went round to his house?'

'He said Michael Winner wouldn't like Meals on Wheels.'

Jim hadn't heard of Michael Winner. 'We've been checking on Bradley's movements before he died. Did you know he'd been living in Britain on and off for over five years?'

'That was when I last saw him, five years ago. He was over here promoting his record.'

'Well, he stayed. He moved around the country quite a bit. We've traced addresses in London and in Leeds.' He said nothing about Harrogate or the Lake District, not to mention the Cotswolds and the Isle of Man. I suspected these were temporary stops while he honed in on his quarries.

'How did he make a living?' I asked casually.

'He was a bloody film star, wasn't he?'

'Not any more he wasn't. I thought he was skint.'

'He was at the end, but I suppose he had a few bob when he first came over.' Burroughs was getting impatient.

'Yet he never came to see his old man in all that time. Strange, eh?'

'I hope you're not holding anything back,' he said suspiciously. 'I don't want to find out you're mixed up in any of this.'

'Jim, I haven't a clue who killed Bradley or Bert,' I answered truthfully. 'And now, I must be on my way.'

'I want to know if anything happens,' he shouted after me.

I walked over to London Road and rang Maria at the Library. 'Any chance you can fit in lunch before you meet Robin?'

'I suppose so,' she said, and sounded happy that I'd phoned. 'You never made it to the Isle of Man, then?'

'No.' I told her about Bert's murder.

'Oh, God,' she exclaimed. 'Look, I finish at one.'

We met in Lucy in the Sky and I brought her up to date with all the week's events, ending with Bert's death.

'He was afraid of something. I said, "I'll be back" and he said, "If I'm not dead by then". Those were his last words.'

'There must be some reason he sent for you in the first place,' Maria pointed out.

'I think he hired me for protection,' I said slowly. 'He felt he was in danger and concocted that story about Bradley being blackmailed.'

If Bert had hired me to protect him, I'd let him down badly. Another point was that, officially, with him gone, my involvement in Bradley's murder was over. Bert had hired me, he was dead, end of story.

Not end of story. I'd promised Bert I'd help him and I owed it to his memory to find his killer.

It hadn't been much of a life for Bert, but at least now, I told myself, he'd be reunited with Mary. Not a sentiment I'd often agree with, *'He's better off dead'*, but Bert had had a pretty depressing existence for the last years of his life.

The Hope family in general seemed to be cursed. Bert and Bradley murdered, Mary killed in a hit and run, Alison dying giving birth to her brother's child. What about the missing member, Norman? Was he cursed too, or could he be the killer? Surely he wouldn't batter his own father to death?

'Bert was penniless,' Maria was saying. 'What possible motive could anyone have for killing him?'

I couldn't think of one. At eighty-one, he could hardly be the victim of a woman's jealous rage, at finding him in bed with her best friend. Similarly, no cuckolded husbands were likely to be chasing him for seducing their wives.

I'd almost have been happy to settle for the sneak-thief theory, had it not been for the chest in the bedroom. What had been stolen from it, and what significance did it have?

'You must find out the truth behind this family secret,' Maria said. 'I'm sure that is where the answer lies.'

I went to the counter to order more drinks and Margie brought them over. 'Hello, love,' she smiled at Maria. 'Taking you somewhere nice today, is he?' I recalled an identical conversation with Hilary a fortnight ago and felt my two lives were converging ominously.

'You know perfectly well Everton are at home,' I told her.

'I don't see you with a blue and white scarf, love.

You want to take him shopping and get him to buy you something nice.' She winked wickedly.

'So what's the next step?' asked Maria when Margie had gone.

'I'm going to find Norman, Bradley's brother. He could be the key to this.'

'What about the blackmail angle?'

'Kirkby's nearer than the Isle of Man. I'll leave the Suttons for later. Besides, I don't see why somebody being blackmailed by Bradley would kill Bert.'

'Perhaps the two deaths are totally unconnected.'

And with that possibility to ponder, we parted. I promised to call her after the weekend if I found Norman, then I made my way to Goodison Park for the match.

The Blues had taken only five points out of a possible thirty-six in their last dozen games, so the prospects weren't good. At half-time there was no score.

'Harry Catterick'd weep at this,' opined the man in the seat next to me. 'What's happened to the School of Science?'

'Joe Royle said we're "dogs of war" now,' I replied.

'He should be running a bleeding kennels then and let someone who understands football take over here.'

The game was devoid of any flair, the players continuously pumping high balls into the air to little effect.

'Perhaps they'd be better joining a basketball league next season,' I suggested.

Just when the game was fading to a nil-nil draw with eleven minutes to go, Dave Watson scored and saved the day.

I didn't go to the Winslow. I was getting bored with the whining of the supporters, not that I didn't grumble myself, but I had other things on my mind.

Where would Norman Hope go to in Kirkby on a Saturday night? It wouldn't be easy to find him: I'd no idea what he looked like. I realised I should have asked Mrs Clarke although she'd not seen him since he was a lad.

I wore my oldest denims and a black leather jacket for the trip.

In the old *Z-Cars* TV series, Kirkby was the 'Newtown' to Liverpool's 'Seaport'. Back in the late Fifties, the city planners had the bright idea of removing whole communities of people from the city centre and rehousing them away from their friends and families in the middle of nowhere in cheap housing projects and high rises.

There were few amenities for them in their new environment and the people felt let down – then the councillors wondered why there was trouble. Industries failed, unemployment was rife, the drug-dealers moved in and the black economy flourished. Another everyday story of urban decay. A Kirkby tower block was just the place for a man like Norman Hope.

Most of the entertainment in Kirkby on a Saturday night was centred round the pubs, social clubs and church clubs, and consisted in the main of bingo, discos, Karaoke and live acts.

I did the grand tour. I played bingo, I drank glasses of mineral water, to the derision of many hardened drinkers at every bar, and I watched some dire turns on-stage in crowded rooms filled with the stench of stale tobacco smoke, spilt beer and sweat.

I noticed that few of the solo singers actually relied on musical instruments any more, preferring to augment their sound with a tape machine and a thirty-six-piece-band backing track. They looked pretty stupid standing alone on-stage against this backdrop of sound, and I didn't give much for their chances if the tapes broke. I also wondered about all the out-of-work musicians around town.

At St Helen of Troy's Welfare and Social Club, I almost got excited when I needed only two numbers for a full house at the bingo. I then watched a morose man sing excerpts from *Miss Saigon* with all the enthusiasm of a dead hedgehog.

'What's the opposite of "charisma"?' asked the man next to me at the bar. 'Because, whatever it is, he's got it.'

The announcement of the Karaoke at St Helen's brought a steady stream of contestants queuing at the stage, egged on by their companions. Unfortunately, it degenerated into a brawl when a man, who bore some resemblance to Elton John without his hair, tried to sing *Amazing Grace* to the tune of Oasis's *Roll With It*. I left before one of the flying glasses hit me.

Everywhere I went I asked if anyone knew Norman Hope but nobody did.

I ended up at St Diana's Catholic Club at eleven o'clock where a DJ stood at the apex of the stage, with his two speakers positioned to face opposite sides of the L-shaped clubroom, playing rap music to an audience too besotted with drink to notice.

The volume was deafening and the dance floor was packed. I treated myself to a cider, my first of the evening in view of the driving, and decided that after this, I'd call it a night.

'You don't know a bloke by the name of Norman Hope, do you?' I asked the barman as he gave me my change.

He thought for a minute. 'Why don't you ask the priest over there? He knows everyone in the parish.' He pointed to a large figure leaning against the bar with a pint in his hand.

'Father O'Brien,' he said as I introduced myself. 'How can I help you?' He had a large round face made ruddy by the number of broken capillaries on his skin – the tell-tale sign of an enthusiastic drinker. He reminded me of an oversized radish.

'I'm looking for a Norman Hope,' I shouted as the music struck a loud passage of tribal drumming.

The Father shook his head. 'I'm not familiar with the name, son. The only Norman we have here is Norman Ericson who helps out during the week, cleaning the drains, moving barrels and the like if you understand me.'

'How old would he be?'

'Let me see now. Norman, he'd not be a pensioner but he'd not be a young man either. Maybe in his early sixties.'

The age was about right. Norman was nine years older than Bradley. 'Is he in here tonight?'

'No, your man doesn't come to the social functions but he'll be down here Monday morning.'

'Perhaps I'll call and see him then.'

'You'd be very welcome.'

Our conversation was interrupted by the DJ who came over to remonstrate with the Father. Apparently, whilst his records were playing, someone had unplugged his leads and connected them to the house speakers. They'd then made off with the DJ's own speakers.

'I never noticed,' he complained, 'because the music never stopped. It was only when someone on the dance floor told me they'd seen two men making off with my speakers that I found out.'

'They'll be well gone now,' I said. 'You won't see them again.'

I left him arguing about compensation with the priest. I didn't give much for his chances. He'd probably be told it was the Will of God.

I wondered if it was the Will of God that I should find Norman Hope. He didn't appear to be a man with many social connections, but it seemed worth a return trip on Monday morning to check on this Norman Ericson.

If the cleaner did turn out to be Norman Hope, I might find out the real Hope family secret and the reason for the two terrible murders.

Chapter Twenty-One

It was after midnight. I didn't feel like going home; I needed some company. Then I remembered I still hadn't told Shirley about buying Princes Avenue so I headed for the Bamalama Club.

She was on the bar as usual. A three-piece band was playing some nice Chicago urban blues music and the place was packed. Kenny Leatherbarrow was at the bar, hands rapping the counter in time to the music. I didn't disturb him.

'Well?' she greeted me. 'What news have you got? I've heard all these rumours about this new landlord.' She poured me a half of the house moonshine, or draught bitter as they label it at the Bamalama.

'I take over next month.'

'Oh Johnny, that's brilliant!' She smiled in delight and kissed me full on the mouth. Her lipstick tasted of strawberries. 'Here, this is on the house. Er, will you be coming over later to inspect your property?'

'I think I ought to, don't you?' I asked. She did.

I took my drink to a stool near the stage and watched the band. They were doing B.B. King's *Sweet Sixteen*. I felt quite content and relaxed, more so than I had the night before in the Masquerade. Shirley made no demands, never asked where I'd been or who I'd been with. We'd only ever spent time together in her flat. We'd never been on a date or even shared a drink, other than in the Bamalama, and that seemed to suit both of us.

One of the regular hookers came over and dragged
me on the floor for a dance. She was in her late thirties
and wore a low-cut leopard-skin mini-dress and leather
boots over her knees. Her hair was ash blonde in contrast
to her sallow complexion. Like the Ford Mondeo, she
was the product of many countries but, looking at her
slanted eyes, I think China had the biggest claim. We
squirmed against one another as the singer tortured the
notes from his guitar.

'Hey, Johnny. You never played no blues music on
your show for ages.' She pressed her groin into mine
mischievously with predictable results.

'Sorry, Misty. I'll play you some on Monday.' I thrust
myself against her, my hand cupping her backside.

'I'll be listening, lover.' She blew in my ear and
followed it with her tongue. It beat line dancing
any day.

The time passed quickly. I had a couple more dances
with the other girls, drank some more beer and listened
to the band go through their Elmore James and Muddy
Waters repertoire as the club got hotter and smokier.

When the band took a break, I went backstage and had
a beer with them. 'Hey, you ain't going to want to get
up and sing, are you?' said the drummer. 'I remember
once when you was drunk . . .'

The singer pushed him aside. 'Johnny, we got a record
coming out soon. If it means letting you sing for you to
play it on the air, the mike's all yours.'

'Memphis,' I told him, 'if I sing, you'll lose the gig.
Give me the record anyway and I'll play it.'

Memphis Chapman had played in a few bands in the
city over the years, although he'd originally come from
St Louis so his credentials as a blues singer were sound.
The current line-up called themselves 'Flip, Flop and Fly'
after the Big Joe Turner record and were rated enough to
have guested at a number of blues festivals around the
country.

At two o'clock, the music finished, the bar closed but the drinking continued. I didn't stick around. Shirley had booked her usual cab and we drove to her place, or my place, as she reminded me it soon would be.

'Am I really getting central heating?' she asked, shivering as we undressed in the bedroom.

'Yeah, a coal fire in the middle of the room.'

'Piss off.' She laughed, grabbed my jeans and started to pull them off. 'I can't wait for you to get it. I'll have this place like a palace.'

'I'll probably make a couple of flats in the cellars,' I told her, as I removed my socks. 'So if you know anyone who's looking for accommodation . . .'

'I'll tell them,' she said, and pulled me on to the black silk sheets, naked beside her. 'I saw you dancing with the whores tonight.'

I grinned. 'I thought you'd hired them as the warm-up act.'

'Maybe I did,' she mused, looking down my body. 'Either way, it worked, didn't it?'

Afterwards, Shirley fell asleep and I lay quietly beside her, my hand cupping her large, black breast as it rose and fell with her breathing.

It had been a hectic week. I'd raced between the Lake District and Cheltenham. I'd nearly been killed and ended up in hospital, and now I found I had two killers to look for instead of one. Or were they both the same?

I could smell the damp in the flat and started to make mental notes of the work that needed doing to the house. Sometimes, you just can't switch your mind off.

I finally fell asleep about four but it was a restless sleep. I dreamed I was on a small boat which was tossing about on the waves, until I came to and found that Shirley was shaking me furiously.

'Quick, get up! Johnny, you've got to get up!'

I peered at her, bleary-eyed. 'What time is it?'

'Ten o'clock. It's my boyfriend. He's on his way upstairs.'

I couldn't recall a boyfriend being mentioned. I'd never asked any questions about Shirley's relationships as she hadn't about mine. But I could see the frightened expression on her face and I didn't feel it was a good time to learn.

She bundled my clothes into my hands. 'Get dressed in the bathroom. Quickly. He'll go apeshit if he finds out. I'll tell him you're the new landlord come to inspect the flat.'

'On a Sunday morning?'

'Can you think of anything better? Hurry up.'

I couldn't. I grabbed the clothes and made it to the bathroom just as he was knocking on the door.

I'd rarely dressed more quickly and emerged a minute later having flushed the toilet and run the taps. I was shaking.

'Has the water pressure always been this low?' I asked, trying to keep my voice steady.

She'd put on her robe and was standing beside him. He wore tracksuit bottoms and a black singlet, showing off his muscles, and looked like a stand-in for Sylvester Stallone. His right arm, which had a proprietorial grip on Shirley's bottom, was covered in tattoos, and the rings on his fingers would have served adequately as knuckledusters.

'This is Rodney. Rod, Johnny Ace, my new landlord.'

'Hi,' I said, and stayed in the bathroom doorway.

He nodded and grunted something indecipherable.

'You only get a trickle on the shower sometimes,' she said. 'It's because there's too many flats in the house for the supply.'

'I'll get that fixed,' I promised. 'The workmen will

be here first thing in the morning.' I moved towards the door. 'Right, I think that's about it. Sorry to wake you. I won't disturb you any more. I can see myself out.'

'I'll come down with you, I want to get the milk in.' She turned to the boyfriend. 'Put the kettle on, Rod. I'll be back in a minute.'

She followed me down the stairs. 'Sorry about this, Johnny. He was away yesterday, watching Liverpool. I didn't expect him back till tonight.'

'Have you had him long?'

'On and off for five years. He wanders off sometimes and I don't hear from him for a few weeks but he always turns up again eventually.'

'But he doesn't live with you?'

'Oh, no. He just stays over sometimes. He's more of a friend, really, I suppose. A bit like you, Johnny. A friend who stays over.'

'Funny I've never seen him before.'

'That's because I'm usually pretty good at arranging things.'

'I've never seen him in the club either.'

'Oh, he doesn't go in the Bamalama. The black people make him nervous. He's afraid they'll think he's stealing their women.' She laughed at the idea. He didn't look the nervous type to me. 'Anyway, he works nights.'

'Doing what?'

'Security guard.' We reached the bottom of the stairs. 'Look, I'm really sorry about this, Johnny. You will come round again soon, won't you?' She opened the front door. 'Oh shit, it's Sunday, there's no milk. Never mind, Rodney won't know. He doesn't notice things like that.'

'I'll be in touch,' I said.

There weren't any taxis about so I walked the short distance to the car, still parked outside the Bamalama, and drove slowly home.

My relationships with women were becoming ever more complicated. I felt like getting away from it all, on my own. Maybe I could book a working holiday in a monastery, tending the herb garden.

Instead, I was offered a day trip on a boat.

The offer took me by surprise. David Warner was the last person I expected to hear from, especially on a Sunday afternoon.

After I'd returned from Princes Avenue, I'd made some lunch, and was enjoying a quiet glass of wine and reading the *Sunday Times* when he rang. Bert Hope's death was mentioned in a short paragraph but it got a whole middle page in the *News of the World*.

'I'd like to have a little chat with you, Johnny. It's about Bradley Hope.'

'Oh yes?' I was suspicious. He'd not been inclined to talk on our last meeting.

'A couple of things have come up that will be of interest to you. What are you doing tomorrow?'

I thought. Kirkby and Norman Hope could wait a day; David Warner might be more important. 'Nothing until I do my programme at six.'

'I've got a boat at the Marina – the *Bilbo Baggins*. What do you say that we meet down there, perhaps late morning? That'll give me time to get my post sorted at the office. I'll take you for a sail up the river if you like, then we can come back and have some lunch at the club.'

I said that sounded acceptable and we fixed on eleven o'clock.

I wondered what had induced this suddenly benevolent attitude. It was hard to believe that his motives could be entirely altruistic. With David Warner, there would be a hidden agenda.

Was he now going to admit that Bradley Hope had

been blackmailing him? Or was he about to warn me off? What if David Warner was behind the BMW attack? He might be planning something else.

I would soon find out.

Chapter Twenty-Two

Liverpool was one of the first British cities to turn the wastelands of its derelict docks into a major tourist attraction. Since then, Cardiff, Bristol, Preston and a load of other places have all done something similar, and London's Docklands speaks for itself but, like I told Bert Hope, take a walk on the south side of the Pier Head past the Albert Dock, and you see a different world compared to the north side end of the city.

I strolled down to the Marina after breakfast. I know little about boats, but I could see that the scores of craft moored there represented a few hundred thousand quid of anybody's money.

David Warner was waiting for me at the Harbourside Club. He wore a navy blazer with grey flannels and a regimental tie. A different regiment from Gordon Sutton's, I noticed. And neither of them had been in the services! Happily, Warner had eschewed the pipe and yachting cap that would have made him look a complete prat.

I wore my jeans, a blue sweatshirt, an anorak and non-designer trainers, more the deckhand look.

'How about a drink before we set off, Johnny?' He shook my hand vigorously and called the barman over.

'My usual, Paul, and something for my friend here.'

I asked for a cider. It was a bit early to be drinking but I didn't like the look of the tea machine and I thought the alcohol might help alleviate any possible seasickness.

'So, what do you want to see me about?' I asked.

'Oh, plenty of time for that once we set sail. Tell me how your programme's doing? You know, we ought to be able to do one another a few favours with the artistes I've got coming into town. After all, we go back a long way, Johnny.'

I could hardly believe the conversation was taking place. In the few times our paths had crossed since The Cruzads' days, we'd never exchanged more than inconsequential chit chat, and he'd never before suggested any sort of business arrangement between us.

'True,' I said. 'I remember working for you once, over the water. For some reason, the audience were expecting The Five Shillings.'

He laughed, brazenly. 'That's how it was in those days, groups always swapping around. I don't suppose the punters noticed.'

'They certainly did. There were only four of us, for a start.'

'They probably thought one of you was ill. Not the full shillings, eh?' He laughed loudly at his little joke then quickly resumed his business voice. 'A bit different nowadays though. Ah, here's the drinks. Thank you, Paul. Have one for yourself.' He slid a ten-pound note across the counter.

Warner collected his change, and picked up his large single malt. 'Cheers.' He downed half the contents in one gulp. 'Yes, it's a bit different nowadays. The industry's gone global.'

He propounded his views on the entertainment world as we finished our drinks then he led me outside to look over the Marina. 'Mine's over there, the cabin cruiser with the red and white stripe.' He gesticulated vaguely into a blur of boats in the distance. 'I call her *Bilbo Baggins* after a group I once managed. Good band – you may remember them. Made me a lot of money.'

I couldn't resist saying, 'Didn't everybody?' He looked at me sharply then decided to take it as a compliment.

'I suppose they did.'

He pointed out a few vessels of interest as we walked over to his boat – large ocean-going craft, a couple of narrowboats that sailed up the Leeds-Liverpool canal, several yachts, power cruisers and tiny motor boats.

The *Bilbo Baggins* was only small. It would have fitted into a lifeboat of the *QE2*. I was surprised. I would have expected Warner to have owned something larger and flashier, suitable to grace the harbours of the French Riviera rather than something that would have looked more at home on Southport's Marine Lake.

'Here we are, jump in.' I joined him in the cockpit and watched as he switched on the ignition, pushed the throttle forward and carefully steered the vessel out of the Marina, through the lock at the south end of the Brunswick Dock, and into the main stream of the river.

'While we're at sea, the radio's fixed on Channel Sixteen and kept open for emergencies but when we come back, we have to radio the lock-keeper on Channel Thirty-seven to let us in. It's all done by computer.'

'Isn't everything nowadays?'

We headed past the Liver Buildings and along the North docks out through the Mersey Bar, where the river widens into the Irish Sea. On the way, he carried on explaining some of the controls to me. I tried to understand what he was saying but I felt he was marking time, making conversation for the sake of it.

'I thought we'd sail along the Welsh coast towards Anglesey,' he said. 'It's a clear day. You'll see Snowdon and the Welsh mountains.'

I could see the Welsh mountains perfectly well from Maria's lounge, and on dry land too, where I felt considerably safer.

'I hope you've got lifebelts,' I said. 'Because I can't swim.'

He smiled. 'Don't worry. The water's so cold, you'd

freeze to death before you drowned, so it doesn't matter.'

As we approached New Brighton, the waves got rougher. I never thought I'd be glad to be on board the *King Orry* again, but it had felt more solid than this light craft.

Warner concentrated on steering out into the open waters; far from staying close to the shore of the Wirral and Wales, he headed away towards the open sea.

'I thought we were staying near the shore,' I said, trying not to sound nervous.

'Can't sail too close, shallow waters. Rip the bottom of the boat.'

This was so patently ridiculous it wasn't worth challenging. Another few minutes passed, neither of us spoke and the coastline receded.

Suddenly, the engine cut out and I turned round in alarm. 'What's happened?'

'I just wanted a little chat,' he said. 'A private chat. Let's go to the back of the boat.' I followed him cautiously. The sea looked very close. 'I had a telephone call yesterday from an old buddy of mine – someone you know, I think. Vezzy Kennedy.'

That was the moment I knew I was in trouble. His eyes stared into mine as he spoke. 'Well?' He barked the word.

'Well, what?'

'Vezzy Kennedy. Do you admit you went to see him in Cheltenham on Thursday?'

'And if I did? I don't see how it concerns you.'

He sighed. 'Oh, Johnny. Why do you have to play these silly games?' I once had a schoolmaster who spoke like that, with an air of weariness and regret, after which he would remove his belt and thrash the pupil concerned with a demonic intensity. I wondered what sort of thrashing Warner had in mind for me.

'Both of us told you to stay out of things but you wouldn't listen, would you?'

'All I wanted to know was if Bradley Hope was blackmailing you. It's not a crime to be blackmailed, is it? Hope was the criminal.'

'The reason a person can be blackmailed is because he has something to hide. That's why he pays, to keep people from finding out about his misdemeanours.'

'But Bradley Hope's dead.'

'Which gives the people he's been blackmailing a very good motive for killing him, as you well know, which is why you were asking your questions.'

The boat tossed about as the wind strengthened. I held on to the side. 'So are you admitting Bradley Hope was blackmailing you?'

Warner sat still. 'When Bradley came to see me five years ago for work, I told him I couldn't use him. He couldn't perform. I told you that, I think.'

'You did.'

'What I didn't tell you was he turned up again a couple of years later, still wanting work.'

I quickly calculated. During those two years, he'd relieved Tony Pritchard and Simon Butterworth of five thousand pounds each. That wouldn't have lasted long.

'I told him to go and see Verity Kennedy because all he was fit for was sweeping out stables,' Warner recalled contemptuously. 'It was intended to mean "piss off and don't bother me again" but he actually turned up at Vezzy's and offered to work at his yard.'

'And Kennedy took him on?'

'He did, as a stable boy. I ask you, from film star to stable boy in ten short years.'

'So what happened?'

'You don't need me to tell you what happened. Vezzy had pulled a few scams over the years – horses not trying, running ringers, the usual things trainers do.'

It's funny how people manage to justify their actions

by suggesting that everybody else is doing similar things. Mrs Pritchard had said much the same.

'I don't think it's the usual thing for most trainers, David. Jenny Pitman wouldn't be too pleased to hear you saying that. You've been reading too many Dick Francis books.'

'You're such a fuckin' innocent, Johnny Ace. Racing's crawling with thieves, just like the antiques game and the art world and football. Anywhere there's big money to be made.'

'Like show-business?'

'Especially show-business.' He laughed. 'I've made a few million over the years that won't see the taxman's pocket, I can tell you.'

'So how did Hope find out?'

'I haven't finished telling you about Verity yet. Somehow, Hope had nosed his way through Vezzy's private papers and armed himself with enough evidence of crooked deals to put him, not only behind bars, but thrown out of the game for good.'

'How much did he ask for?'

'Ten grand.'

Double what he'd demanded from Pritchard and Butterworth. Obviously, even crime suffered from the curse of inflation. 'And did Vezzy pay?'

'He did. Like everybody else.'

'And did you know about this?'

'Not at the time. Once he'd had the money, Hope left the stables and came back up North.'

'To you?'

'That's right. To me. Still wanting work, but now he'd given up the idea of performing and offered to help in the agency.'

'Funny no one locally ever knew about it.'

'He asked for it to be kept quiet. He didn't want people he knew to find out he'd sunk to this level.'

I smiled to myself. Warner couldn't see the irony of

describing a job in his organisation as something to sink to.

'But how could they not know? They'd see him in your office.'

'He worked in a back room and I let him sleep on the premises. There's another floor above my office that I use as a storeroom for old records and paperwork. He must have lain up there in his sleeping bag night after night going through my contracts until he'd amassed enough evidence to blackmail me.'

'But everyone knows you're a crook.' The words came out involuntarily.

He corrected me. 'Everyone knows I pull a few strokes now and then, and I have a reputation for getting back at people who upset me, but the really big scams I keep quiet about.'

'But Bradley found them?'

'Yes.'

'So what did you do?'

'When he came to me with a demand of fifteen grand, you mean?'

Another increase. Perhaps Bradley had started operating a means test on his victims.

'Did you pay it?'

'Not there and then. I stalled him. The first thing I did was ring Verity, which was when I found out he'd been done as well. We had a talk about it and both of us decided we'd too much to lose. Fifteen grand wasn't a big amount in the scheme of things. He'd not been back to Verity for any more so I paid up.'

'And he disappeared.'

'As if he'd never been near the place.'

'How soon before he came back?'

'He didn't. Not until this January.'

'Oh.'

'He'd been to Vezzy's again though.'

'Another ten grand?'

'Fifteen. Last year, that was. Vezzy told him that
was it. He'd shoot him if he ever came near his
yard again.'

The wind was getting stronger all the time and once
or twice I nearly lost my balance. Warner was obviously
used to it and he remained still.

'So which of you killed him in the end?' As I said
the words, I realised I didn't want to hear the answer.
Once I knew that, I'd have to be silenced. And then I
knew why I'd been brought out here: I wasn't booked
for the return trip.

'I gave him another five thousand in January. I told
him it was all I could get my hands on for a few weeks.
The cheques from the Christmas and New Year period
take some time to come through. He knew this from
working with me so he accepted it.'

'And when he came back?'

'He wanted the other ten. I arranged to meet him one
evening by the Pier Head. It was dark. I took him down
to the Marina and we went for a sail.'

'I'm surprised he came with you.'

'I told him we were going to collect the money from
a hiding place along the river.'

'And he believed it?'

'He'd no choice. I brought him out here, approxi-
mately the area we are in now, strangely enough.' I
looked around. I could see an oil rig in the distance and a
couple of ships, but well outside the range of hailing and
I'd not brought a megaphone with me. I could imagine
it being pretty bleak on a February night.

'And you stabbed him?'

'Through the heart. He wasn't expecting it. And
then I tied weights to his legs and dropped him over
the side.'

'You've certainly moved on from hanging people out
of windows.'

He smiled. 'You remember that? If I had my time

again I'd probably drop them. They can't come back then. But with regards to our late friend Bradley, if those weights hadn't come off the chains, he'd still be down there and you'd have every chance of reaching your hundredth birthday.'

I didn't miss the significance of the remark but there were other things I wanted to know.

'What did you do with the knife?'

'I was a bit clever here, I thought. I wiped my fingerprints off the handle, wrapped it in a plastic bag and took it back with me. The next day, I went across to Birkenhead on the ferry and dropped it in a litter bin near where all the winos and druggies hang out.'

'Why go to all that trouble? Why not just drop it in the sea?'

'When the knife was found, it would be connected with all those homeless halfwits and piss artists and drug addicts so the police wouldn't bother looking for anyone else. That is, if they ever found Hope at all.'

It had nearly worked too. Once the body had been found, Mitchell was soon in the frame for his murder. Warner was unlucky that the police themselves had provided Mitchell with a cast-iron alibi for the time of death.

And, of course, as all the blackmailed victims had paid up, the police didn't know of anyone with a motive to murder Bradley Hope so a mugging seemed as good as anything.

Something, however, didn't add up. Bert Hope's death.

'Why did you kill Bradley's father?'

He looked puzzled. 'His father? I didn't kill him. Why should I?'

'You tell me. Someone killed him.'

'It wasn't me. I never met the man.'

'You knew he was dead?'

'It was front page in the *Daily Post* this morning.

Beaten to a pulp, but not by me, I'm afraid. Sorry, Johnny, you'll have to look for someone else for that one, except you won't be looking anywhere.'

And, from the inside pocket of his blazer, he produced a small revolver.

Chapter Twenty-Three

'I hope you brought the weights,' I said.

'Don't worry. I've planned this very carefully.'

'But I've told people I'm out with you today.'

'So have I – you're in my diary. You're going to have an unfortunate accident.'

'Like the accident I nearly had the other night, you mean?' I suddenly realised he must have been behind the BMW attack.

He smiled. 'If you want a thing doing properly, do it yourself. Isn't that what they say?'

'Aren't you afraid I've left notes with somebody about the blackmail?'

'I'll take that chance.' He seemed totally confident.

'Does Verity know what you're doing?'

He didn't reply. Instead, he took a step forward, still pointing the gun at me. I looked round. If I jumped overboard, I'd drown. The sea was rough and the most I'd ever been able to swim was two breadths of the public baths.

My only chance was to launch myself across at Warner and hope he missed his shot, but then I looked at the distance between us, a mere six feet, and I knew I hadn't got a chance.

It was the sea that saved me. He was standing facing me, presumably fixing a bullseye on my forehead, when a big wave suddenly caused the boat to lurch sideways at the very moment he pulled the trigger. The bullet shot into the sky, inches over my head. Warner lost his balance and fell backwards, his head and the top half of his body hanging over the side of the boat. The gun fell from his grasp and was swallowed up by the swell.

He leaned forward and tried to scramble back into the boat but I quickly jumped across to grab his legs and, before he could regain his balance, I tipped the rest of him into the sea.

He struggled in the water, arms threshing, his fingers straining to gain purchase on the side of the boat, but all the time, the boat was drifting away from him. He tried to swim but, hampered by his blazer, he couldn't quite keep up.

He shouted at me to help him but I couldn't risk it. He might try to pull me into the water. He realised what I was thinking.

'Help me . . . won't harm you . . . give you . . . word . . . can't . . . swim.' His words were becoming disjointed against the roar of the wind and sea and his struggles for breath.

'I wouldn't . . . shot you . . . I was . . . trying . . . frighten you . . . give me . . . arm . . .'

It wasn't a chance I was prepared to take.

Already he was outside my reach and his cries were becoming fainter.

I watched him as he eventually slid beneath the surface . . .

I wasn't proud of myself for letting David Warner drown but I knew it was a choice. One of us would die, and that made it no contest.

However, it was going to take some explaining when I got back. Some juries would undoubtedly class it as murder and, in many ways, they would be right to do so. Yet, I didn't feel any sense of guilt. Warner had killed Bradley Hope and I knew he would have killed me without compunction, which I felt justified my action. Even without the gun, he'd have had the upper hand. All I'd done was level the playing field. In my favour!

First of all, I had to establish some credibility about the accident. There was a lifebelt secured to the back of the boat. I untied it and threw it overboard.

The important thing was, there were no witnesses. Not even the strongest telescopes on the distant ships, the oil rig or the shore could have revealed the struggle that led to Warner's death. As far as the world was concerned, nobody would be able to dispute my story that he fell overboard by sheer accident as the boat lurched in the strong waves.

I went back to the controls and remembered what Warner had said about the emergency channel. I picked up the microphone and screamed, 'Help!' in a frantic voice, followed by, 'Man overboard!'

A coastguard station answered immediately and asked for my position. I looked around for dials and compasses but they meant nothing to me. 'Somewhere off the Welsh coast. I can see the mountains in the distance.'

'Stay there, we'll get the New Brighton lifeboat out. They'll find you.'

I wasn't going anywhere. I waited. The *Bilbo Baggins* rose and fell with the waves until I thought she would tip over. My mouth was dry and I was starting to feel sick.

Within a quarter of an hour, I heard the sound of a helicopter above. I realised it had probably come from RAF Valley, the one you see on all the television newsreels. Now I was the news.

I took off my coat and waved it in the air. The chopper came down low and I pointed vaguely to where Warner had fallen.

We'd drifted so far, by this time, that I wasn't sure within a mile where the spot was or, indeed, in which direction.

The helicopter was still hovering when the lifeboat pulled alongside.

'I've searched the best I can,' I shouted to the crew, 'and there's no sign of him.'

'Just hang on there.' They set off in the direction I'd left and I watched them fade into the distance. Suddenly, I was terrified that Warner would appear from the depths like the Loch Ness Monster and accuse me. I shivered and realised I was cold. Or was it shock? I put my anorak back on and zipped it up.

The lifeboat returned. 'No sign, I'm afraid. Can you handle that thing?'

'I'm not sure.' I'd watched Warner at the controls but I wasn't over-confident. I wasn't even sure how far out we were, probably halfway to the Isle of Man. 'I'll have a go.'

For a second, I entertained the thought that I could have gone across and questioned the Sutton brothers. I was curious to know if they'd been blackmailed too, only now it was academic. They hadn't killed Bradley Hope as I now knew only too well.

'Don't worry. We'll lead the way and the Hoylake boat's out there searching for your friend.'

I tried to remember what Warner had told me about the controls. I turned on the ignition to start the engine. To my relief, it worked. I slowly pressed the throttle and the boat moved forward. I was glad the *Bilbo Baggins* had a steering wheel rather than a rudder, and I was soon heading back towards the mouth of the Mersey behind the lifeboat.

The wind was still strong and I wished I'd brought warmer clothes. I checked my watch. It was nearly four o'clock. In two hours, I had my show to do.

Never had I been more glad to see the Liver Buildings as I sailed up the river past the Pier Head toward the Marina. I radioed the lock-keeper on Channel Thirty-seven and found he was waiting for me to guide me into the Marina. My main problem was finding the berth that we had earlier vacated. There weren't many spaces so I picked the one that looked the likeliest, steered the *Bilbo Baggins* in and switched off the engine.

The police were waiting at the quayside, two officers I didn't know, but I had my story ready.

My longtime friend and sailing companion, Mr David Warner, the well-known local impresario and business-man, had tragically fallen off his boat into the rough seas and drowned. He had been drinking. Not too much though, the autopsy might prove otherwise. I'd tried to save him but in vain.

They didn't seem suspicious – why should they? I looked suitably distressed, I was still shivering from shock, the barman came across with a brandy for me, and the whole experience had obviously had a devastating effect.

My immediate worry was that Warner might turn up alive but I told myself this was impossible. I'd seen him disappear under the water.

'Perhaps you should go along to the hospital, sir,' one of the policemen suggested after they'd finished taking down my statement.

'I'll be fine,' I assured them.

At five o'clock, I managed to get away, leaving my phone number for the police to contact me if they needed anything further.

I got through the show somehow, although I can't say it was the most sparkling one I'd ever done. Afterwards, I went straight back to the flat and rang Jim Burroughs. 'Jim, it's Johnny Ace. Can you get down to my place as soon as possible? I've just solved your case for you.' And before he could reply, I put down the phone.

He arrived within the hour, giving me time to micro-wave a vegetable casserole with herb dumplings that I had in the freezer. I'd not eaten since breakfast and I wanted to be alert for the questions that were sure to follow.

'Which case is this, then?' I sat him in the lounge with a can of ice-cold Newcastle Brown in his hand. I was on mineral water.

'The Bradley Hope case.'

'I didn't know you were handling the enquiry.'

I ignored his sarcasm. 'Get ready for this, Jim. David Warner killed Bradley Hope.'

'Warner? Warner that we knew in the Sixties – the agent?'

'The very same.'

'But he's a prominent local businessman!'

'John F. Kennedy was quite well-connected but that didn't save Marilyn Monroe.'

'Where's Warner now?'

'At the bottom of the Irish Sea. He went scuba-diving without his scuba.'

'Come on, Johnny. Stop bloody playing around. Tell me what happened.'

'Bradley Hope was blackmailing Warner.' I forebore to mention the other victims. I didn't give a toss about Kennedy or the Sutton brothers, but I didn't see the need to turn Simon Butterworth's life upside down. 'He'd been working for him in his office and he discovered evidence of a few naughty deals. He saw it as a chance of making some money so he threatened Warner with the police unless he paid up.'

'He picked on the wrong man there.'

'Precisely. Mind you, he paid at first but Bradley became a little too demanding so our Mr Warner decided to take him for a one-way ride on his boat.'

'There used to be stories of Warner dangling people out of his upstairs windows if they owed him money. That was way back in The Beatles' days.'

'Nowadays, he drops them. Or rather he did. His dangling days are over.'

'But Bradley Hope was a big name. What was he doing, working as a gash hand in Warner's office?'

'Like you said the other day, he was skint. All washed up. It happens.'

'I know it does. Remember P.J. Proby? He was in the big time too, but he ended up cleaning out stables in Huddersfield.'

'Not a good example, Jim. Proby's back in the big time. He played to fifteen thousand people in Manchester last Christmas in *Quadrophenia* and he's got a new CD out with Marc Almond. You forget you're talking to a music man.'

'All right, smartarse.'

'Ah, but Proby stopped drinking, Bradley Hope didn't – that was the difference.'

'So how did Warner kill him?'

'Took him for a ride, just like the old Chicago gangsters – except this ride was on water.'

'And Warner just knifed him and threw him overboard?'

'Got it in one.'

Burroughs looked suspicious. 'Who told you all this?'

'Warner himself. I was out with him on his boat.'

'The same one that he took Bradley out on?'

'The very same. The *Bilbo Baggins*. Do you remember them?'

'I'll say I do. Had a brilliant keyboard player who was always eating fry-ups after every gig.'

'That's the one. Well, Warner named the boat after them.'

'How come you were out with him? I didn't know you and he were friends.'

'He had a business deal he wanted to discuss with me. Nothing heavy, just about putting his artistes on the show. Anyway, we got to talking about Bradley. I told him I thought Bradley was a decent guy who'd fallen on hard times. Warner had had a bit to drink and said he could put me right about that asshole, as he called him, and he told me about the blackmail.'

'Did he admit killing him?'

'He said he stabbed him through the heart and chained him up with weights before throwing him into the sea somewhere off the North Wales coast.'

'So it was premeditated?'

'Definitely. Next day, he took the knife across to Birkenhead and dropped it in a litter bin near the winos to put your people off the scent. So your Mr Mitchell turned out to be telling the truth.'

Jim Burroughs didn't look too pleased to receive this information. 'I don't suppose you've got any of this on tape?'

''Fraid not. It all happened unexpectedly.'

'Hang on, you say Warner's dead. How did that come about? I take it this tragedy occurred when you were out with him?'

'Yes, just this afternoon. I've given a statement to the police. They had the coastguard and the helicopters out but they didn't find him. He fell overboard, Jim.'

'A likely fucking story. More likely you threw him over.'

'Why should I?'

'Why didn't you save him then?'

'I can't swim,' I explained, 'so I could hardly jump in after him. I threw him a lifebelt but he couldn't reach it.'

'He didn't ever hang you from his windows, did he?'

'No, why?'

'Might have given you a motive. I assume there were no witnesses to Mr Warner's sad demise?'

'None.'

'I thought as much.' He took a long swig out of the can. 'You'll have to come back to the station in the morning and make yet another statement.'

'I've already made one.'

He grimaced. 'I'd like to know what's going on with you. You're involved in this affair somewhere, aren't you? Who are you working for?'

'No one,' I answered. It was true. My one-time employer was dead.

'This trip you took with him – it was at his invitation, I presume?'

'Obviously. It was his boat.'

'Could he have intended your trip as a single-ticket-only job – a bit like Bradley Hope's excursion?'

'Come on, Jim, do you think I'd have gone if I'd thought there was any remote possibility of that?'

'I don't know, you're crazy enough. Was there any reason why he might want you out of the way?'

'Don't be silly. I hardly knew the man.'

'Of course, once he'd told you about killing Hope, you became a witness. You could have blackmailed him yourself after that. He might have felt he had to kill you too.'

I shrugged my shoulders. 'Not an easy one to prove, I would've thought.'

Jim Burroughs stood up and paced the room. 'Who killed Bradley Hope's father?' he asked. 'Tell me that.'

'I don't know, Jim, honestly.'

'It must be connected with Bradley's death. Did the old man know his son was a blackmailer?'

Just the opposite, I thought. And he'd not believed me when I'd told him. 'If he did, he never said anything to me.'

'Could they have been in it together, father and son?'

The idea was ludicrous and I said so.

'Somebody must have had a reason for staving in the old bugger's head.'

I thought so too but I didn't think it had anything to do with Bradley's crimes. My guess was that Maria was on the right track. Bert's death had something to do with the Hope family secret.

Tomorrow, I planned to get to Kirkby and St Diana's and continue my search for the elusive Norman Hope.

Chapter Twenty-Four

The *Daily Post* carried a big story on David Warner's fatal accident. As someone who likes to keep a low profile, I wasn't too thrilled about the headline: *Radio DJ in Drowning Tragedy*.

The consequence of my involvement was a number of reporters and cameramen turning up at the door. I gave them all the same story: 'Terrible accident, old friend, couldn't save him . . .' whilst trying to give the impression, without actually saying so, that we'd been on a drinking binge and that Warner had toppled over the side whilst fooling around.

I escaped to The Diner for breakfast, putting on a suit in the hope of merging unnoticed among the accountants and insurance men.

The *Post* quoted the police as saying there were no suspicious circumstances regarding Warner's death, which I was glad to read, although I knew nobody should believe anything the papers said, and much less any statement from the police.

My mobile phone rang as I ate the last of my toast and marmalade. It was Hilary.

'Whatever are you doing now? I've just read this morning's paper.'

'Just an accident,' I said, trying not to get marmalade on the phone.

'Another accident! It's not a week since you got run over. Then there was your policeman friend looking for you in the Masquerade on Friday. What's going on?'

'Coincidence, Hil,' I assured her. 'Everything's fine. How about the movies one night?'

She backed down. 'Why don't we go and see *Elvis* at the Empire? It's supposed to be brilliant.'

I'd seen it back in the Seventies in London and it *had* been good. 'Yeah, nice idea. What night?'

'I'm off on Thursday.'

'OK – come to the station at seven. We can have a quick bite to eat first.'

Hardly had I put the phone back in my pocket when it rang again. This time it was Maria.

'Are you all right?' she asked anxiously. 'I've just heard about the accident.'

'I'm fine.'

'It wasn't an accident was it, Johnny?'

'I'll tell you all about it,' I said. I've never trusted the security of mobile phones, even digital ones. 'Are you free tonight?'

'Yes. Robin's gone back now. Why don't you come over to mine and I'll cook something?'

'That sounds wonderful. Eight o'clock?'

'I'll see you then.'

I wiped the marmalade off the phone with a napkin dipped in the remains of the tea. Going to Maria's would get me away from my flat and possible further visits from the press until the story died down. Which wouldn't be until Warner's body floated ashore somewhere.

The sooner the better. I'd feel safer when the inquest was over. Assuming, of course, they went for accidental death. I didn't care to dwell on any alternative.

I left the Royal Liver Buildings and walked through the Cunard Building to my parking meter. I'd brought the car out to save going back to the flat and more confrontations with the press. I knew now how poor Princess Di felt.

The drive to Kirkby took me less than half an hour. St Diana's looked deserted as I pulled up outside the club.

I tried the door and found it unlocked. A cleaning lady was polishing the stainless steel sink behind the bar. She was probably the same age as the hookers in the Bamalama Club but infinitely less glamorous. Her hair was tied in a pony tail with an elastic band, she wore no make-up and her slacks were baggy all the way down to her ankles.

'Excuse me,' I said, 'have you seen Norman anywhere?'

She looked round startled and the ash from her cigarette dropped on her nylon overall. 'You gave me a fright. I never heard you there, luv. Norman Who do you want?'

'Norman that cleans the drains.'

She looked puzzled. 'Never heard of him,' she said. 'We come here twice a week and I've never seen him. Elsie!' she shouted to her colleague somewhere on the other side of the clubroom.

A stout, older lady shuffled round the corner, a brush in her hand. 'What is it?'

'Do you know anyone called Norman?'

'Only Greg Norman the golfer. Why?'

'This gentleman is looking for him. Says he cleans the grids here.'

Elsie shook her head. 'Doesn't ring a bell. Who is he?'

I said, 'He's like the odd-job man. It was Father O'Brien who told me about him. Norman Ericson his name is. He reckoned I'd find him here Monday morning.'

'It's Tuesday today,' pointed out the first cleaner.

'I wonder if he means that old fella that empties all the rubbish,' said Elsie. 'You know the one, Doreen, with the limp that's always blowing his nose on the side of his hand, the dirty beggar.'

'I know the one you mean now. Is his name Norman, then?'

'Dunno. Could be.'

'Where would I find him?' I asked.

'He just turns up occasionally, no special time. I've not seen him today, have you, Else?'

'Do you know where he lives?'

Doreen shook her head. 'No idea.'

'Wait a minute,' said Elsie. 'Didn't I hear him say once that he was on the eighth floor of somewhere, 'cos we was talking about gardens and I said he ought to get a window box if he wanted to grow things.'

'He must be in the Stafford Cripps block then,' Doreen reckoned. 'That's about a mile away – look, you can see the top of it over there.'

I looked through the window at a concrete slab stuck against the midday sun. 'Pretty hideous, isn't it?'

'You want to go inside,' Doreen sniffed. 'It's a disgrace. I keep my lot well away from there. All drug-dealers and scallies.'

'If this Norman turns up,' Elsie asked, 'who shall I tell him was looking for him?'

'He doesn't know me,' I said. 'Thanks for your help,' and I went back to the car.

The Stafford Cripps tower block was every bit as awful as Doreen had suggested. The lifts weren't working and the stone steps were littered with empty cans, cardboard trays with half-eaten meals stuck to them, crisp packets, the odd syringe and intermittent piles of dogdirt. The stench of stale urine vied with the smell of tomcats and the combination almost choked me.

'Streets in the sky' the council had called them when they were built. I thought of Raymond Chandler's words, 'Down these mean streets a man must go . . .', only in this case it was 'up'.

I was gasping by the time I reached the eighth storey. Perhaps I needed to go round to Denis McKale's gym for a few workouts.

There seemed to be eight flats grouped on each floor.

I tried the first door I came to. It was painted a bright green and had three security locks fitted. There was no bell so I banged hard with my fist.

The curtain at the side twitched and I could hear faint sounds of a television set from within but nobody answered. I realised I'd come badly prepared for this excursion. By wearing a suit, I'd be mistaken for someone in authority, like the rent man. Landlords weren't popular in many places as it was, but in venturing into a highrise like Stafford Cripps, they took their life in their hands. At best, doors were unlikely to be opened to them.

I tried the second flat but with the same result so I gave up. Halfway down the staircase, I met two kids on their way up.

'You don't know where Norman Ericson lives, do you?' I asked.

'I wouldn't tell you if I did, so fuck off.' He was about seven or eight and had two earrings in each ear and shaven hair, but the look of menace was dissipated by his ears, which stuck out on either side of his head like teapot handles.

His friend spat at me as they ran off and I looked forward to the day Tony Blair would come to power to introduce his promised curfew, although it would be unlikely to start as early as one o'clock in the afternoon.

I decided my best chance would be to go back in the evening wearing different clothes. Now, however, it was Tuesday afternoon, a time when I usually went down to the office to touch base with Geoffrey.

'We're well into Princes Avenue, boss,' he announced before I'd even shut the door behind me. 'Jack had the lads there at eight sharp yesterday morning.'

It was a pity they hadn't been there on Sunday morning and woken me before Rodney's arrival at Shirley's flat.

'Great,' I told him. 'Have we anyone for Livingstone Drive yet?'

'A couple of people have rung. I've made appointments for you to meet them at five if that's OK.'

I remembered the last time I'd waited to meet someone at that house and it reminded me to thank Geoffrey for saving my life.

'Goes with the job, boss,' he said shyly. 'You did say you wanted a minder. What's all this business with Warner? Seems like you managed without my services there.'

'That was an accident, Geoff, and don't ever think anything else.'

'Better him than you though, eh?' and he winked.

I said nothing. I didn't feel a hero although Geoffrey made me sound like one. I was more of a hero risking a visit to the Stafford Cripps highrise at night, but it would have to be tomorrow night as tonight I was going to Maria's.

I had a few minutes to spare when I arrived at Livingstone Drive so I rang Pat's bell.

'Johnny, are you all right? We saw the accident last week when that car nearly hit you.'

'I'm fine, Pat, thanks.'

'And what about yesterday on the boat? Trouble seems to follow you.'

Or I went out looking for it, one or the other.

'Is your Mum up and about? I wanted a quick word.'

I was taken up to see the old dear, sitting by the window in a wheelchair reading a copy of *The Lady*.

'I suppose you read about Bert Hope, Mrs Lake?'

'A terrible business. Who'd do that to an old man?'

'I was hoping you might have some idea yourself. Did the Hopes have any enemies you know of?'

'No, but then I didn't live in the neighbourhood. I only knew Mary through work, as it were, and she was a lovely woman. Deserved better than him.'

I risked telling her a little of Bert's secret. After all, he was dead now. 'Bert told me there was some shameful event took place in the family years ago. I wondered if you knew what it was.'

She thought for a minute. 'I've no idea, but if there was anything, I'm sure it had nothing to do with Mary.'

Neither of the people turned up to look at the flat. I gave them ten minutes then drove to the station to do the show.

'The press have been looking for you.' Ken looked displeased. He hated interruptions. 'You never mentioned this accident last night.'

'Didn't want to worry you, Ken.'

'Bit tasteless playing *Endless Sleep*, wasn't it?'

'My sense of humour. Besides, I've always liked Jody Reynolds.'

'I thought it was Marty Wilde did that.'

'He did, but you should know by now that we always play the originals on this show.'

I dedicated a Dinah Washington song, *Big John*, to Misty at the Bamalama and played Big Joe Turner for Memphis and the boys. I thought about *Sea of Love* for David Warner but I knew where to draw the line.

I was half an hour early at Maria's but she was pleased to see me. She wore a lemon top with matching scarf and a short black mini-skirt. She had the legs to get away with it.

'I hope you don't mind,' I said, 'but I didn't want to go back to my place this afternoon with all the reporters, so I wondered if I could have a shower here before we eat.'

'Don't be silly, you don't have to ask. Look, I'll run you a bath. Did you bring a change of clothes?' I pointed to my overnight bag. 'OK. I'll finish the meal while you have a good soak. Later you can tell me everything that's been happening.'

I lay in the foam-filled hot water and closed my eyes
and recalled the giant bath at the Crown Hotel. Harrogate
was only ten days ago but it seemed like an age away.
Ten days since I'd first learned that Bradley Hope was
a blackmailer instead of a victim.

Since that time I'd uncovered three more blackmail
victims, been nearly run over, and killed the man I'd discovered to be Bradley's murderer. Hardly a quiet week.

Now, though, I was left with a greater mystery. Who
had killed Bradley's father, and why?

'Like I said before, it's got to be someone from the
past,' reiterated Maria, as we sat beside her lounge
window overlooking the Bay, drinking the last of the
red wine. The meal had been delicious – duckling with
nectarines followed by Maria's strawberry flan.

'But who?'

'Bert must have had a good idea who, that's why he
was terrified.'

'It's got to be Norman,' I said. 'Revenge for being
thrown out all those years ago.'

'What does your policeman friend think?'

'Jim Burroughs? He doesn't know about the Hope
secret and he's never traced Norman.' I told her my
fleeting idea about Bert having a love-child.

'Even if he did, why should he or she murder him?
No, I don't go for that.'

'Mrs Lake said they were a very private family. Mary
idolised Bert.'

'I still don't know why Bert said Bradley was being
blackmailed. Why didn't he just ask you for protection
if he was afraid?'

'I don't know.' Maria hadn't drawn the curtains and
I looked out of the window. The skies were clear and a
half-moon illuminated the sea where David Warner had
drowned. I shivered at the thought.

'What happened with David Warner?' asked Maria,
as if reading my mind.

I told her about the boat trip. 'Do you think I was wrong?' I asked, after I'd finished. She was probably the only person I would ever tell, and somehow it was important to me that, even if she disapproved, she wouldn't condemn me.

'I think,' she said carefully, 'it was the only thing you could do. He tried to kill you. If that bullet had been a few inches lower . . .' She left the words unspoken. 'Has it upset you?'

'Morally it has. I think I've done a terrible thing but, like you say, I don't feel I had an alternative and I don't feel guilty in the sense I should allow the Law to punish me. It was something between Warner and me. I'm not going to be a danger to other people.'

'It's pretty certain Bradley Hope was blackmailing the others, isn't it?'

'I'd say so. Not a nice person, our Bradley.'

'None of them are very nice, not even the victims. After all, they were all on the make.'

'Is there anyone nice in the whole case? Bert, I suppose.'

'Probably not,' said Maria, and I looked at her.

'Oh, come on, Bert's harmless.'

'He's never sounded very nice to me. He disowned his own son, didn't he? And he wanted you to kill somebody for him. Besides, we both agree now that he was probably lying about Bradley.'

I had to admit she was right. 'He had had a hard time of it though.'

'Bradley was making a fortune at one time, when he was a film star. It's funny Bert never saw any of it. They hadn't fallen out, had they?'

'I once asked Bert why Bradley didn't buy his parents a big house and he said he didn't want to move from Bootle, especially after Mary died.'

'That's another thing. You say she was knocked down and killed by an off-duty policeman. Wouldn't there have been an insurance payout? I mean, the driver would be bound to be insured if he was on the Force.'

'You're right. I never thought of that.'

'So where did that money go?'

'It must have gone to Bert originally.'

'Whatever did he do with it? Perhaps he had a nest-egg stashed away after all.'

'And was killed for it.'

'Who inherits?'

That was the question I'd asked Jim Burroughs. 'It's got to be Norman, with Bradley dead. He's the only one left.'

Maria looked thoughtful. 'There's another possibility. Bradley was blackmailing Bert and that's where his insurance money went.' She waited to see my reaction.

'His own father? That's crazy.'

'Why? He was blackmailing everyone else he knew.'

'But what would he have on Bert?'

'I don't know. You're the detective.' She smiled and put her arm round me. 'Come on, it's late. Shall we go to bed?'

It was the first time since Harrogate and it was good. She made no mention of demands or commitments, and afterwards we had a long and peaceful sleep. I felt fitter the next morning than I had done for a while; the stresses of the past week had eased away.

'What's the plan of action now?' asked Maria over breakfast.

'I'm going to find Norman Hope,' I replied. 'He's the only person who might have the answers to all this.'

'Be careful, Johnny. If he did kill Bert, he'll be dangerous.'

I smiled ruefully. 'I'm getting used to dangerous people in this case.'

'Let me know what happens when you've seen him.'

'I will.' I knew she really meant I should let her know I was safe, and I was glad of her concern.

'I was thinking about Bradley getting money from his father,' she continued. 'He needn't have been blackmailing him. He could have just demanded it.'

'With menaces, you mean?' I laughed. 'Charming family.'

'That's all I can think of.'

'We'll know more when I've spoken to Norman – if and when I can find him.'

Chapter Twenty-Five

Wednesday evening found me back in Kirkby. I was wearing an Everton replica football shirt, faded blue denims with holes in the knees, an old pair of trainers and a baseball cap and I looked like every other middle-aged slob on the estate.

The Stafford Cripps building appeared even more forbidding in the dark. I parked on the street outside and ventured on to the stairwell. It was eight o'clock and nobody was about.

On the eighth floor, I walked around the block trying to guess which flat Norman Ericson might occupy. I still didn't know if Norman Ericson was Norman Hope, but it was the only lead I had.

I was looking for signs that indicated a man living alone, although I didn't know that to be the case for certain, but this time I ignored flats with broken toys, skateboards and children's debris outside the door.

By the time I'd completed a circuit of the building, I'd eliminated five of the eight dwellings. I knocked on the wooden door of No. H2. A woman peered through the side window then came to the front door.

She wore a blue towelling dressing gown that ended above her knees and she held a hair dryer in her hand. She was probably in her early thirties but the deep lines on her face and flecks of grey in her straggly wet hair made her look ten years older.

'Yeah?'

'Sorry to bother you, luv. I'm looking for a Norman Ericson.'

'Never heard of him.' She started to shut the door but I persisted.

'An old bloke, in his sixties. He does some cleaning round the clubs. Walks with a limp.'

The door stayed half-closed. 'And he lives up here?'

'So I'm told. On this floor.'

She peered at me suspiciously. 'You're not doing drugs, are you?'

'No.'

'And you're not the police?'

'Do I look like the police?'

'You could be. They're all in plain clothes these days. If you see a copper in uniform round here, you know it's an actor on *Brookside*.'

'I suppose you're right but I'm not an actor or a copper, I'm just an ordinary bloke looking for Norman Ericson.'

'You don't want a bit of company, do you?' She opened the door wide again and licked her lips invitingly.

'Are you on the game then?'

'No, I'm not,' she retorted angrily, then her voice softened. 'But I have a few gentlemen come round sometimes, help with the housekeeping, like.'

'I see.'

'Only ones I know, mind you. The housing benefit and income support doesn't go far.' I looked over her shoulder at the twenty-eight-inch television and the video recorder. 'I've got some blue films if you'd like to watch those,' she offered, seeing my glance.

'Is Norman one of your gentlemen?' I asked.

'God no, not if he's sixty odd. I'm a bit particular.'

'Who lives next door but one, the one with the cardboard where the hall window used to be?'

'Number four, is that? I don't know. People keep

themselves to themselves round here. It can be dangerous to get involved, if you know what I mean.' She allowed the dressing gown to fall open a few inches to reveal her breasts which were flat and drooping, like white pancakes against her sun-tanned skin. 'Are you sure you won't come in for a bit? I'm not expensive.'

She wouldn't have to be, I thought. 'Sorry, dear. Maybe another time. I've got to find Mr Ericson.'

'Well, sod you.' She banged the door shut and I moved on to No. H4. My knock brought no reply. The place was in darkness and I could hear no sounds.

My last possibility was H7 round the opposite side. This had a glass-fronted door, not a sensible choice in this area, I felt. It also boasted a bell and one long ring brought someone almost immediately to answer it.

'Me Mam and Dad's out. There's only me and me baby sister here.' He was about nine years old, with blond hair and blue eyes and he wore an Everton replica shirt like mine, a coincidence he quickly noticed. 'Hey, are you an Evertonian?'

'Yep.'

'Crap this season, aren't they?'

''Fraid so.'

'I wouldn't tell my mate that, though. He supports Liverpool and they're a load of gobshites.'

'"Overpaid nancy-boys" someone called them on David Mellor's show.'

'Do you listen to that?' I'd obviously made a friend for life. He had a cheeky face, freckled, and his hair was long over his collar. He'd need to be tough, with his looks, to survive in a neighbourhood like this.

'Never miss it, and Richard Littlejohn during the week.'

'I listen to that as well. It's good, innit?'

'I'm looking for an old man called Norman Ericson.' Anyone over forty would be an old man to a boy his age.

He screwed up his face. 'Who's he?'

'Some old guy that's supposed to live on this floor.'

'Don't know him. Sure you've got the right block? There's Clement Attlee Tower across the way.'

'Who lives in H4 on the other side? The one with the cardboard in the window.'

'Dunno. Could be him. I dunno. Never seen no one go in there.'

So much for the council's talk of 'neighbours in the sky'. Mind you, it probably was just as bad in the old terraced houses though, at one time, every street would have some spinster or housewife who was a busybody and knew everything that was going on in the neighbourhood. That's all gone now like sawdust in butchers.

I thanked the lad anyway. 'Do you think we'll go down?' he asked me anxiously.

I didn't like to even think about it. 'No chance,' I lied. 'We're not good enough for the first division.'

I retraced my steps to No. 4 and banged again on the door. No answer. Making sure nobody was watching, I pushed the cardboard out of the window frame and peered through into the hall.

I couldn't make out too much in the dark but I thought I saw a man's raincoat hung up on a hallstand.

I checked the lock. It was a Yale-type, the sort that burglars are supposed to open in five seconds with any plastic credit card. I've tried it many times and it's never worked for me. At least, here, there was an alternative means of illegal entry.

I thrust my left arm through the gap and reached for the lock on the door. It was a couple of inches out of my reach. I edged closer to the wall, stood on tiptoe and tried again. This time I was able to pull back the catch and the door opened.

I quickly stepped through, closed it behind me and switched on the light. The naked low-watt bulb allowed me to see through to a small living room, a bedroom, a tiny kitchen and a bathroom.

I tried the bedroom first. The bed was unmade and covered with an old grey blanket, the sort you put round horses, rather than a duvet. The pillow case had brown grease stains.

I opened the old oak wardrobe. A pair of men's trousers hung there, still with the braces attached, and a couple of old suits. Two pairs of worn black shoes and some trainers were on the floor. On a bedside table was a copy of the *Sun* dated Saturday, March 15.

If the man who lived here had battered Bert Hope to death, he'd been here the day afterwards.

In the kitchen, a pile of unwashed crockery lay in the sink. I opened the fridge. Half a pint of milk was starting to go sour. Other than that, the only occupant was a cabbage. On the badly stained electric cooker was a pan half full of water. There seemed to be no kettle. On the work top lay a collection of unmatching cutlery, a big old tea caddy, a full jar of Marmite and a few cans of Boddingtons draught bitter. There was a white sliced loaf in the bread bin.

All the indications were that a man lived here alone. There were no flowers, no women's clothes, no ornaments.

An old patterned moquette three-piece suite took up most of the space in the living room. On a teak draw-leaf table, a football coupon, biro, an ashtray full of cigarette stubs, a lottery ticket and an electricity bill lay next to a mug of half drunk coffee.

I picked up the electricity bill and read the name on the top. It was Norman Ericson.

I went over to a large chest of drawers and opened them one by one. Two were full of clothes – pyjamas, jumpers, shirts and underwear. The rest were empty.

I tried the bathroom last. Stood in the bath were an assortment of mops and brushes and a cardboard box with cleaning materials. Obviously the tools of his trade.

Well, I knew I was in the right flat. I'd found Norman Ericson, but how could I connect him to Norman Hope? I needed some evidence – a birth certificate, family documents. Jim Burroughs had told me that papers had been stolen from Bert Hope's bedroom chest. If Ericson *was* Norman Hope then those papers could be here . . .

I searched the kitchen cupboards, just a few tins of food, mostly beans; the bathroom cabinets, a razor, shaving foam and a toothbrush and paste; and through the clothes, but I found nothing.

I didn't hear the door opening. I just felt someone behind me as I stood with my back to the living-room door and, as I turned, I saw the shape of a large man, his hand raised.

'I've got you, pal, good and proper,' he said, and before I had a chance to move, he hit me on the side of the head.

Chapter Twenty-Six

I fell to my knees as the pain stunned me but managed to instinctively hold up my arm to ward off the next blow. Mercifully, my assailant's punch had missed the bruised area on my skull. As he struck out, I rolled to one side and grabbed his ankles. He fell over and we wrestled on the floor until I was able to pin one arm behind his shoulders and hold him down with my knee in the small of his back.

'Right,' I told him. 'You move now and I'll break your arm. Understood?' I yanked his arm an extra couple of inches upwards to reinforce the message. He grunted. 'I've got a few questions for you. For a start, is this your flat?' I gave another little jerk to encourage a response.

'Yes, and you've no right to be here.' It wasn't the voice of a young man.

'Maybe not, but I am here so let's get on with it. What's your name?'

'Look, let me get up, you're hurting me.'

'All right, but don't try anything or you'll know about it.'

He slowly got to his feet and turned round. He looked older than his sixty-two years. His skin was loose and fleshy, thick hairs grew out of his nose and ears and his cheeks were rough like weathered bark. He wore an old greatcoat over some crumpled slacks and a thick workman's shirt in a red check. His hair was grey and seemed to grow in thin patches over his head.

I motioned him to sit on one of the armchairs. He limped slightly as he stepped across. 'Your name,' I repeated.

'Norman Ericson.' He spat the words out. 'Though what it's to do with you . . . You've broken into my home and then you start asking me questions.'

'I've been looking for you for days.'

'Why? You don't know me.'

'That depends. Was your father Herbert Hope?'

His jaw dropped. 'How do you know that? Who are you?'

'Just tell me.'

'Yes, the bastard was my father and I hope he rots in hell.' He spoke viciously as if the words alone could not express his venom.

'So you know he's dead. Did you kill him?'

He said nothing but stared into space with a malevolent expression. I carried on with the questions.

'I saw your father last week. I know all your family history, Norman. About you and Alison and the baby.'

'He told you, did he?'

'He did, but not the whole picture so you can fill me in with the details.'

'Like what?'

'Like how old you were when you first slept with your little sister.'

'Twelve,' he declared in a firm voice.

If that was meant to shock me, it worked. *'Twelve?'*

'That's right. She was ten. We just messed about at first, you know, like kids do. But we soon learnt what to do to each other. Instinct really, I suppose. Nobody teaches animals how to shag. They just get on with it.'

'But you knew it was wrong?'

'Our parents told us fuck all about sex. It was never mentioned. Of course we knew we weren't supposed to do it, but it was the shagging we thought was wrong, not the fact that we were a brother and sister doing it with each other.'

'When did your parents find out?'

'They never did until Alison got pregnant.'

'How far gone was she then?'

'Over five months. She'd not dared to tell them before that, but she was starting to show.'

'What did your mother say about it all?'

'My mother was never allowed to have an opinion of her own. My old man spoke for her. That's how things were in those days.'

The pendulum had swung the other way now, I thought. Norman Hope was right, though. You wouldn't say Mary had been a downtrodden woman. She just knew her place.

'How soon after the baby was born did he send you away?'

He shrugged his shoulders. 'No more than a couple of weeks. As soon as the blood tests came through.'

'And what then?'

'Got a cigarette and I'll tell you?'

'Sorry, I don't smoke.'

'There's a packet on the table under that coupon. Pass it me, will you.'

I picked up a squashed packet of Benson & Hedges and threw it across. He took out one cigarette and lit it with a battered Zippo lighter from his coat pocket. He then proceeded to recount his life story after leaving Liverpool.

He'd lived rough, at first, in London, moving in with a crowd of beatniks in the Notting Hill area. He started calling himself Norman Ericson to avoid National Service.

He worked as a cleaner, caretaker, porter and on building sites to earn enough money to buy his food and drink, mainly drink.

When the Sixties came, he got in with the CND

left-wing crowd and was arrested a couple of times during student riots. In 1967, when it was all flower power and Free Love, he joined up with some hippies and travelled to Cornwall where he'd lived for a few years in a commune.

Times had become hard by the Seventies. The commune broke up and he ended up in a bedsit. He turned to petty crime to survive and eventually landed in jail. When he was released, he headed back to the city, this time to Manchester, where he resumed his career of burglary, shoplifting and theft, alternating his abode between cheap lodging-houses and Strangeways Prison.

'What brought you back to Liverpool?' I asked. 'And when did you arrive?'

'Just a minute,' he said. 'You've been asking all the friggin' questions. Now it's my turn. Who the hell are you? Why are you so interested in my business?'

'My name's Johnny Ace. I'm a private investigator. I was working for your father.'

'What would he want with a detective?'

'It was after your brother Bradley was killed. He contacted me to find out who murdered him.'

'Weren't the police doing that already?'

'Yes, but Bert knew something the police didn't. Bradley was being blackmailed.'

'Who by, did he say?'

'That's what he wanted me to find out because he was afraid the blackmailers, whoever they were, would try to kill him next.'

'That's a good one.' Norman Hope looked amused. 'And what did you think of all this?'

'Bert was afraid of someone, that's for sure. But I found it hard to believe Bradley was being blackmailed. Just the opposite, in fact. I subsequently found out that Bradley himself was a blackmailer and had made a considerable sum of money over the last five years.'

'Did my father tell you how they were able to blackmail Bradley?'

'He called it the family secret. He said Bradley had paid up because he didn't want his Dad to be exposed to the shame of the world if it got out his son had fathered a child by his own sister.'

For a moment there was quiet then Norman burst out laughing, but it was a bitter laugh. 'Is that what my father told you? And you swallowed it?'

'I found it hard to see Bradley as a victim, but then I couldn't see the point of Bert lying. After all, he's the one that hired me in the first place. In the end, I decided he really wanted protection and the story was just an excuse.'

'Why do you think he needed protecting?'

'I never found out, but seeing as how he ended up being bludgeoned to death, he obviously did.'

'Not a good result for you, eh?' Norman laughed again. His father's violent death seemed to amuse rather than horrify him.

'I asked you before, did you kill him?'

This time he answered. 'No, I didn't but I would have been quite happy to have done. The bastard ruined my life and a lot of other people's.'

'But he didn't deserve to be beaten to death at eighty-one.'

'Why not? Though I agree, thirty-one would have been better.'

'You're one to talk about ruining people's lives. What about poor Alison?'

He smiled. 'Odd how Alison becomes *poor* Alison in this story, like she was a helpless little girl led astray by her wicked brother.'

'Wasn't she?'

'Listen, pal, we grew up in the Dingle when times were hard and kids were rough. We went shoplifting and thieving and Allie was the most nimble at it of

all of us. We ran gangs and had fights and sagged off
school. A right shower of scallies we were, Alison 'n'
all. She wasn't no angel.'

I remembered Mrs Clarke's comments about the Hope
family.

'That doesn't justify what you did.'

'What I did?' He shook his head sadly. 'You've got
your facts all wrong, you know. All wrong.'

'How do you mean?' I got the feeling that he was
going to tell me something momentous.

'For a start, Bert wasn't lying to you when he said
Bradley had told him he was being blackmailed. He did
tell him that and the old man paid up because Bradley
had a bigger hold on him than you know.'

'On Bert?'

'Oh yes, on Bert.'

'What could Bradley possibly have on his father?'

'The real family secret, Johnny Ace – the *real* family
secret. You see, I wasn't the father of my sister's
child at all.'

'But the blood test . . .'

'A load of bollocks. That could only prove that
I *wasn't* the father, if it was negative. If it was
positive, it meant I could have been the father, but
only along with a million other people with the same
blood group. There was none of this DNA malarkey
in those days.'

'Then who was the father?'

He straightened in his chair. 'Are you ready for this?
I'll tell you who it was. The father of Alison's baby
was my old man. Bert bloody Hope slept with his own
daughter!'

Chapter Twenty-Seven

It took me a minute to digest this startling information. 'When did you first find this out?'

'Not until five years ago. I met Bradley by chance in Manchester. I was living rough as usual and drinking in a pub one lunchtime when Bradley came in. I'd not seen him for over forty years – since he was seven, in fact – but I recognised him, of course, because his photo was always in the papers. Mind you, he looked pretty ropey himself by then.'

'I know. I saw him around that time.' It was when I'd had him on the show. It was also about then that he started his career in blackmail.

'I went over to him,' Norman continued, 'and introduced myself and we got on fine.' He laughed ruefully. 'Like long-lost brothers. He seemed upset at the way I'd been treated, and it was then that he told me about my father's little trips to Alison's room when everyone else in the house was asleep.'

'But he was only a kid at the time.'

'He couldn't get to sleep one night, saw the old man creep into Alison's bedroom and followed him.'

'And what did he see?' As if I couldn't guess.

'The old man on top of his big sister, humping away. He didn't realise what it meant at the time, of course, being a kid. But he did later. Bradley was always a cunning little bastard though. He said nothing then, just saved it up for future use. "Knowledge is power," he told me, "and power brings money."' An appropriate motto, I thought, for a blackmailer.

'So how did Bert fix the blood tests?'

'He didn't need to. Clever, the old man, wasn't he? You see, he knew I'd been shagging Alison too, so he saw how he could put the blame on to me, because we both had the same blood group.'

'How come he said nothing earlier on when he knew you were doing it with your sister?'

'Perfect cover for him, wasn't it? He was just biding his time before he had a go at her.'

'So you don't know for sure the baby wasn't yours? It could have been either of you.'

'No. I'd stopped doing it with her months before. I'd got myself a girlfriend by then and I was shagging her instead. I'd not been near our Allie. But I was too young or too stupid to realise it couldn't have been my kid and the old man was quick in having me sent away before I could work it out.'

'How do you know Alison wasn't having it away with half the lads in the street as well?'

'She wasn't. She never bothered with lads in that way. She was a tomboy. Played football and cricket with the lads, drank and swore with them, but no shagging or anything like it.'

'Kept it in the family, eh?' I said drily. 'Did your mother never know the truth?'

'You're fuckin' joking. Never. She thought the sun shone out of my old man's arse and anything he said she accepted without question. Once I'd been thrown out, I never saw her or heard from her again. Or any of them.'

'What happened to the child?'

'According to Bradley, it was adopted. He never saw it and it was never referred to again.'

'What about when your mother died – did you not hear about that? It must have been in the papers.' Although I hadn't seen it.

'I never read the papers. I didn't know about it until

I saw Bradley that day in Manchester. That was when
he told me about the money.'

'What money?'

'The insurance the old man got from my mother's
accident. The bastard copped for twenty-five grand.'

'Twenty-five grand?' So Bert did have a nest-egg after
all. 'What happened to it?'

'What do you think? Bradley was no fool. He went
round to my father's with his story about him being
blackmailed and he'd run out of money, exactly as the
old man told you he'd said. Bert wasn't lying to you,
you see. Bradley told him if he didn't come up with ten
grand, this mystery blackmailer was going to spill the
beans about Alison's baby being his. But, of course, there
was no mystery blackmailer, it was Bradley all along.'

Maria had been right. Bradley was blackmailing his
own father, although we'd never have guessed what the
hold was that he had over him.

'Hang on though, that was five years ago. Bert only
hired me at the end of last month.'

'He paid up five years ago but, last Christmas, Bradley
had been back for more. He refused to pay, at first,
so Bradley put the fear of God in him. Told him
these people would kill him if he didn't pay and then
they'd come after the old man. So, you were right,
he hired you for protection. He must have been shit-
ting himself when Bradley got killed. Thought he'd
be next.'

'Never mind him, it must have been a shock to you
when Bradley got killed.'

'Not really. Any one of a dozen people could have had
it in for him. I knew all about what he was doing with his
blackmail scams. God, he was shacking up here some of
the time. It was always on the cards that someone'd have
him seen to.' Norman didn't seem too concerned about
his brother's demise.

'Why should Bert pay up anyway? There was no one

left who'd bother whether he'd fathered Alison's child
or not.'

'But there was. Me, for a start.'

'But you knew.'

'He didn't know that, did he? He'd always been
terrified that one day I'd find out. He thought that if
I ever knew how I'd been stitched up, I'd come back
and see to him. He didn't know that Bradley had already
told me everything.'

'And he didn't know that both his sons were blackmailing
him either.'

'There's no need for that holier than thou stuff. The
bastard threw me out of my home when I was just a kid.
He ruined my life just to save his skin. He deserved all
he got.'

'Even a fatal battering?'

Norman held out his hands. 'Maybe.'

'Did Bradley split the money with you as well?'

Norman looked shifty. 'Let's say he gave me a
fair share.'

'And after Bradley died, did you go back to Bert's
for more money?'

'And did I kill him? That's what you mean, isn't
it?'

'You already said you didn't.'

'That's right, and I've even got an alibi.' I was
surprised. 'It said in the paper he was killed on Friday
afternoon, didn't it? Well, on Friday afternoon, I was at
St Diana's helping clear rubbish out of the basement.
Just ask the priest, he'll vouch for me.'

'In that case, who do you think did kill him?'

'Fuck knows and who cares?'

I supposed I did. However odious a person Bert Hope
had turned out to be, he had been my client. He'd been
looking for protection, however obtusely, and I'd let
him down. I'd every intention of finding out who had
murdered him.

I gave Norman my card and told him to ring me if anything happened. I didn't know what was likely to happen, but it seemed a good idea at the time. I left him sitting in his armchair, beer in hand, and drove back home in a reflective mood.

I was no nearer to finding Bert's killer, but the disclosure that Bert was the real father of Alison's child was surely a relevant factor in his death.

I wondered where the child was now.

The only people I knew who had known the Hope family in the early days were Mrs Lake, who knew them before Bradley was born, and Mrs Clarke, who'd remembered Alison's pregnancy and had told me where I might find Norman in Kirkby.

I needed to talk to both of them again.

I was making my breakfast the next morning when I heard the news on Radio Merseyside. David Warner's body had surfaced at Formby Point, where more often it was dead sheep and used syringes that were washed ashore.

It was discovered by a local woman, Mrs Partington, walking her Labrador on the beach. The cause of death was confirmed as drowning and police did not regard the death as suspicious.

Warner was described as a major figure of the Sixties' Merseybeat scene, and my name was mentioned again as his companion on the boat when he fell overboard.

I rang Geoffrey as soon as the office was open to get Mrs Clarke's number.

'Nothing gone wrong with the sale, has there?' he asked anxiously. 'We've nearly got the new roof on.'

I assured him the Princes Avenue house was fine.

'While you're there, I've got someone wants to see Livingstone Drive. Can you show them if you're going to be around today?'

I wanted to see Mrs Lake in the flat above so I said I would.

'It's a Miss Barrie,' said Geoffrey. 'She's a student at John Moores.'

'Right. Any other news?'

'How's your head?' It was exactly a week since I drove to Cheltenham after my 'accident' with the BMW. It seemed like a year.

'Fine.' It had survived last night's altercation with Norman Hope.

The appointment with Miss Barrie was at midday so I drove over an hour earlier, hoping to catch Pat Lake and her mother in.

'This is becoming a habit,' Pat said, as she answered the door. The sound of rock music filled the flat.

'I take it your mother's in bed, or has she become an Ozzy Osbourne fan?' I asked, as I stepped into the hall.

'Mother prefers Al Bowley. She's still got a wind-up gramophone in her room to play her old seventy-eights on. Come on in.' I followed her into the lounge and she turned the volume down on the stereo. 'Tea?'

'If you've got chocolate biscuits.'

She went into the kitchen and I looked through her collection of CDs until she returned with a tray.

'There we are, tea and biscuits as requested, complete with tea strainer.' She saw me examining her albums. 'Found anything you like?'

I've never been keen on rock music, I prefer rock 'n' roll, but there was no sign of Jerry Lee Lewis or Jack Scott in her collection, or even Elvis Presley. 'Bryan Adams isn't so bad.'

'Don't you like Metallica?'

'I think I'd rather have Al Bowley.'

We drank our tea beside the bay window where I could keep an eye open for Miss Barrie.

'To what do I owe this visit?' asked Pat. 'Or is it Mother you've come to see again?'

''Fraid so,' I replied. 'What time will she be up?'

'She's up now, but she likes to sit in her room. I've told her you're here, but finish your tea first. I see they found your friend's body.'

'David? Oh yes. He was more of an acquaintance really.'

'I don't suppose he had anything to do with your "accident" with the car the other night?'

I looked at her sharply. I was sure I hadn't imagined the sarcastic way she'd pronounced the word. She was an astute lady. What was she doing wasting her time stuck up here?

Mrs Lake was sitting in her wheelchair beside the bed. She wore a peacock-blue shawl round her shoulders, which matched her hair, and a long, pleated frock. Once again, the room she sat in was stifling hot and I took my jacket off before I sat down.

'It's about the Hope family,' I began. 'You were telling me the other day about Mary not being able to have any more children after Alison.'

'That's right. There was some complication, I don't know what, but after that she never . . .'

'Had relations with her husband, I think you said.'

'That's what she told me. How true it was, I don't know. She certainly mentioned she'd been sterilised so she couldn't bear any more children.'

'I wonder how Bert took this.'

'It's not for me to comment on other people's lives, but I wouldn't imagine Mr Hope would have deprived himself of his carnal pleasures.'

'Another woman, you mean?'

'Or women.'

'Anyone in particular?'

'There was talk of a Mrs Critchley who lived in the next street. Her husband was away in the Army, and rumour had it that Bert Hope was a frequent visitor to the house.'

I wasn't sure what I was seeking. Perhaps a love-child

fathered by Bert who might have resurfaced after all these years to claim his share of the family fortune, and killed Bert when he found he'd missed out.

'You said Bradley was adopted. Do you know who his real parents were?'

Mrs Lake looked round. 'Is there any more tea in the pot, by any chance?' and she held out her empty cup and saucer.

'I'll get you some.'

When I returned, she'd wheeled her chair to the window. 'I know who they were supposed to be,' she said carefully. She paused and looked at me. I waited for the revelation to come.

Chapter Twenty-Eight

'Bradley was the child of Mr and Mrs Critchley.'

'The same Mrs Critchley that Bert Hope was supposed to have been having it away with?'

Mrs Lake ignored the colloquialism. 'The very same. Only Mr Critchley was in a German prisoner-of-war camp at the time and had been for the last two years.'

'So the child couldn't have been his.'

'Precisely. But Mrs Critchley was certainly the mother.'

The implication hit me. 'And you're saying, the father was Bert Hope?'

'It's more than likely.'

So Bradley *was* Bert's own son, after all. I had been right in suspecting a love-child but this one hadn't come along from nowhere. Bradley had been there all along and he had helped himself to the family fortune, or the insurance money as it was.

But Bradley was already dead when Bert was killed so my theory of the love-child as a murderer was a non-starter.

'How terrible for Mary,' I said to Mrs Lake. 'Do you think she knew she was bringing up a child that her husband had fathered by another woman?'

'If she did, she didn't say anything. They brought Bradley up as if he were their own. But Mary would be loyal like that.'

I suspected that today's women would regard that as loyalty stretched to the point of idiocy, but Mary maybe felt her husband was justified in seeking solace elsewhere if she was unable to accommodate him herself.

I guessed she wouldn't have been so understanding if she'd known he was abusing their only daughter.

'Did Mr Critchley return from the war?'

'I don't know. We'd lost touch by then.'

I wasn't sure how this new information affected things. I suspected not much. Bradley Hope had been happy to blackmail the old man, whether or not he knew he was his biological father.

As for Norman, he and Bradley had been in cahoots. No suggestion of jealousy between them. They'd robbed their father in tandem.

I looked at my watch. Five to twelve. I thanked Mrs Lake and Pat and went to inspect the empty flat downstairs before Miss Barrie arrived.

Geoffrey had put the new furniture in, a Regency striped suite, black ash display cabinet, bookcase and dining furniture. The wallpaper was blue and yellow with a matching border, to tone with the light blue carpet which made the room look bright and spacious.

I'd almost given up on her when Miss Barrie turned up at ten past in a taxi.

'Sorry I'm late,' she said breathlessly. 'Is the flat still available?' She looked little older than sixteen. She had short blonde hair and wore a mini-skirt and a black top. A ring flashed on her bare midriff, secured to her navel.

'You're just in time. I'd given up on you.' I showed her round and she seemed impressed.

'It's just what I want,' she said. 'Can I have it?'

I felt something wasn't quite right about Miss Barrie but I didn't know what it was. Her credentials were adequate. She handed me references from her tutor and last landlord. She had a bank account to enable her to pay the rent by Standing Order and a cheque written out already for the deposit. She had no animals or children and wasn't on housing benefit.

'My father is subsidising me through university,' she explained, when I queried her sources of income.

Other than an irrational feeling of disquiet, I could think of no reason not to accept her. There were no other prospective tenants in view and she was very attractive.

'OK. It's all yours.'

'Great.'

I spent the next ten minutes sorting out the paperwork then I gave her the keys. 'Any problems, ring this number and ask for Geoffrey.' I handed her a card with the office number.

I'd hoped to arrange a meeting with Mrs Clarke, but although I tried several times during the day, there was no reply from her number.

I was in the studio at six for the programme, dressed ready for the evening at the theatre with Hilary. I played Elvis singing *Don't*, to publicise the show we were going to see, and followed it with a new version of the song on P.J. Proby's new CD. I also put on *Love Is The Sweetest Thing* by Al Bowley for Mrs Lake and a Bryan Adams track for Pat.

Hilary was waiting for me in the foyer when I'd finished and we walked across to the Not Sushi. It's a new Japanese fast-food noodle bar that opened up in Fleet Street a few weeks ago and seems to have caught on. You sit at long wooden tables to eat and they have Unisex toilets. Liverpool goes cosmopolitan!

Hilary had the *kake udon* and I tried the vegetable *cha han*.

We'd only forty minutes to spare for the meal before we took a taxi across town to the Empire. The theatre was packed and some of the audience were dressed in Fifties' outfits, the men in velvet-collared drapes and drainpipes and the women in layers of petticoats and stiletto heels. They jived in the aisles during the rocking numbers and it was a lively, colourful show.

The guy playing Elvis looked a bit like him, but so did a million other Elvis impersonators up and down the country.

'Good, wasn't it?' Hilary squeezed my hand as we came out of the side Lord Nelson Street exit.

'Yeah, great.' It had been good but it had nothing like the excitement of seeing Clyde McPhatter, Duane Eddy and Bobby Darin in the same theatre one night back in the Sixties. They were the real thing.

I suppose punk fans will feel the same when Radio Two trots out the Cliff Adams singers performing Johnny Rotten and Clash songs. Not the same as hearing the originals at Eric's.

We went back to the flat. 'I see they found your friend who fell off the boat,' said Hilary. 'He took his time floating ashore.'

'His wallet probably weighed him down.' I tried to be flippant but it wasn't a subject I wanted to discuss. I didn't feel I'd ever be comfortable with it.

'How's the holiday packing coming on?' I quickly changed the subject.

'It's only March,' she laughed. 'We don't go for another ten weeks. On the other hand, I did see this bright red thong I was going to treat myself to, to wear on the beach.'

'Sounds interesting.'

'Put it this way, I think if I wore it, I'd still get an all-over suntan.'

'Get it.'

'Come to think of it, I might get you a matching one. How'd you like that?'

'You'll want to make sure you get the right size. Why don't you measure me for it now?'

'All right, I will.'

She did, and David Warner wasn't mentioned again.

I tried Mrs Clarke's number in the morning after Hilary had left. This time I was successful.

'Have you got an hour to spare?' I asked.

'Nothing going wrong with the deal, is there?' Her rough Dingle tones carried overtones of alarm.

'Nothing at all. It was something else I wanted to talk to you about.'

'That's all right then because I've already spent the money. I can't see you until four this afternoon, though.'

'That'll be fine.'

Mrs Clarke lived in Grassington so we arranged to meet in the Dormouse Tearooms in Smithdown Road.

'What is it you want to ask me?' She was sporting a different wig which I found rather disconcerting. This one was a dark brown creation styled in a bob cut more suited to a woman half her age.

'It's about Bradley Hope and his family.'

The waitress brought the tea and toasted teacakes and Mrs Clarke picked up the pot. 'Shall I be mother?' She poured out the tea and milk and handed over my cup and saucer. 'Right, what is it you want to know about them? Bad lot they was.'

Little did she know how bad. 'I'm curious about what happened to the baby that young Alison had.'

'Ah, him.'

'Oh, it was a boy, was it?' I couldn't recall that being mentioned before.

'Yes, didn't you know? They called him Sydney.'

'They christened him before he was adopted then?'

She frowned. 'I'm not sure. No, I don't think so. I think it were his new parents what named him. Sydney Arthur he were called, after her father.'

'Whose father?'

'Why, his mother's father, of course – that is, the woman what adopted him.'

'Did you know her name?'

'Didn't I tell you? It were a couple who lived in the next street. A Mr and Mrs Critchley.'

Chapter Twenty-Nine

Mrs Clarke munched her teacake as I tried to assimilate this new piece of information.

The way I read it, Mrs Critchley, having given away the child she'd borne to Bert Hope (i.e. Bradley), had now accepted, in return, the child Bert Hope had fathered with his own daughter, Alison. Sydney.

It was hard to credit. Was this baby a sort of consolation prize for Mrs Critchley for magnanimously relinquishing the first child?

What did Mary Hope think about the arrangement? More to the point, what about Mr Critchley, the father of an adopted baby? Why had he agreed to adopt it? Did he know about the first one? If so, what had he done, if anything, about his wife's flagrant infidelity?

Mrs Clarke was talking again. 'The Hopes left shortly after that, and good riddance I said.'

'But the Critchleys stayed?'

'As far as I know. I got married myself soon after and me and my husband moved to Aigburth.'

'What were they like, the Critchleys?'

She looked puzzled at the question. 'Just ordinary folk. He'd been in a German prison camp – not Colditz, the other one – and not all of him came back, if you catch my drift.'

I didn't, so she explained in some detail. The gist of it seemed to be that Mr Critchley, due to injuries sustained whilst on active service for his country, had returned to his wife infertile. He could possibly have been impotent as well but Mrs Clarke seemed unsure of the subtle difference.

'So that's why they adopted,' she said. 'The Hopes knew the Critchleys were wanting a child so when poor Alison died, the baby having no father, it seemed the perfect solution.'

'No legal forms or anything? Just handed it over?'

'That's how it was in those days. The less the authorities knew the better.'

'So the Critchleys were friends of the Hopes, were they?'

'They knew one another – that were enough, weren't it?'

'What did Mr Critchley do when he came back from the war?'

'I don't know. I think he was something with the Corporation – Borough Treasurer's it might have been.'

I poured us each a second cup of tea. 'I've heard rumours,' I said in a lowered voice, 'that Mrs Critchley had had a baby herself, years earlier, whilst her husband was away. Do you know anything about that?'

'I can't say I do. What year was that?'

'Nineteen forty-four.'

'I'd be sixteen then. It probably passed me by. Whose baby was it?'

I saw no reason to reveal to her that it was Bert Hope's and the baby was Bradley. 'I thought you might have been able to tell me,' I said, and went back to the matter in hand. 'I don't suppose you know where the Critchleys are now?'

'Probably in the cemetery. They were getting on then. Mrs Critchley must have been over forty when they adopted Sydney so she'd be nearly ninety now, and Mr was older still.'

'What about young Sydney?'

'Not a clue what happened to him.'

There wasn't any more to say about it. We moved on

to talking about Princes Avenue. She'd seen the workmen at the house and seemed quite content with the situation. The tenants had been informed I'd be taking over at the end of the month. None of them had given notice.

'You'll be glad to be rid, won't you?' I said. 'When do you leave for Gran Canaria?'

'May.'

I said I'd get in touch with her if I had any problems with the house and we parted. I drove straight to the station to do the show. On the way, I tried to think through everything I'd been told and work out what my next move should be.

Sydney Critchley must now be the number one suspect for Bert's murder, probably because I knew of nobody else connected with the old man. I had to admit, however, it wasn't the best of reasons.

On the other hand, he did have a motive. Two, in fact. Firstly, he might have felt abandoned at having been given away by the Hopes, especially if he learned the truth about his origins. His mother, a mere child, abused by her own loving daddy, *his* father, who promptly palmed off his newborn son on his ex-lover, whose own bastard child was set to inherit the family fortune such as it was.

Secondly, there was the question of money. If he'd got wind of the insurance pay-off or he thought there might be an inheritance from Bradley, then he'd only got Bert standing in his way.

And Norman.

The realisation hit me. If the second scenario was true, and he'd already killed Bert, then Norman Hope's life was in danger from his half-brother who was also his nephew.

He wasn't on the phone. I couldn't get to Kirkby until I'd finished my programme. I just hoped that wouldn't be too late. Maybe I could get a message to him somehow.

I played the first record for Norman Hope of Stafford Cripps Tower in Kirkby. 'And a message for you, Norman,' I announced on air, 'from Father O'Brien at St Diana's. He wants you to go down to the club right away. It's urgent. OK?'

It was the best I could do. An hour had never passed so slowly. At seven o'clock, I dashed past a startled Ken and hurled myself into the driving seat of the RAV4.

I did a Damon Hill through Walton, leaving a trail of blasting horns, waving fists and shouted threats behind me, but luckily, no police. These days, they're not even there when you don't need them.

I screamed to a halt outside St Diana's Club and ran inside. Father O'Brien was sat on his usual stool at the bar, pint at hand.

'Have you seen Norman?' I almost shouted the words. 'The drains man.'

He shook his head. 'Not all day, why?'

'No matter.' Then, as an afterthought: 'You don't happen to remember if he was with you last Friday, clearing out the cellar?'

'Let me see, Friday. Yes, he was. He was helping to tidy the basement in readiness for storing the new furniture.'

'All day?'

'From lunchtime till evening.'

So Norman's alibi was confirmed. I just hoped he'd live to need it. I jumped back into the car and sped off to Stafford Cripps Tower. A few kids were playing football against the graffiti-covered wall and I threw one of them the obligatory fifty pence to watch my car.

I took the steps two at a time, hardly noticing the stench, until I reached the eighth floor. Good job I was fit.

I hammered on Norman's door. There was no reply. I thrust my hand through the cardboard side window and reached up to turn the latch. I pushed the door open and ran into the lounge.

I only needed one glance.

Norman was lying sideways across the floor. The side of his head had been cut open, possibly by an axe, and the blood had gathered in a cloying mass on the frayed carpet.

I felt the side of his rough cheek. It was cold. His eyes were wide open with fright. He'd obviously seen what was about to happen to him. I gently closed them. I've never known why people close the eyes of the dead but they always do, and I somehow felt it respectful to do the same.

I went into each room to make sure the assailant wasn't still there but he was obviously long gone.

It had to be Sydney. But where was he now?

As I was coming out of the bathroom, I noticed a cupboard behind the cylinder that I'd missed the first time I'd searched the flat. I opened it and looked inside. Behind some towels was an old biscuit tin. I pulled it out and opened it. Inside were piles of papers, some gathered together and held by elastic bands.

At the top were birth and marriage certificates and various official letters and documents. These might well be the ones stolen from Bert's bedroom.

I took a glance at the tied bundles. Most of them were photocopies. One lot mentioned Tony Pritchard and contained various house plans and planning permission documents. Another had copies of contracts signed by David Warner.

I'd obviously unearthed the source of Bradley Hope's blackmailing operation.

I replaced all the papers in the tin for future inspection and carried it out with me, pausing for one last look at Norman. I passed nobody on my way down the stairwell, which is not to say that nobody saw me. In that neighbourhood, eyes were everywhere.

The kids playing round the car had disappeared
when I reached ground level and I drove away without
encountering anybody.

At the first public phone box I came to, I stopped
and dialled 999. 'Go to Flat H4 in Stafford Cripps
Tower in Kirkby,' I told the police operator. 'You'll
need to break in.' Then I put down the receiver and
drove away before they had time to alert the near-
est patrol. They're pretty quick at tracing calls these
days.

I didn't go back to the flat. Instead, I rang Maria
at home. 'I've just found Norman Hope,' I told her.
'Battered to death like Bert.'

'Where are you?'

'On the mobile somewhere on the M57 outside Kirkby.'

'Are you coming round?'

'Is that OK?'

'Course it is. I take it you haven't eaten?'

'No, have you?'

'Yes, but I'll make you something. How long will
you be?'

'About twenty minutes.'

Maria had opened a bottle of red wine and a mushroom
and onion pizza was in the oven.

She greeted me with a kiss on the lips. 'Twice in a
week! I *am* doing well.' She smiled to let me know she
was teasing.

I sat down and told her the story of Sydney Critchley.

'I can't believe it,' Maria said. 'It's incredible. And
you think it's him who's murdered Norman?'

'And Bert.'

'He'd probably have killed Bradley too if Warner
hadn't beaten him to it.'

'No, I don't think so. I think it was Bradley's death that
alerted him to the prospect of a possible inheritance. He
probably expected Bradley would leave a fortune. Most
people did.'

'And as his half-brother, he'd be first in line if Norman and Bert were out of the way?'

'Don't you agree?'

'There's two snags to that theory,' complained Maria. 'He's too obvious a suspect for a start.'

'Most murderers are. It doesn't seem to stop them.'

'And what about Bradley's wives and children?'

'I've been looking into that. I don't think he had any official children, as it were, although rumour has it there were several born on the wrong side of the blanket. As for the wives, they all seem to have been long since divorced.'

'And young Sydney would have found that out.'

'Not so young. I make him forty-five.'

'How are you going to find him?'

'Legwork, I suppose.' There was a faint chance Mrs Critchley would still be alive at ninety-one. If she was, the odds were she'd be in a nursing home. I'd need to ring round all the homes in the area. I'd given up on her husband. Not many married men make it to ninety-six. They tend to lead the way to the grave by several years, thus giving their wives time to enjoy the facilities of the Widows' Association.

'I can check the voters' register at the Library for you.'

'Would you?'

'Of course.'

'What would I do without you?' I put my arms round her and kissed her. She sighed.

'In the roulette wheel of life,' she said, 'somebody had to get you. I guess I was the lucky one.' She kissed me back.

I wasn't keen on the analogy. If I were to be a prize, I'd prefer it to be one everybody could share. Like sunshine.

'What about the police?' she continued. 'Won't they be looking for you?'

'I don't think anyone saw me going in the flat.'

As it turned out, they didn't need to. I'd left my card with Norman on my previous visit and it was the first thing the officers at the scene found when they went through his pockets.

I'd been back in my own flat less than ten minutes next morning when Detective Inspector Jim Burroughs knocked on the front door. He wasn't a happy bunny.

Chapter Thirty

'Breakfast for two, is it?' I greeted him brightly. His new sidekick, Sergeant Page, was with him. Neither of them smiled.

'All right,' began Jim. 'Tell us your side of the story.'

'What story's this?'

'Every time we find a dead body these days, your telephone number turns up at the scene. Now I know there's a simple answer, like you've bought a funeral parlour and you're touting for custom, but Sergeant Page here thinks it's very suspicious and I ought to arrest you.'

Sergeant Page blushed and looked at the ground.

'Whose body have you found this time?'

'As if you didn't know. Norman Ericson, real name Norman Wilfred Hope, son of the late Herbert Hope. Battered to death in his highrise flat with your visiting card in his coat pocket. Who do you think you are? The Saint?'

'Before my time, old thing,' I smiled, trying to sound like Roger Moore and failing miserably. I don't look like him either.

Jim Burroughs looked grim. 'Was he already dead when you called?'

'What makes you think I called? Why couldn't I have met him at Mass on Sunday and given him my card then?'

'When we showed your photograph to the neighbours

this morning, one of them identified you as the man who called round on Wednesday looking for a Mr Norman Ericson.'

'Not a lady in a bathrobe offering her services to gentlemen callers?'

This time it was Jim Burroughs's turn to blush.

I looked at my watch. 'Is it that time already? I'll be late for the match.'

'You're not going to any match till you've answered some questions.'

I realised I wasn't going to be able to put him off any longer. 'Sit down, Jim, and I'll tell you the full story.' I pulled across another chair for Carol Page and gave them a brief, expurgated résumé.

'Right. For starters, Bert Hope hired me to find out who was blackmailing Bradley.'

'So you admit you are involved in the case?'

'I guess so.'

'In your capacity as private detective?'

'Investigator, enquiry agent, I don't know what you'd call it. But, whatever, I discovered that it was Bradley himself who was doing the blackmailing, which was why Warner killed him. Warner mistakenly thought I knew about the murder, so he took me out on the boat, but he was thrown overboard by a freak wave before he could harm me.'

Jim Burroughs's expression changed from mild disbelief to incredulity as I continued.

'Bert had copped for a few grand insurance when his wife was killed so I reckoned that, as the only surviving relative, Norman was the obvious suspect for killing him, hoping the money would be his. I found out by chance where he lived but he had an alibi for the time of Bert's murder. He couldn't have done it.'

'If Norman Hope didn't murder his father, who did? And who killed Norman?'

'One at a time. I can't be sure of this, but the favourite is Bert's other son, Sydney.'

'Who? There's no record of another child.'

'He was adopted at birth. The certificate was probably amongst the papers stolen from Bert's bedroom.' I didn't mention that I had them in my possession. 'Norman told me about him.' Norman wouldn't be around to contradict me.

'And how come you're so sure this Sydney's the murderer?'

'Process of elimination, Jim. Apart from the fact there's nobody else on the scene, he had the two best motives – money and revenge. He'd been spurned by his family and he was hoping to inherit once he'd got rid of everyone.'

'His own father and brother. A nice man.'

'Hang on, Jim, before you judge him. It's not quite as simple as that.' I briefly outlined the details of Sydney's conception.

Jim struggled to get to grips with it. 'So his mother's really his fifteen-year-old half-sister and his father . . . hang on, does that make Bert Hope his grandfather as well?'

'Half-grandfather maybe,' interposed Sergeant Page.

'Either way,' I said, 'you can't blame him for being slightly aggrieved, especially as he doesn't seem to be in line for any of the cash floating about.'

'You mean the insurance money?'

'And Bradley's lost fortune. Sydney probably didn't know he'd squandered it on drugs, high living and alimony.'

'There was the money from his criminal activities as well. You said Bradley Hope had been blackmailing David Warner. Was Hope blackmailing anyone else?'

I had to tread carefully here. 'Nobody's come forward to admit to it if he was.'

Burroughs turned his attention back to Sydney. 'What

name does this other son go under? And where will we
find him?'

'Critchley's his name, Sydney Arthur Critchley, but
I've honestly no idea where he'll be. With your resources
though, Jim, it shouldn't be too difficult.'

'Our resources! Don't make me laugh. Do you know
how many men I've got for this job? We've had three
armed robberies, one drug killing, a missing teenager
and a ram raid in the last twenty-four hours.'

'A quiet day for a change. Don't worry, if I find him,
I'll let you know. We can work together on this.'

'Any other time I'd tell you to keep your nose out of
police work.'

'But you've so much on . . .'

'If you do find him, I want to know immediately.
I don't want you tackling him yourself, do I make
myself clear?'

'Of course.'

I saw them to the door. As he followed his sergeant
out, Jim Burroughs turned to me. 'Remember what I said
– be fucking careful, Johnny. If he's killed two people
already, another won't matter to him and I don't want
to have to come round to scrape you off the pavement.
Shovels come expensive these days.'

'And you're on a tight budget, don't tell me,' I said
and shut the door.

I felt weary. For over three weeks, I'd hardly stopped
and I felt I needed a break away from it all before I
embarked on my search for Sydney Critchley.

I picked up the phone and rang Manx Airlines. They
had a plane leaving at 19.55 hours for the Isle of Man
– plenty of time for me to make it and still go to the
match first. I booked myself a ticket and went on to fix
up the hotel and the car hire.

Then I rang Gordon Sutton and said I needed to see
him and his brother urgently. He didn't sound overjoyed
to hear from me.

'I know it's short notice,' I said, 'but I'll be arriving at Ronaldsway Airport at twenty past eight.'

'I take it it's about this Bradley Hope business. We've already helped you all we can.'

'You've got it wrong. This time I'm going to help *you*.'

'We're going to a dinner dance tonight with our wives.'

'Where at?'

'At the Sefton Hotel, as a matter of fact.'

'That's lucky. I'm staying at the Sefton. Make it nine-thirty in the upstairs bar. You can slip away for five minutes. It won't take long, and you might regret it if you don't hear what I have to say.'

The combination of veiled threat and assertive closing had the desired effect. If I ever give up detective work, I could perhaps make a fortune selling double glazing. He agreed to meet me.

I got out the biscuit tin and sorted through the papers Bradley Hope had collected.

After a quick sandwich, I threw some things into an overnight bag and drove over to Goodison Park. Manchester United were the opposition so there was a big crowd to see the champions in action.

I wasn't expecting much from Everton so I wasn't disappointed. We lost 2–0. The new goalkeeper played abysmally, Schmeichel saved our one shot on goal, from Unsworth, and with eight home defeats, we were well on course for relegation.

'I give up.' The man next to me rose from his seat in exasperation five minutes before the end. 'I think I'll start watching Southport instead. You might get a decent game there and even the odd win as a bonus.'

I stuck it out till the bitter end then drove out along the dock road towards the airport at Speke, passing the Marina. Only five days had gone by since the fatal trip with David Warner. I hadn't even found

Norman Hope then. Now they were both dead. Who would be next?

I hoped it wouldn't be me.

I stopped at the Brittania, by the old Garden Festival site, for a meal. From the window, I could see the Mersey flowing past and I was glad I was flying across to the island. After my experience on the *Bilbo Baggins*, I never wanted to set sail on the Irish Sea again.

I had the liver and onions with chips and two veg, followed by the sponge pud and custard and a pint of cider. I felt I needed filling up.

At the airport, I bought the *Football Echo* to read on the plane but the journey was so short, I hardly had a chance to open it. By the time they'd served the tea and biscuit, we were circling Castletown.

There was a blue Micra waiting for me this time and I was in Douglas and the Sefton by nine o'clock. I had a quick shower and got changed then went down to the Harris Café Bar where I bought a glass of cider and took it across to an empty seat by the window. I could see a large boat at the landing-stage but couldn't make out whether or not it was the *King Orry*.

I checked my watch. It was nine-thirty. I'd done my bit and was here on time – but where were the proprietors of The Isle of Man Bespoke Horseless Carriage Company?

Chapter Thirty-One

Roy and Gordon Sutton entered the bar at 9.31, both in evening dress and looking anxious.

'Glad you could come,' I said genially, extending my hand to each in turn.

'What's all this about, Johnny?' Roy could hardly conceal his annoyance. He remained calm on the surface but a pulse under his left eye was beating with unusual vigour.

I motioned them to join me at my table and offered to buy them a drink but they declined. 'We're in the middle of a dinner,' Gordon fretted. 'You said it would only take a few minutes.' He consulted an ostentatious Rolex watch on his wrist to emphasise the point.

'And so it will. You remember when I came to see you a couple of weeks back, I asked if you knew anything about Bradley Hope being blackmailed?'

'And we told you we didn't.'

'Exactly, and you were speaking the truth. I found out that Bradley Hope himself was the blackmailer and he had chosen many of his ex-colleagues as his victims.' The Sutton brothers exchanged wary glances. 'The question I should have been asking you was, were you being blackmailed by Hope?'

'I told you before, we haven't seen Bradley Hope in thirty years,' asserted Roy.

'You may say that, Roy, but I'd like to bet that, far from not seeing Bradley Hope, you actually employed him for a period during the last five years,' I held up my hand to silence their protests, 'and whilst he was with you, he came across certain information that could have proved very embarrassing for you if it had been made public.'

Roy Sutton's face went white, but before he could speak, Gordon broke in. 'That's ridiculous!' His voice was angry. 'Bradley Hope work with us?'

'Before you deny it, I can tell you I've seen the evidence.'

'What evidence?'

'The evidence he threatened to hand over to the police if you didn't pay him.'

Gordon stared, speechless, and this time it was Roy who opened his mouth.

'OK Johnny. I'll admit it. Bradley Hope was over here and, yes, he did ask for money and we paid him.'

'Not five thousand pounds, by any chance?'

'You know that too. And five thousand the next year and the next.'

'Until?'

'Until somebody did us the favour of killing him.'

Gordon spoke again, through clenched teeth. 'So what are you going to do about it?'

'First of all, I want you to tell me what you did that was wrong.'

Gordon snarled, 'I thought you said you knew . . .' but Roy hushed him up.

'We did nothing terribly wrong, Johnny. We were two young lads from Liverpool, scallies you'd probably say, trying to build up a business from scratch. Yes, we clocked a few motors, sold a few patched-up wrecks and not all our "one lady owner" ads were strictly accurate, but,' he stopped to wave his finger for emphasis, 'we never sold a car that wasn't in good mechanical condition. Nobody was ever injured driving any of our vehicles because of faulty brakes or whatever. And that is how we were able to build up this business, through our good reputation.'

Gordon joined in. 'And just because this snivelling bastard found some old documents that could have incriminated us, we had to pay up or lose everything.'

'"A good reputation takes a lifetime to build and a second to destroy",' quoted Roy. 'We wouldn't have been prosecuted but the publicity would have ruined us.'

Not to mention being thrown out of the Golf Club and the Rotary, I thought. Before either of them could speak, I took from my inside pocket a bundle of papers tied with an elastic band.

'I found these papers in a flat in Kirkby where Bradley Hope had been living for a time. I haven't opened them but I saw your name on the front page and I thought they might well belong to you.'

Roy Sutton reached forward and almost tore the papers from my grasp. He ripped off the band and shuffled through them, his brother helping him.

I took another sip of cider. 'I hope they are what you wanted.'

'Have the police seen these?' It was Gordon who asked the question.

'No. I managed to remove them before they arrived on the scene. Nobody has seen them.'

They carried on examining the documents till they reached the last one. 'I needn't tell you how very grateful we are,' Roy said carefully.

'What exactly is your role in all this?' asked Gordon. 'Are you wanting money for these papers, because if so . . .'

'I don't want any money. They're yours. As for what my role is, I've been working as an enquiry agent hired by Bradley Hope's father.'

'But you're a disc jockey,' said Roy.

'It's a new sideline,' I said.

Gordon grinned suddenly. 'You've been on one of

those courses advertised in the papers, haven't you?' He
turned to his brother. 'You know them, Roy. "Train to
be a private detective in sixteen weeks".'

I'd seen them too. The country will soon be full of
private eyes, not to mention counsellors, debt collectors
and chiropodists.

'No, I haven't been on a course. It's just something I
fell into.'

Roy said, 'But wasn't Bradley's father murdered as
well? I saw it on the television news.'

'Bert's death was nothing to do with all this. It was a
family matter. As for Bradley, I can tell you that he was
killed by David Warner. Remember him – the agent?'

'God, we worked for him years ago, in The Suttons.
Was Bradley blackmailing Warner as well?'

'Yes.'

Roy laughed. 'He picked the wrong one there.'

'Who else was there besides Warner and us?'

'Tony Pritchard for one, the Baronets' keyboard player.
Tony killed himself. You may have read about it in
the paper.'

'Poor bastard.'

'Warner's dead as well, isn't he?' said Roy. 'A boating
accident or something.'

'I believe so.' It wasn't something I wanted to dwell
on. 'I think my five minutes are up,' I said, rising to
my feet.

'Is that it, then?' asked Gordon. 'Is that all you came
for, to return these papers to us?'

'Believe it or not, yes. I thought it might give you
some peace of mind.'

'We appreciate it,' said Roy, holding out his hand.
'Don't we, Gordon?'

'Are you staying on the island?' Gordon asked. 'You
must come round for a meal with us.'

I thanked him but declined. I wanted some time to
myself. They told me once again how grateful they

were, and how I could have the use of one of their cars anytime I was on the island. I extricated myself before their gratitude became maudlin. We said our goodbyes and they returned to their dinner in the Atholl Lounge.

I finished my drink and decided to go for a walk along the Promenade. There was a sharp wind that blew spray from the Irish Sea over the rails.

I wasn't sure how I stood legally in all this. I suppose, by the letter of the law, I should have handed all the documents over to the police.

Somewhere along the line, I'd decided to make a moral judgement. Had I felt the Sutton brothers had been seriously cheating people, selling dangerous cars or something equally dishonest, I wouldn't have given them back the papers. But I probably wouldn't have handed them to the police either.

I still had the papers belonging to Simon Butterworth which I intended to post to him. I didn't feel he'd done too much wrong either.

Tony Pritchard maybe had, but he'd got his come-uppance as Ken would say. As much come-uppance, I would have thought, as you could get. I'd send his incriminating contracts back to his widow.

I didn't know if David Warner had a widow or not and I didn't much care.

As for Verity Kennedy, he'd been so offensive when I'd tracked him down at Cheltenham, that I decided to let him sweat. I wasn't so vindictive that I'd send the evidence of his misdeeds to the Jockey Club, but I didn't feel inclined to return them to him either. In the end, I'd probably burn them.

I reached the landing-stage and crossed over the road to walk back on the opposite side. There were *Vacancies* signs hung on the doors of most of the six-storey Victorian hotels. No wonder they'd started changing them into offices. A slight drizzle was falling and I passed nobody on the walk back to the Sefton.

In my room, I switched on the TV for *Match of the Day* in time to see the Manchester United goals in slow motion. It wasn't an experience I wanted to endure again so I zapped off the set and put out the light.

Sunday morning dawned bright and dry. I tried the Manx kippers for breakfast, recommended by the waitress, before setting off in the Micra for a trip round the island.

At Peel, I walked through the narrow streets up to the Castle, and felt as if I was back in medieval times, then I drove across the deserted mountain roads past Snaefell to Ramsey where I parked the Micra and went for a walk round the quayside.

I came across the Trafalgar Hotel, which seemed a grandiose name for a small pub, but it was a Cains Brewery house, which made me homesick for Liverpool, so I went in.

The small bar was packed with fishermen. I ordered a cider and a toasted sandwich and took them outside to a wooden bench where I could watch the boats in the harbour. One, the *James Lee*, reminded me a bit of the *Bilbo Baggins* and David Warner, and I was glad I was returning by plane.

I felt very much at peace and contented and I thought about my conversation with Tommy McKale at the Masquerade, the night Jim Burroughs came to see me about Bert Hope's murder.

Maria had wanted to come with me to the Isle of Man but I'd chosen to come alone which bore out Tommy's theory of my being a 'free spirit'.

I reckoned he had a point. I need the company of other people, for an audience, or for sex, or just the stimulus of their conversation and company. But, in the end, I function best on my own. That way I get the choice of what I do, when I do it and with whom I do it.

When I'd finished my drink, I collected the Micra

and went back through Douglas to Silverdale Glen near Ballasella.

The pleasure gardens at Silverdale are straight out of the nineteenth century. An old water-wheel still drives the kids' roundabout next to the lake where the ducks vie with the paddle-boats. I walked beyond the playground through the woods and out into the countryside beyond.

I thought how nice it would be to live somewhere like this, quiet and peaceful, away from the rat race, but I knew it could never be for me.

I'd miss the buzz of living in a city and I'd need the network of people I'd built up over the years in Liverpool. They were all part of my life, interconnected like microchips on a printed circuit board, so that, in some strange way, I could only exist when they were all switched on.

I had a cup of tea at the craft-shop café before driving the couple of miles back to Ronaldsway Airport.

The plane left at ten to seven and I was back in the flat for eight o'clock, just in time for Maria's phone call.

'I think I've found Sydney Critchley,' she said.

Chapter Thirty-Two

'I've been trying to ring you since yesterday, but you've been out and the ansaphone wasn't on. At least I didn't have to listen to that awful song.'

My ansaphone plays *Pledging My Love* by the late R & B singer who shares my name. Maria has poor taste in music. In football parlance, you've got to ask questions about someone who owns a Tony Hatch CD.

'You've got something?' I asked excitedly. I didn't care to tell her I'd been alone to the Isle of Man so I let the unspoken question about my whereabouts pass by without comment.

'Could be. I started going through all the voters' lists at work yesterday, and so far, I've found two Sydney Arthur Critchleys – one in Gateacre and the other in the Dingle.'

'The Dingle's got to be favourite, hasn't it?'

'That's what I thought. Do you want the address?' I scribbled it down. It was only two streets away from where the young Sydney had been raised.

'I'll go round there first thing tomorrow. Does he live alone?'

'He's the only name down for that address.'

'Fine.'

'The Gateacre one has three ladies listed as well, all Critchleys. I'll give you that too, should I?'

'Yeah, might as well although it doesn't look likely. I don't see the Sydney we want as a family man.'

'Let me know what happens, Johnny.'

'I will.'

I put the phone down, checked my watch and decided I might as well try the Dingle address immediately. I'd nothing else planned for the evening.

Cars were parked all along Gwydir Street and I drove slowly past them as I searched for the right number. I wasn't sure how I was going to tackle this. If Sydney had had any sense, he'd have long since fled the area. But if he'd any sense, he'd never have killed his father and brother in the first place, knowing he'd be the main suspect. I had to assume, therefore, that he was stupid. Or incredibly confident.

I left the RAV4 at the end of the street and walked back to the house. Through the front-room curtains, I could see the shining glare of a television set. Somebody was in.

I rang the bell and heard the shuffle of feet and a door opening inside. A voice called out from the hall: 'Who is it?'

'I'm looking for Sydney Critchley.'

'He's not in.' By the height of his silhouette and the timbre of his voice, I judged the speaker to be a boy in his late teens.

'When will he be back?'

'Don't know. He didn't say.'

'Is there anywhere I might find him?'

'You could try the pub down the road, he might be in there.'

I could, and he might, but as I'd no idea what Sydney looked like, I knew I'd be wasting my time.

'Thanks,' I said, and walked back up the road to fetch the car nearer to the house. I parked on the opposite side, with two wheels on the pavement, where I could keep an eye on the front door whilst allowing other cars to pass. Then I waited.

This, of course, was what real private-eye work was like. Hours of sitting and waiting and watching. Boring.

I struggled to keep awake and didn't dare read in case I missed something.

I put an old Rolling Stones album, *Out of Our Heads*, low on the CD player. The Stones were about to embark on another world tour, which must have given new hope to every fifty-four-year-old Mick Jagger wannabe from Brazil to Stockholm.

The CD was starting its third circuit and I was getting cramp in my right leg when a man came strolling up the road towards the car. In the inadequate streetlight, I could make out his height, about five eight, and his bulk, considerable, but precious little else.

I switched off the music, got out of the car and started walking down the road. He stopped outside the house I'd been to, and fumbled for his key. I rushed across to him. 'Mr Critchley?' I asked.

He looked startled. 'Who wants to know?' He seemed younger than forty-five.

'Sydney Critchley?'

'Yes. Who are you?'

'My name's Johnny Ace.'

'Not the radio chap? I listen to your show in my cab.'

'You're a lorry driver?'

He laughed. 'No. Taxis is my business.'

'It was actually your father I wanted to ask you about.'

'My father? Not wanting a loan, are you?'

'I'm sorry?' I was fast losing control of this conversation.

'He's a bank manager. Or rather, he was. He was made redundant eighteen months ago. Fifty-four and on the scrapheap.' He shook his head in disgust.

'He's still alive then?'

'He was at lunchtime. What's all this about?'

'I think you're the wrong Mr Critchley.' I explained I was looking for a Sydney Critchley who had grown up a couple of streets away in the Fifties.

'Christ, you're talking forty years ago.'

'You've not heard of him then?'

'No. I'd've remembered if I had, wouldn't I?' He laughed again. 'With a name like that.' This Sydney Critchley seemed to find it very amusing.

I walked back to the car. There was always the Gateacre lead but it was too late to call now. The Bamalama Club was only a few minutes away and I thought I might go there, until I remembered my encounter with Shirley's boyfriend the week before.

In the end I went home alone.

I was up next morning at seven, ready to hit the phone and scour all the nursing homes and rest homes listed in *Yellow Pages* for Sydney Critchley's parents. It was a monumental task. Even supposing I got through to them all first time, and took only a couple of minutes for each call, I reckoned it would take me at least two days to get the job done.

I started at eight o'clock. By nine o'clock, I'd spoken to just nine homes. None of them had a resident called Critchley.

Out of curiosity, I found the phone number for the Sydney Critchley in Gateacre and tried that. A lady answered and informed me that her husband could be found at his office in town and gave me the number. The secretary there answered, 'Critchley and Co, Chartered Accountants' and I knew I'd run into another dead end. 'Sorry, wrong number,' I told her.

I made a pot of tea, more than anything to lubricate my voice, and continued with the nursing homes, keeping a careful list of the calls I made. The twenty-sixth one brought a brief glimpse of hope at nineteen minutes to twelve.

'We have a Mrs Emily Critchley,' the Matron informed me. 'Would that be the lady your client is looking for?' My pitch was that I was an enquiry agency searching for a missing relative for a solicitor client.

'Has she any children who visit her?'

'Let me see. No, I have no record of any. She came to us from the hospital. She'd lived most of her life abroad; her husband was in the colonial service. He died several years ago.'

'I don't think it's the lady I want.'

I carried on. I missed lunch completely, I was so engrossed in the work, but at three-thirty, with my voice reduced to a croak and my head aching, I decided to call it a day.

I made one final call, to Maria.

'No go,' I told her. 'One's an accountant, the other's the son of a bank manager.'

'I've not found any more, either, and I've come to the end of the electoral register.'

'So it's back to the nursing homes. I must have done over sixty today.'

'No luck?' Maria sounded sympathetic.

'Just one Mrs Critchley, but her husband was in the Raj or something.'

'Many more to go?'

'I'm about halfway through but I've finished for today because I've got the show to do at six and I've not had lunch yet.' I suddenly felt starving.

'Why don't I just check out the electoral role like I did with the others?' Maria offered.

'The turnover in nursing homes is so high and often patients get missed out. It's a bit like the bedsit world, really. Besides, you'd need to look in *Yellow Pages* to find out which were the nursing homes anyway.'

'Tell you what, then. I finish at five – why don't I take over where you left off in the *Yellow Pages*? I should be able to ring a dozen or so whilst you're doing your programme, then you can call for me at mine after the show and we can go for a meal? There's a new place in Formby opened called the B'Stro.'

'Sounds like a good idea.'

I picked her up just after eight and we drove out to Formby. 'I remember this,' she said as I drew up outside the restaurant. 'It used to be called the Lighthouse.'

'Nothing stays the same for long any more. Now it's the B'Stro.'

They'd done it out well. Continental murals decorated the cream walls, and the tables and chairs were unmistakably French.

'How'd you get on with the phoning?' I asked Maria when we'd ordered.

She pulled a face. 'Awful. I made thirteen calls, it took me ages to speak to the right person and half the time I never managed it. Now I know what hell all those telesales people go through. I'll never scream at them again when they ring in the middle of dinner to sell me a new kitchen.'

'I will if they ring me. They've no right interrupting people in the privacy of their homes in the evenings.' She'd got me on one of my pet hates or maybe it was the frustration of the day getting to me.

Maria patted my hand. 'Now then, dear. No need to get so worked up.'

I bridled when she spoke the words, but although I said nothing, the mood of the evening was changed for me. I'd seen women treat their husbands like lapdogs in public. They were usually women of over fifty, often wearing extravagant costume jewellery, and more likely than not, fat to the point of obesity.

Maria was none of these things but, given the way she patted my hand and called me 'dear', I could easily see it happening in another ten years. I didn't want to stick around to see it happen.

'So are you going to carry on with them tomorrow?' she continued, oblivious to my disquiet. 'The nursing homes, I mean.'

'I'll have to. I've no other leads.'

'If you want me to do any more, I will.'

'Thanks. I'll see how I get on.'

I couldn't deny how helpful she was to me and how I needed her. And, of course, how I enjoyed her company. Yet, after the meal, I excused myself from staying at hers on the excuse of getting an early start on the phone.

It was only eleven-thirty when I dropped her off in Blundelsands but I didn't feel like going home. I ended up at the Masquerade Club.

Dolly was at her old position on the desk and I told her I was glad to see her back. She pulled out her paperweight from under the counter and waved it at me with a grin of triumph.

Inside, a new DJ was working the decks. He stood at five foot nothing and had black hair moussed up in a quiff but half of it dropped over one side of his face like a curtain, enabling him to sneer at the dancers unseen when they approached him with their requests. He wore a maroon jacket and black trousers and could have been mistaken for a cocktail waiter.

'Who's the new guy?' I asked Vince, as I ordered my drink at the bar.

'Some freak Tommy found. I think he came to get rid of the rats and Tommy was short of a jock.'

'Big Dave left then?'

'Dave S., you mean? Oh my dear, what a commotion! Here we go, one cider.' He put down the drink, took my money and put the change into a small pot pourri jar beside his till. 'Thank you, dear, now where was I? Oh yes, the odious David. They took off his wheels, ripped out the seats and put the whole lot on the roof for when he came out. You should've seen the old sod's face.'

'If it isn't one of the Water Babies.' Tommy McKale came up to the bar and put his arm around my shoulder. 'Been fishing lately, Johnny?'

'Not me, Tommy, I've got an abject fear of water.'

'No wonder. A little bird tells me that if the celebrated Mr Warner hadn't recently gone on a one-man search for Atlantis, we might not have seen you in here again.'

'It's a fair guess, Tommy, though it's not something I'd say myself. Are you joining us?' I asked Vince to fetch him his usual tipple.

'I don't think your young lady's too happy with your private-eye career,' he said.

I was surprised Hilary had mentioned it. She'd said nothing to me. It wasn't a subject we discussed.

'Only because I think she worries about you. Little things like cars running you over, people getting knifed, the odd drowning, that sort of thing.'

I had to admit it didn't look reassuring.

'Seriously, if you need any help,' Tommy offered. 'Like last time.'

'I don't think so but I'll let you know.' Things might change. I might find Sydney Critchley. I moved the conversation on. 'Who's the new DJ then?'

'He's not a DJ, he's a ratcatcher. Did Vince tell you about that Dave S.?' I nodded. Tommy laughed. 'I didn't mind his style myself, I feel like telling some of the punters to fuck off too on occasions, but it doesn't do to upset the types we get in here. This lad, Vernon, seemed to know a bit about music so I thought I'd try him out on a quiet night.'

'Good, is he?'

'For a ratcatcher.'

Actually, Vernon was OK. He played quite a bit of old Tamla material, mainly the smoochy stuff, Temptations, Smokey Robinson. The Monday crowd is an older crowd. I had a couple of dances with two of the regulars, Asian girls called Maisie and Susie, who had a trade going with visiting seamen.

'No boyfriends tonight?' I asked Susie as we gyrated to Mary Wells's *You Beat Me to the Punch*.

'Why? You asking me back to your place?' she smiled teasingly. I must have looked horrified because she threw back her head and laughed. 'Another time, Johnny, but I got a client coming in later, big bucks.' She rubbed her fingers together to emphasise the point and giggled. 'Another time.'

As the record finished, she shouted after me as I turned away: 'Hey, but you can play me a record on your show, right?'

'Right.' I went over to the bar to finish my drink. Ronnie Richmond was sitting in a corner, drinking alone. I waved my glass in acknowledgement and he nodded back.

On the dance floor, I recognised Vinny Hall looking like a Santa Monica beach bum in a short-sleeved Hawaiian shirt and white slacks. He didn't see me, which was as well as I still owed him £280 from our last meeting. He was groping a young girl whom I took to be a student and probably one of his tenants. Vinny was a notorious Liverpool landlord.

Everyone seemed to be in tonight. The place was buzzing.

I looked around and saw a woman I thought I knew. She was slim, about forty and wore tight denims, a baseball cap and a black Harley Davidson T-shirt which barely covered a tattoo of a peacock on her upper left arm.

She was dancing with a Hell's Angel, a burly figure whose long black hair hung well over the fur collar of a leather flying jacket emblazoned with patched slogans. I had him down for early middle age. In another ten years, he'd be eligible to join Status Quo.

Vernon was playing *Needle in a Haystack* and they were giving it some of the old Northern Soul on the dance floor. At first, I couldn't place her, then I realised with a shock it was Pat Lake. So much for the Miss Brodie image. She waved across as her partner threw her energetically over his shoulder.

I wondered who was sitting with her mother.

I wondered, too, where Sydney Critchley was at this moment.

'Another cider, Johnny dear?' I was dazzled for a moment as a light flashed in my eyes but it was only Vince's jacket that seemed to be made out of tinfoil and reflected the disco lights as he moved round the bar.

'No thanks, Vince. I've got work to do in the morning.'

I was enjoying myself and would have stayed longer but I remembered the nursing homes. Tomorrow there was more legwork to be done. I hung around another ten minutes, finished my drink and called it a night.

I made my first phone call at nine o'clock prompt next morning and I worked up to a good rate as I went along. By ten, I was motoring. I'd done fourteen in all and was well down the alphabet, albeit with no success.

It was on the fifteenth call of the morning that I hit paydirt.

'Troy Rest Home, Matron speaking.'

'Good morning. I wonder, do you have a Mrs Critchley in your establishment, by any chance?'

'Yes, we do. Who is it calling?'

'I'm from Ace Investigations. Our clients are solicitors who are trying to trace a Mrs Critchley on behalf of a relative.'

'Have you got the right one? Ours is a Mrs Norah Critchley.' I cursed the fact that I hadn't asked Mrs Clarke for her full name.

'This Mrs Critchley is about ninety years old and has a son of about forty-five called Sydney.'

'I don't know about the son, she never gets any visitors, but she is about the age you say.'

'Can I come down and see her?'

'I don't see why not. You have the address, do you?'

It was a Victorian redbrick detached house in one of

the streets off the north end of Southport Promenade. Most of its neighbours had become holiday flats or bedsits, with cars parked on the front tarmac, but the Troy Rest Home still retained its original lawn and gardens plus a set of new wrought-iron gates.

'You had no trouble finding us then?' the Matron enquired when I presented myself at the front door. 'You could have brought your car round the back. Didn't you see the sloping entrance at the side?'

I'd missed it completely. 'Too busy admiring your garden,' I explained. 'Is Mrs Critchley able to see me?' I was anxious to get down to business.

'I've told her you're here and she's looking forward to seeing you. Like I said, she doesn't have visitors.'

'None at all?'

'Nobody since she's been here, which is over three years. Do you know any of her family?'

'I used to know her son, Bradley.'

'Really? I'm Mrs Hyman, by the way. I don't believe I introduced myself.' She was a small woman, dumpy with plump red cheeks and old enough to be considering moving into one of her own rooms.

'Johnny Ace.' We shook hands. Up close, she smelt of disinfectant. Probably I'd interrupted her emptying the bedpans.

She led me to a lounge at the back of the house. Around a huge marble fireplace, with a gas-fire blazing in the middle, sat five old ladies on utility armchairs, staring silently into space.

I was reminded of the expression, 'God's Waiting Room'.

One of the ladies, her hair fine enough to reveal most of her skull, dribbled on to the pink cardigan pulled over her shoulders. Next to her, a woman lay with her head back and her mouth open, snoring loudly and displaying a set of shrivelled gums uncluttered with teeth. A faint

smell of vomit pervaded the air, despite a liberal spraying
of a floral deodorant.

Dolly from the Masquerade Club was probably around
the same age as some of these women, but I couldn't
imagine her in a place like this.

'That's Mrs Critchley, on the last chair,' the Matron
whispered. She ambled across and touched her shoulders.
'You've got a visitor, Norah.'

Mrs Critchley turned round. I'd seen people as thin
as her before but only in those documentaries they
have on periodically, the ones about Belsen or the
Burma Railway. Her skin, stretched over her bones,
was translucent and unlined but her blue eyes shone out
with a startling radiance that made me understand what
Bert Hope might have seen in her half a century ago.

'Her mind wanders sometimes, she tends to live in the
past a bit, but she's all there,' whispered the Matron but
she'd no need to tell me. Mrs Critchley started chattering
away as soon as I was introduced.

'A friend of Bradley's, you say? I haven't seen Bradley
for years. He's in America, you know, making motion
pictures.'

'It's Sydney I came about, Mrs Critchley, your son
Sydney.'

'Yes, Sydney comes to see me regularly. He's local,
of course, that helps. Not like Bradley. Bradley's so far
away, singing with the stars I tell people, but he's a star
himself now, isn't he? I often wonder where he got it
from, it's not from my side of the family.'

Hardly from Bert, I thought. 'Sydney's local, you say,
Mrs Critchley? Where does he live?'

'He's in one of those apartments, is Sydney. Bradley
has a villa, of course, but then Bradley's a star and they
have to have them, don't they, to keep up appearances.
Mae West wouldn't have been seen dead in public in a
raincoat.'

'Which apartments are they, that Sydney lives in?'

'I used to know the name. It was the same name as that Prime Minister they used to have.'

Couldn't be Major. They wouldn't name a lavatory after him, never mind a whole apartment block. 'Churchill? Thatcher?' I couldn't call to mind too many recent leaders of note. 'Disraeli? Pitt?'

'She was in a film with Bradley once.'

'Pardon?'

'Ingrid Pitt. She was very good. I think it was about vampires.'

I sighed. 'Think again, Mrs Critchley. Sydney. Which town does he live in?'

'He makes a few of those sort of films nowadays, does Bradley. Spine-chillers, we used to call them. I preferred it myself when he was singing, when he was in Las Vegas.'

'Has Bradley not been to see you for a while?'

'It's a long trip across that big sea. He comes when he can.'

I knew all about long trips on seas. 'I'm sure he does.'

I felt sorry for her because she obviously regarded Bradley as her own son, which, of course, he was, but she'd never been able to acknowledge him. To the world, he belonged to Mary.

She rubbed her hands together as if she was cold. The veins on the back of them stood out visibly. 'He'd had his name down for years for that apartment.'

'In Las Vegas?'

'No, silly. Kirkby.'

'You're talking about Sydney now?'

'Attlee, that's who it was named after.'

'I beg your pardon?'

'That's where Sydney lives. You asked me where Sydney lived. He's at Clement Attlee Tower in Kirkby.'

Chapter Thirty-Three

'It's in Knowsley not Liverpool, that's why I never found him in the voters' list,' explained Maria.

We were having lunch at the Café Renouf in Rodney Street and were halfway through the pasta dish of the day.

It's a good spot for a café, in the middle of a street of Georgian houses, all occupied by lawyers, accountants and other professionals but, most importantly, doctors. Rodney Street is the Harley Street of Liverpool. Remember what Charles Forte used to say: 'The three most important things when opening a business are location, location and location.'

Maria had rung through to a helpful lady at Kirkby Library who'd confirmed that a Sydney Arthur Critchley resided at Flat G3 in Clement Attlee Tower.

'I'll go round tonight after I've done the show,' I told her.

'Do you think that's wise? Why don't you just tell the police?'

'I could be wrong. He might be totally innocent and I'd look stupid. And he'd probably sue me for defamation of character.' But that wasn't the real reason and I couldn't fool myself. I wanted to get there first.

'But you don't think you're wrong, do you, Johnny?'

'No, I don't. If Sydney Critchley didn't murder Norman and Bert, then I'd be totally lost. I wouldn't have a clue where to look next.'

'And if he did kill them, what will you do?'

'Play it by ear, I guess.'

I'd no plan of action at all. My aim, I suppose, was to hand him over to the police once he'd confessed, but I hadn't really considered the finer details of how I would carry this out.

'You want to take someone with you. You could get hurt.'

I said I'd think about it. Maria went back to the Library and I drove across to the office to see Geoffrey.

'All coming on at Princes Avenue, boss,' he said. 'When do we take over?'

'Officially May first, but the way things are moving, it could be a couple of weeks early.'

'Jack's been measuring up for the central heating.' Shirley would be glad, I thought. 'And the roof's coming on nicely.'

'No word from the new tenant at Livingstone Drive?'

'That Miss Barrie? Snotty little cow, she is. On the phone wanting to know where the washing machine was and would we be supplying her with a freezer. I soon put her right. She's not been in there a week.'

'Yeah, I had a strange feeling she might be trouble but don't worry. I'll go and see her as soon as I can and sort her out. I'm sure you can find a spare fridge-freezer somewhere.' My mind was on more important things. 'Are you doing anything tonight, Geoff?'

'Nothing special, why?' Sometimes I worry about Geoffrey's lack of social life.

'Do you fancy a trip out to Kirkby?'

He looked at me cautiously. 'Is this another of those minder jobs?'

'Could be.'

His face broke into a big grin. 'Suits me. I feel like a bit of fun.'

I didn't expect it to be much of a fun evening but why

spoil his anticipation? 'I'll pick you up at your place after the show.'

Ken was already in the studio when I arrived at the radio station. 'Is your throat better?' he asked. I'd nearly lost my voice the night before after a day on the phone.

'I thought it sounded sexy with that husky growl.'

'Sexy?' Ken scoffed. 'Bronchial maybe but sexy, no way.'

I played *Susie Darlin'* by Robin Luke for Susie at the Masquerade and a track from the new Oasis CD. They'd just won this year's Ivor Novello Awards and I like to be topical sometimes.

At half-past seven, I picked up Geoffrey at his house in Aintree. He lives near the Grand National course off Melling Road. I wondered if Verity Kennedy would be coming up for this year's race, a little over a week away.

'All ready, boss.'

'Bloody hell!' I exclaimed. Geoffrey was dressed in combat uniform, those leaf-coloured camouflage garments you see in ex-Army stores. 'We're going to Kirkby not Bosnia.'

'Like it?' Geoffrey beamed.

'I thought minders wore smart penguin suits.'

'Not with the price of cleaning at Johnsons these days. I couldn't afford to get one dirty.'

We set off on the short trip to Kirkby and on the way, I gave Geoffrey a brief rundown on the reason for our visit.

'Very nice,' he commented when I'd finished. 'He's battered two of them to death and now we're going round on a social visit.'

I parked the car behind the Clement Attlee Tower and we walked up the stairwell to the G section which was on the seventh floor. It was every bit as malodorous as the Stafford Cripps Tower which we could see,

less than a quarter of a mile away, from the landing
balconies.

I wondered if Norman Ericson née Hope and Sydney
Critchley had known they lived so near to one another?

'Here we are,' said Geoffrey. 'Floor G.'

'Number three must be round on the left,' I said.
'Here's number one.' We walked round to the third
front door which had one of those butterfly knobs
that you turned to ring the bell. I turned it. We
waited. Nothing. I turned it again and the door was
pulled open.

The man who stood in front of me looked like an extra
from a Hammer horror film. His skin was Warhol white,
his dark hair plastered to his head and he was dressed in
black from head to toe.

In the room behind him, Gothic posters covered
the walls and a three-pronged candelabra filled with
incense-burning candles stood on an old oak sideboard.
A red bulb shone in the overhead light. The walls and
ceilings were painted black.

'I'm looking for Sydney Critchley.'

'What for?' It was an unexpected reply.

'Are you Sydney Critchley?'

'What if I am?' His voice had none of Norman's
Scouse accent.

'Your mother's Norah Critchley who used to live in
Rhiwlas Street?'

He fixed me with a malevolent glare. 'My mother
is Alison Hope and she hasn't lived anywhere for
forty-five years.' He placed special emphasis on the
word 'lived'.

'Oh, Christ,' exclaimed Geoffrey, under his breath.
'A nutter.'

At least I had the right man at last. 'When did you
last see Bert Hope, your father, Sydney?' I noticed my
tone had changed to the hushed whisper one uses when
asking dogs to give up their bone.

'Not recently.'

Geoffrey interceded. 'You live here on your own?'

'What of it?'

'Tell me about your brother Norman,' I continued.

'Half-brother.'

Geoffrey decided to try shock tactics. 'You killed them both, didn't you? Your father and your brother. You battered them to pulp.'

The shock tactics worked, although not in the way I would have chosen. Without speaking a word, he reached behind the door, picked up a wood-handled axe and felled Geoffrey with one blow to the head. Luckily the blade must have been blunt or it would have cleaved his skull open. As it was, Geoffrey lay unconscious with blood seeping out of the wound and trickling over his temple and over his ear on to the floor. An inch to the left and he could have ended up like Norman Hope.

He brought the axe up to strike again, but I jumped across, pushed him into the room and tried to wrestle the weapon from him. He was too quick for me. As I grabbed hold of the axe, he brought his knee up savagely into my groin and I collapsed, writhing, on the floor.

Sydney ran into a back room and brought back a reel of twine and proceeded to tie my legs and ankles together. By the time I'd got back my breath, he'd secured my hands behind my back. Geoffrey was still unconscious in the doorway. Sydney went across the room, dragged Geoff in by his feet, and locked the door.

'I don't know who you are, but I'm going to kill you,' he said, matter-of-factly.

'Why?'

'Lots of reasons. I don't like you. You know too much. If I don't kill you, you'll kill me. You might hand me over to the police. Want any more?'

I said it was enough to be going on with.

'I'm registered crazy, you know. When I kill you, my social worker will be able to confirm I hadn't taken my medication and I'll get off. Maybe spend a few weeks in hospital but I've been sectioned before . . .' His voice trailed off as if he'd lost interest in the conversation.

I wasn't sure it was as easy as that, but I wasn't prepared to argue. Either way, there seemed to be no deterrent to his intentions. Would the prospect of capital punishment have made a difference? I couldn't tell. I tried another tack.

'My girlfriend knows where I am,' I pleaded. 'If I don't return safely before nine o'clock, she's ringing the police.'

'Why didn't you bring them with you in the first place? It would have been easier.' I had to concede he was right. I was beginning to wonder which one of us was mad. He picked up a telephone from the coffee table and placed it on the floor beside me. 'Pick it up and call her.'

'You'll have to untie my hands or I can't dial.' He hesitated. 'Look, I can't get away or anything. My feet are tied.'

For a moment, it could have gone either way. I don't know whether there's anything in that mind-control business but I know I consciously willed him to untie my wrists. He could have made me dial with the bonds on, it would have been clumsy but not impossible, or he could have dialled himself.

But he didn't do either. He took a penknife from his pocket, leaned down and cut the twine. I rubbed my hands and arms to restore the circulation.

'What shall I tell her?'

He stood over me, the axe back in his right hand. 'Tell her you're here on your own, your car has broken down and to come and pick you up. Tell her you'll wait in this flat. Tell her the flat is empty. Say a word out of place and I will kill your friend.' He went over to Geoffrey who hadn't moved since the blow.

The phone was a red plastic one. I picked it up, prayed there would be an answer, and dialled the mobile number of Detective Inspector Jim Burroughs.

Chapter Thirty-Four

I could hear the ringing tone – once, twice – then a man's voice answered. 'Jim Burroughs.' I vowed to go to church every Sunday for ever.

'Is Maria there, please?'

Hesitation. 'I think you've got the wrong number.'

'Tell her it's Johnny Ace.' I looked across at Critchley, barely two feet from me and whispered, 'It's her mother.'

'Johnny! What's going on?'

'Hi Maria, it's me. Listen, I'm in a bit of trouble . . .'

'Maria? What's going on? What sort of trouble?'

'Serious. The car's broken down and I'm in Kirkby.'

'What the fuck are you doing there?'

'At Sydney Critchley's.'

'What!' I was frightened Critchley had heard his exclamation but he gave no indication. He just glared at me, axe in hand. Geoffrey still hadn't moved and I was beginning to worry about him.

'I'm in his flat now. He's not here.'

'He's with you in the room, right?' Jim wasn't an inspector for nothing.

'That's right.'

'He's holding you?'

'Yes.'

'What's she saying?' Critchley hissed at me.

I moved the phone away from my mouth. 'She wants to know if she should come and fetch me.'

'Tell me the address, we'll be right over.' Jim Burroughs's voice was now sharp and alert.

'Say yes,' instructed my captor.

'If you can, love. You know the address, don't you? Flat G3, Clement Attlee Tower.'

Critchley whispered, 'Tell her to come alone and tell nobody. And what make of car is she driving?'

'Maria, are you there?'

'Yes,' answered Jim.

'You're coming in the Fiesta, are you?'

'He can see the road from where you are?'

'Yes. And come on your own, won't you. Don't tell anyone where you're going.'

'Johnny, keep him talking and stay clear of the door if you can. Is anyone else with you?'

'Geoffrey had an accident trying to change the wheel,' I said before Critchley could stop me.

Critchley immediately slammed his hand on the cradle and cut off the call. 'Why did you say that?' he screamed.

'He's still unconscious. He needs attention.'

'What's the point? You'll all be dead by tomorrow.' He moved over to the window and looked down to the street below. 'I'll be able to see your girlfriend arrive from here. She'd better be on her own, otherwise . . .' He left the threat to my imagination.

I looked around the room for a possible weapon but there was none. Critchley stood there, still holding the axe, looking at me as if I were an exhibit in a zoo.

'What are you doing here?' His voice had changed back to a conversational tone.

'Looking for you.'

'Why bother looking for me? Nobody will miss them.' I knew he was talking about Bert and Norman.

'Your father, Bert, hired me. I think because he thought someone was trying to kill him. The funny thing was, it was Bradley who was the person behind it and Bradley was already dead. He'd certainly no idea it was you.'

'Oh yes, he had,' said Sydney, surprisingly.

'What do you mean?'

'I'd been to see him myself a few times. I told him I'd go to the police and expose him for raping my mother.'

'Unless what?'

'Unless he paid me.'

I let this new piece of information sink in. 'So you were taking money off him as well?' What a charming family. They were all at it.

'Why not? He deserved it.'

'Why kill him?'

'I didn't.'

'You said you did.'

'No. I said I was the person behind it. One of them, anyway.'

'Of course you killed him. Who else was there?'

'Norman killed him. He hated him. We all hated him. Bradley hated him too. He'd rejected Bradley's mother.'

'Norman told me he didn't kill him. Besides, Norman had an alibi. He was with the priest all the afternoon when Bert was killed.'

'Norman tells lies. Father O'Brien was totally inebriated by three o'clock when Norman crept away. He decided to go round to his father's to retrieve some family papers. Don't ask me why.'

I could imagine Bert's terror at seeing his eldest son return, the one person he most feared.

'Bert wouldn't have let him in. He was frightened of Norman.'

'He'd let anyone in. You only had to shout "Gasman" or "Meals on Wheels" and he'd open the door.'

So much for all the locks.

'Anyway, when Norman saw his father again, it brought it all back, what he'd done to my mother.' It was strange to hear this middle-aged man talk of the young Alison as his mother. 'It was the first time he'd

seen him since he threw him out as a teenager. All those
emotions were too much for Norman. A classic case of an
impulse killing.' Sydney sounded like a psychiatrist.

'How do you know all this?' I said.

'Norman told me.'

'Norman gave me the impression he'd never known
you.'

'He would, wouldn't he? Seems you were taken in by
our Norman.'

'How well did you know him?'

'We all lived up here, me, Bradley and Norman,'
revealed Sydney, surprisingly. 'On and off over the
last five years. We swapped between flats, of course,
if strangers came, like my social worker or Norman's
rehabilitation officer.'

'Why did you kill Norman? I mean, that must have
been you.' There was nobody else left.

'It was. I was sick of him. Bert and Bradley had gone,
God knows who killed Bradley, but who cares? I thought
that'd be the last of the Hopes.'

'You're the last of the Hopes. Was it for the money,
not wanting to share it with Norman?'

'There was precious little money left, I tell you and
I should know. No, it was time to finish the line.' He
started singing, in an unnaturally high voice: '"Our
Father, Which art in Heaven."' Then he giggled. 'Good,
eh? Very appropriate, I thought. He was father to us all,
you see – me, Norman and Bradley. And now the tainted
line can die out.'

'But *you* are the line; you're a Hope by blood, not a
Critchley.'

'Then I shall die too. We can all go together.' Without
warning, he ran over to the window and flung it open
wide. 'When the mysterious Maria arrives.'

For God's sake, let Jim Burroughs hurry, I thought. I
tried to struggle to my feet, holding on to the side of
the coffee table but he jumped back and swung the axe

sideways. I heard the bone in my arm crack on impact and a violent pain brought bile into my throat.

'You first,' he said, and this time raised the axe. 'Then your sleepy friend.'

I rolled aside as he smashed it down again on the spot where I'd lain. In desperation, I scrambled to my knees and hoisted myself up with my left arm, my legs still tied together. He pulled up the axe and stood back to launch another attack. Holding my broken arm close to my side, I hurled myself head-first into his solar plexus.

The impetus carried us both across the room and he landed against the window, winded. The axe fell to the floor. Instantly, I reached down, grabbed his legs with my good arm and forced his body up on to the windowsill.

And then, using my head and one arm, I pushed.

Chapter Thirty-Five

He screamed as he fell. The drop seemed to take an eternity but they do say only the last half-inch counts.

All I could think of was David Warner, toppling over the side of the *Bilbo Baggins* into the sea. This was getting to be a habit.

I didn't look to see the corpse. I'd read about jumpers before and I just knew they made a mess.

I reached for the axe and rubbed it against the ropes on my legs until they frayed and snapped. It seemed to take an age. I massaged the circulation back into them then hobbled across to Geoffrey who was still lying motionless on the floor. I turned him on his side and felt his pulse. It was still beating but faintly. The blood was still oozing from the wound but it was darker now and had congealed on his hair.

'The ambulance should be on its way,' I told him. I was never quite sure whether or not people in comas could hear but I thought I'd say it anyway.

I went back to the window, in time to see a Ford Fiesta slide cautiously round the corner. It stopped below the window and a woman got out and went over to the remains of Sydney Critchley. I recognised her as Detective Sergeant Carol Page.

She ran back to the Fiesta and must have radioed to someone because, within seconds, three police cars surged into sight, sirens blazing.

Out of the first one stepped Jim Burroughs. I shouted

from the open window and waved until I eventually
caught his attention. My right arm was throbbing badly
and I held it close to my chest.

He shook his finger at me, indicating I should stay
where I was, and he disappeared round the corner towards
the entrance.

Another siren sounded and an ambulance came into
view.

I turned unsteadily away, a wave of nausea sweeping
over me, and glanced around the room. Sydney appeared
to have had an unhealthy interest in the occult, judging by
the posters, books, Satanic videos and other paraphernalia
in the place.

No wonder he'd turned out strange after a family
history like his.

A bang at the door indicated the arrival of Jim
Burroughs. I let him in. He didn't waste time with
pleasantries. 'Who did it?'

'What?' I asked innocently.

'Another fucking stiff. Trouble follows you, Johnny
Ace.'

'Never mind that for now. Can you get hold of the
paramedics for Geoffrey?'

He took a quick shufty at the figure on the floor and
pulled out his radio. 'Ambulance up here and quick.
We're in G3, seventh floor.' He turned back to me.
'What happened?'

'He took an axe to Geoff as we walked through the
door, then he kneed me in the balls and, before my eyes
had stopped watering, I was tied up like one of Miss
Whiplash's best.'

'That was when you phoned me, right?'

'Right.'

'And in the . . .' he checked his watch, '. . . in the
ten minutes we took to get here, you've miraculously
done a Houdini and Sorry Sydney, I presume that *is*
Sorry Sydney doing his imitation of tomato soup out

there, Sorry Sydney had taken to paragliding without his glider.'

'That's a point,' I said, diverting his flow. 'How come you did get here so quickly? You must have been close by.'

'We were at an enquiry at St Diana's. Some DJ had a load of gear stolen when he was gigging there last week and his old man's a friend of the Chief Constable so we had to put in an appearance.'

'Did you find the stuff?'

'What? You must be joking. Total waste of time but a good exercise in toadying. The police force today is forty per cent administration, forty per cent politics and twenty per cent crime busting.'

'That's why you need people like me to solve your cases for you.' I winced as a pain shot up my arm.

He noticed the gesture. 'Looks like you need a doctor, never mind anything else. Is that arm broken?'

'I think so.'

'Sydney?' I nodded. He returned to his tirade. 'The trouble with you, Johnny, is you tend to act as judge and jury as well. That's two in a week you've sent to the Chair, metaphorically speaking.'

'Pure accidents, Jim. This last fellow lost his balance at the wrong moment. Don't they call it vertigo?'

'Crap, I call it.' He sighed. 'Roll on my pension.'

'You could've taken it a dozen times by now.'

'I'm taking no chances after Robert Maxwell. Anyway, enough of that. I want to know how you found Sydney.'

I told him about hunting down Sydney's real mother in the Southport nursing home, and recounted the conversation before Sydney's fall.

Jim Burroughs scratched his chin thoughtfully. 'In the end, it's all about chickens, this case.'

'Chickens?'

'That's right. They always come home to roost in the end.'

'In Bert's case, with a vengeance. The whole Hope clan has been wiped out.'

'Revenge of the family, eh?'

A knock at the door interrupted us and two paramedics ran in to attend to Geoffrey. Behind them was Carol Page and a couple of uniformed officers.

'Look, get in that ambulance with your mate, will you,' Jim said. 'I'll catch up with you tomorrow.'

'What about my car? I can't leave it here.'

'Sergeant Page can drive it back to the station and you can have it picked up tomorrow.' I smiled gratefully at her and gave her the keys.

The paramedics were already taking Geoffrey by stretcher down to the waiting ambulance and I followed them. Geoff still hadn't moved and I was very concerned. I'd got him into this and he didn't deserve it.

At Walton Hospital, I was escorted to Casualty to have my arm set in plaster and Geoffrey was rushed to Intensive Care.

I didn't want to go home but they insisted there was nothing I could do at the hospital and a taxi was sent for. I rang the ward as soon as I got home and was told that Geoff was critical but stable.

I felt no remorse for Sydney's death but I knew I couldn't handle the guilt if anything happened to Geoffrey.

For the second time in little over an hour, I prayed.

Next morning found me back at the hospital and sitting in the corridor outside the Intensive Care Unit. I'd been there since six. I'd not been able to sleep. I'd refused the painkillers. I was never keen on the side effects. I feel the same about cannabis or heroin. And look how many people septrin killed.

'We'll let you know as soon as there's any change,' the Sister had told me when I rang again at five, but I couldn't stand the wait. I had to be there.

His mother was by his bedside. I realised I knew surprisingly little about Geoffrey. He wasn't married, although he was in his thirties. His father was dead and he lived with his mother in the semi in which he'd been born. He wasn't gay but he didn't have any special girlfriends that I knew of. Most of his time was spent running my property business and I knew what a mess I'd be in without him.

At eleven o'clock, a nurse came out of the ward. 'Mr Ace?'

I jumped up. 'That's me.'

'Mr Molloy has come round and he's asking for you.' I don't think I'd ever heard Geoffrey called by his full name before. 'Would you like to come in?'

He looked enormous, lying in the small single hospital bed, a drip attached to his arm and a bandage round his head. His mother sat beside him, holding his hand. She had curly hair, jet black, and was so tiny I wondered how she'd produced someone of Geoffrey's size. She smiled at me. 'So you're the famous Johnny Ace? Geoff's told me all about you.' She noticed my sling. 'Oh dear, you've been hurt as well.'

'I'm OK.' I shook her hand with my left hand; something I'd have to get used to.

'Don't get up. It's nice to meet you at last.' I turned to the nurse. 'Will he be all right?'

'He'll have a headache for a few days, but he'll live.'

'Some minder youse are,' Geoffrey whispered, his accent more noticeable than usual. 'Good job it wasn't a BMW.'

'I'd have saved you if it'd been a BMW,' I replied, and leaned over to hug him. His mother looked pleased.

'He's always saying how good you are to him, Mr Ace.'

'Couldn't do without him,' I told her, 'but this doesn't mean you're getting a rise,' I added to Geoffrey. 'I'll expect you back in the office this afternoon.'

The nurse was about to protest until she realised I was joking. Before I left, I rang Hilary at the Royal Liverpool Hospital and asked her to check out Geoffrey for me to make sure the doctors weren't hiding anything. They tell you nothing in hospitals, but I thought that Hilary, being a nurse, might have connections at Walton.

'What's happened now?' she asked despairingly.

'He had an argument with a woodcutter who thought his neck was a tree.'

'Johnny, be serious. All these accidents, what's going on?'

'Nothing, Hil. It's all over now, honest. What do you say we go out tonight?' Weary though I was, there was nothing I wanted more now than to go out and forget about everything that had happened since Bradley Hope's death, and Hilary was the best person to do it with.

'Where shall we go?'

'I don't know. Surprise me.'

'Wait a minute, I don't finish till ten. I've got a split shift.'

'Tell you what. I'll meet you in the Costa Coffee shop in Lime Street Station at quarter past and we'll go on from there.' I love railway stations at any time but especially at night. There's a sense of adventure and excitement about them that airports don't have. Perhaps it's something to do with seeing *Brief Encounter* so often.

'I'll be there. Take care.' She blew me a kiss.

Next I rang Jim Burroughs. 'Lunch at the Grapes?' I suggested.

'In Mathew Street?'

'That's the one. Where we used to go in The Cruzads' days.'

'Twelve-thirty,' he commanded.

Mathew Street was packed with shoppers plus a few sightseers crowding round the new Cavern Club and all the souvenir shops cashing in on The Beatles. We found an empty table and ordered a bottle of red wine and sandwiches. I wasn't ready for a knife and fork job with one hand.

'All wrapped up, then?' I said after we'd finished eating.

'Just about. Warner killed Bradley Hope and now he's dead. Norman killed Bert and he was killed in turn by Sydney who's also dead. I suppose you'd call that all wrapped up.'

'I like a nice tidy end to a case, don't you?'

Burroughs said nothing but took out one of his tablets and washed it down with a mouthful of wine.

'Still getting indigestion?' I asked him.

'It's right across here.' He indicated the upper part of his ribcage. 'Like a belt tied too tightly round my chest. It's nothing. It goes away after a while.'

'You want to go to a doctor's. Sounds like it could be heart trouble to me.'

'Thanks a million. Just what I want to hear.'

'Seriously, Jim. I'd have a check-up if I were you.'

'Getting back to the case . . .'

'Tell me the run-down on Sydney – I know about the rest.'

'Not much to tell, really. He was always a bit odd, judging by the social workers' reports.' He shook his head. 'Bloody social workers. Why do we have 'em? They don't stop the buggers committing the crimes.'

'How did he first find out about his origins? The Critchleys surely wouldn't have told him.'

'His father, Mr Critchley that is, died when Sydney was fifteen. That sent him off the rails a bit, but he'd always been a problem child. He left home less than a year afterwards and then it was the usual story – juvenile courts, probation, young offenders' hostels. Somewhere along the line, the trick-cyclists stepped in, and he was in and out of a few institutions until he finally ended up behind bars.'

It was in prison, five years ago, that the meeting took

place that changed Sydney's life, for that was where he first ran into Norman Hope. They got talking and the bizarre relationship between the two of them was revealed. Understandably, they both shared a violent hatred of Bert Hope and, when they came out, decided to do something about it.

'Sydney had found accommodation through the Community in Care homefinders service. Probably a similar organisation for ex-cons did the same for Norman. Either way, they ended up next door to one another in Kirkby.'

'Five years ago was when Bradley came back to England, Jim.'

'Yes. My guess is, they sought him out. After all, he was still a bit famous then and easy to track down.'

'They probably thought he had money.'

'And when they found out he didn't, they recruited him to the team.'

'The Brothers Three, eh?'

'What?'

'Never mind. Go on.' For a professed musician, Jim Burroughs was strangely ill-informed about music.

'That's about it, really.'

'I would think that Bradley kept most of his blackmail scam exclusively for himself,' I suggested. I didn't mention the other victims.

'I'd accept that,' agreed Jim, 'although he probably contributed some of the money to their communal upkeep, such as it was.'

'It wasn't exactly Chatsworth House up there, was it? My guess is Bradley had some stashed away in a safe deposit box somewhere.'

'In which case, we'll find it. There'll be a receipt somewhere. I wonder who'll inherit that?'

'Mrs Critchley, I imagine. She's his mother. A pity it will have come twenty years too late for her to enjoy it.'

'Never mind,' said Jim. 'Look on the bright side. It'll save the council a few bob on her nursing home fees.'

'Great,' I said bitterly. 'But will it put our council tax down? Anyway, tell me – what's the official line on Sydney's demise?'

The policeman raised his eyebrows quizzically. 'You would want to know that. He fell accidentally from the window, didn't he? Or so you said, and you should know as you were the only witness.' He shook his head. 'Two accidental deaths in little over a week.'

'Is a little careless, I know.'

'I hope you don't get the same coroner, that's all.' He indicated my nearly empty glass. 'You'd better finish the bottle. I'm on duty.'

'Go on. I'm not driving with one arm.'

He poured out the last half glass of wine. 'You're serious about this enquiry agent business then?'

'Detective agency, I think, Jim. Enquiry agent sounds like a branch of the Citizen's Advice Bureau.'

'That's probably what it'll be most of the time. Are you going to open up an office in town and do it properly?'

'I'd not thought about it, to tell you the truth.' And I hadn't. Cases seemed to have come to me so far, without me doing much looking. 'It's an idea though.'

'There's a few firms in town already. Mainly they do industrial espionage, bad debts, divorces, tracings, that sort of thing. Not too much criminal work. Not too many murders, anyway. It's not like the television, you know. I can't understand why you want to do it. You've got enough on with your flats and your radio show, haven't you?'

'No such thing as single careers nowadays, Jim. Lateral employment, that's what it's all about.'

'That's what they call it, do they? Lateral employment. Jack of all trades, master of none, more like.'

'I wouldn't say master of none. I found all your murderers for you, didn't I?'

'All right, I hold my hands up. You didn't do badly, but . . .'

'In fact, your lot will come out of this pretty well, I'd say. A high-profile case, all tied up in three weeks and I know my name won't be mentioned anywhere in despatches. I shouldn't be surprised if you don't make Chief Inspector.'

His face reddened. 'You can cut out that bullshit for a start.' He stood up. 'I'm off. Some of us have work to do.'

'And I'm going home to bed,' I said. 'I might get four hours' sleep in before I do the show.' The wine was already making me sleepy.

'Don't forget to move your car from the police station car park before it gets stolen.'

Before I put my head down for the afternoon, I rang Maria at the Library and ran over the scene at Kirkby with her. She was horrified.

'Are you sure that's all you've done, broken your arm? He could have killed you. And Geoffrey too.'

I agreed with her that that was probably his intention.

'Do you want to come round later?'

Tonight I was meeting Hilary. 'I'm worn out, Maria. What about Friday?'

'Oh, Johnny, in case you hadn't noticed, it's Easter this weekend and I've promised to take Robin to Venice.'

I hadn't noticed. 'Will a nineteen-year-old want to go away with his mother?'

'If it means a free trip to Venice, he will. I've booked the tickets and everything.' For a moment, I felt rather sad, as if I was missing out on something. 'How much I'll see of him when we get there's another matter.'

'When do you get back?'

'Tuesday. Why don't you come to mine on Wednesday night and you can tell me the whole story properly?'

'I'd like that.'

I put down the phone and was in bed and asleep within ten minutes. The alarm clock woke me at five-thirty and I took a taxi to the radio station. Ken looked worried when I entered the studio.

'What now?' he sighed, eyeing my sling. He'd read the tabloid accounts of the *Bilbo Baggins* accident, he knew about the BMW attack – and now this!

'Not my fault, Ken. A group of Irish vegetarians attacked me when I was shopping in Dewhurst's.'

He ignored my comment. 'Will you be able to do the programme?'

'No problem. Good job I'm ambidextrous.' It's all done by computer these days and I can operate a mouse with one hand.

'I don't know,' he grumbled. 'If you had a nice wife at home and a couple of kids, you wouldn't get into these scrapes.'

'But would I have as much fun?'

I played Sly and The Family Stone's *Family Affair* in the show and dedicated it to Norah Critchley, the only one of that particular family left – and who would miss them?

Afterwards, I went to the Shangri-la for a Chinese. I used a fork. I took my time over the meal until, at nine-thirty, I walked up to Lime Street Station. The coffee shop was closed. So much for the late-night travellers. I stood outside, read the arrival screens and watched the passengers come and go.

Hilary arrived at ten past ten, wearing a long brown raincoat. She ran the last few yards and threw her arms round me then stopped when she saw the sling and plaster.

'What's happened?'

'It's a long story. I'll tell you later.'

'Are you sure you're OK?'

'Promise. Where'd you like to go?'

'You told me to surprise you, right?'

'Did I?'

'Yes. So, follow me.'

She led me out of the side entrance of the station into
Lord Nelson Street. 'My car's parked in the Gladstone
Hotel car park,' she said. We walked up the hill.

'Do you remember that silly game we used to play?'
asked Hilary. 'Where one of us did a mime or something
and the other had to guess what song it was.'

'Course I do. I threw one of Shady Spencer's odes
across the room . . .'

'And I got *Poetry in Motion*. That's it. And you
gave me a bus ticket for *Ticket to Ride*. Well, I've
got one for you now.'

'Go on.'

'Wait till we get in the car.' We reached the car
park. Her Peugeot was parked in an unlit spot by the
far wall.

'Well?' I said, as I sat beside her at the front and we
shut the doors. 'What's my surprise?'

'I thought of something that might appeal to you.'
Hilary smiled seductively, and slowly she undid the
buttons on her raincoat.

She wore nothing underneath.

I lowered my lips to her nipples and licked them.

'Come on,' she said, 'what is it, the song?'

I stopped and tried to concentrate. 'I don't know,' I
admitted, and carried on caressing her boobs.

'Keep going.'

I explored further down her body until I came to a
red lace garter around her thigh.

'*Lady in Red*, Chris De Burgh?'

She shook her head. 'Nope. Try again.'

I ran my hand back up from the garter to between her
legs and back again. She shivered.

'Got it!' I exclaimed. 'The Big Bopper – *Chantilly Lace*.'

'Correct,' laughed Hilary, pulling the coat back round her. 'Now I'm taking you home to give you your prize.'

'Oh baby,' I cried, 'you *knooooooooow* what I like!'

Skinner's Round

Quintin Jardine

By the blade, by water, by the fire, by lightning, shall the desecrators perish . . .

A four-day tournament involving the world's leading golfers is being staged to mark the opening of Witches' Hill, a new country club created on his East Lothian estate by the Marquis of Kinture. But on the Sunday afternoon preceding, one of Kinture's business partners is found dead in his private jacuzzi in the clubhouse – with his throat cut.

The next day an anonymous letter is received by the local newspaper, containing a fragment of a legendary witches' curse upon anyone who desecrates their place of worship.

For Assistant Chief Constable Robert Skinner, the key to the murder is surely to be found in the here and now rather than in East Lothian's grisly past as a notorious centre for witchcraft. But then a second murder occurs, this time by water, and soon Skinner is facing the most challenging case of his career.

0 7472 4141 4

HEADLINE

The Jump

Martina Cole

Donna Brunos worships her husband and is devastated when he is jailed for eighteen years on a charge of armed robbery. Georgio swears he's been set up and – terrified he won't survive the rigours of Parkhurst – persuades Donna to help him escape.

Implementing the daring plan takes Donna into a twilight world she never believed existed – a world of brutal sex and casual violence. And the more she sees of the sordid underbelly of Georgio's business dealings, the more she comes to suspect that her beloved husband is not the innocent he claims to be . . .

'A big powerful read with a climax that will knock your socks off' *Today*

'Gritty realism . . . Martina Cole's star is in the ascendant' *Sunday Express*

'A major new talent' *Best*

'Gritty, atmospheric stuff!' *Today*

'You won't be able to put this one down!' *Company*

0 7472 4821 4

HEADLINE

If you enjoyed this book here is a selection of other bestselling titles from Headline